OF SCALES & FIRE

NATALINA REIS

HOT TREE PUBLISHING

ALSO BY NATALINA REIS

M/M Stand-alone Romances

Infinite Blue

Lavender Fields

Of Magic & Scales Series

Of Magic and Scales

Of Scales and Fire

Of Fire and Bone

M/F Stand-alone Romances

Loved You Always

Blind Magic

Fictional-ish

Her Real Man

The Jewel Chronicles

Desert Jewel

Rebel Jewel

Snow Jewel

For information, contact the publisher, Hot Tree Publishing.

www.hottreepublishing.com

Editing: Hot Tree Editing

Cover Designer: BookSmith Design

E-book ISBN: 978-1-922359-56-8

Paperback ISBN: 978-1-922359-66-7

Para o país que me viu nascer, obrigado.
For my native country, thank you.

ONE

OF MERMEN AND WARLOCKS

IF LOOKS COULD KILL, I WOULD HAVE ALREADY decimated Antonio Silva, the cop warlock who insisted on dating my best friend and employee, Cristina. My stomach churned as I watched the magical bringing her hand to his lips and placing an intimate—and yes, sexy, I'll admit it—kiss on the inside of her wrist. Cristina giggled like a sixteen-year-old, her amber face lighting up with a toothy smile.

"Don't look if it bothers you that much." Fouchard came to stand beside me in the small café kitchen and looked out the service window into the coffee room where the couple was saying their good-byes. "If I didn't know you were gay, I'd be jealous."

I shrugged, stealing a brief glance at my hot boyfriend. The corner of his lips twitched upwards. "She's my friend, and he is—" Sleek? Stunning? A damned magical? "He's too old for her." I was grasping at straws.

"He's like five years older than she is," Fouchard said with a snort. "Hardly an abyssal gap. You just don't like the fact he's a magical creature." Bingo! Heat rose to my cheeks. It was ridiculous how much I mistrusted magicals, when it turned out I was one of them myself *and* dating a merman. Longtime habits are hard to break. "You have to grow out of that, Aiden. It's not healthy to hate your own kind."

Of course he was right, but it was hard to break that cycle of mistrust after spending a lifetime running away from magical creatures while getting in all kinds of trouble because of them.

"I don't want him to hurt her," I said, still eyeing the warlock in hopes he could feel my threatening glare. With all my newly discovered powers, why couldn't I have Superman's heat vision? "He's too sleek."

Fouchard turned to the small sink and began drying the dishes I had washed a few minutes before. "I think he's fucking hot. She'd be stupid not to bed that one."

I swung away so fast, I heard the bones of my neck creaking. "Oh, really? So I guess you'd like to tap that too, right?" Red-hot jealousy overtook my whole being, and I probably looked like one of those white English tourists after a couple hours under the

Portuguese sun. "If that's what you want, go ahead. Who am I to hold you to promises made in the dark while we made love?" Man, was I besotted and stupid!

My boyfriend laughed, carefully setting the plate he was drying on the stainless steel counter. "First, he's straight and most likely wouldn't appreciate me propositioning him," he said, taking a couple steps toward me and crossing his arms over his chest. "And second, why would I want that when I have the sexiest man on earth at my disposal?"

I couldn't help it: a smile crept to my lips, and the jealousy melted away as quickly as it had flared. "And who might that man be? Do I know him? Is it the King of the Fae?"

Fouchard rolled his eyes. "Alabyron be damned. He may be pretty and ooze sensuality but you, my sweet and insane whatever-you-are, are the one I dream of." Aw, I knew it was cheesy, but I loved it when he said those things. I never tired of hearing him sing my praises. "Granted, you can be a stupid idiot sometimes, but you're my idiot, and I love you." I loved him too, even though he swung a little too easily between praise and insult.

He drew me into his arms and kissed my forehead. "Leave Cristina alone," he said. "She's fully capable of taking care of herself." I knew that, but I couldn't help worrying about her. She was a regular, a mere mortal woman who didn't have a chance against magical glamors and compellings. "And if something happens, she has you, a powerful whatever, to protect her."

It had become a running joke with us—the fact that I had no clue who or what I was. It was painfully obvious I was a magical of some kind, but no one seemed to be able to identify which one. I had lived my whole adult life thinking I was just a Joe Schmo, only to find out that was far from the truth. I was still pretty ambivalent about it. It was nice to have powers other humans could only dream of, but on the other hand, it also meant I was forever linked to a group of creatures I had fought so hard to stay clear of.

I pushed him away, pretending to be mad at him. "Well, I am very poorly acquainted with my own powers, and until I learn how to better control them, I'm not much help to anyone." I took another quick peek at the couple now walking out the door.

Fouchard slapped me with the kitchen towel. "Those powers were what saved my sister two months ago." It was true; I had helped rescue his sister from the hands of a serial killer bent on getting rid of all magicals who didn't fit the traditional mold. My boyfriend took a couple steps until his lips hovered over mine, his heady scent invading all my senses. He was the one who held all the magic. "Stop being so down on yourself and own it. You do with everything else, why not with this too? It's part of who you are."

True, except I really didn't know who I was. Fuck, I didn't even know my own birthday. "Besides, you have magic in those fingers of yours," he whispered, a wicked smile spreading on his lips. "You're a true sorcerer with that mouth." He brushed a thumb along my lower lip. Then he looked down at my crotch and licked his lips. "And other magical parts." He let it hang as he lifted his eyes to mine.

Shit. How did he do that? I had been walking around with a hard-on since I met him.

"Stop it now, or I will have to show you how magical I can be right here in the kitchen, and it wouldn't look good for the customers," I said, swallowing the giant knot in my throat. "You're truly wicked, you know."

Fouchard laughed out loud and took a step away from me, throwing the towel over his shoulder. "You love it." I did. "Right, Pinocchio?" he asked with a pointed glance at my crotch. Wicked, truly wicked.

"*Meu Deus*, you're at it again." Cristina erupted through the swinging doors, her usual look of mock disgust on her face. "Get a room already. With two homes between the two of you, why do you have to bring your raging hormones into the coffee shop?"

I snorted and returned to what I was doing before getting derailed by her and the sleek cop. "Bicas R Us is my coffee shop, after all," I said, drying a coffee cup. "If I want to have wild monkey sex in here, it's my prerogative. Unlike you, my friend, who is cavorting with the enemy."

Cristina flipped me the finger. "Tó is not the enemy." Oh, so Antonio Silva now was simply Tó, was he? It seemed as they had moved from the flirting stage into a more intimate one. "He's been an ally, and you know that. He covered for that whole mess with Pescado and Vee, no one the wiser. Thanks. To. Him."

"He's a fucking warlock," I exclaimed, almost dropping the cup. Yes, he had covered up when the serial killer had kidnapped and almost killed Vee, and yes, he had been a great help with the "cleaning up" afterward. But he was a magical, and Cristina was not. "He can make you do… things." *Lame, seriously lame, Aiden.* "Things you don't want to do."

Cristina frowned and slid some crockery onto the tray she was holding. "He hasn't made me do anything I didn't want to do, idiot." It was lovely to have friends who had no trouble calling you out. "Get used to the idea, because I'm dating him and that's that."

"Leave the girl alone," Fouchard interjected with a chuckle. "She's a grown woman and doesn't need you mothering her."

I huffed, annoyed that I seemed to be alone in my concern, and exited the kitchen to go take an order. As I left, I heard my boyfriend say, "You know he only does that because he loves you, right?" My heart melted. The tough, obnoxious merman had such a sweet, soft center. One of the reasons I loved him so much.

Summer was in full bloom, and so was business. The crowds washed by and through my coffee shop like the tides, in and out in predictable waves. The height of business was around lunchtime and then later in the afternoon and into the evening. We were so busy that Fouchard volunteered to give us a hand while his sister was at a summer camp aptly targeted at extraordinary girls. Of course, that only meant girls with the potential to be great, not those who were mermaids like Vee was. It didn't matter, the camp visited the beach daily, which satisfied his sister's pull to the sea and left him with ample free time to focus on other things, mostly me. I was not complaining; my merman—or merrow, as he preferred to be called —was very creative and enthusiastic with ways to keep us both blissfully happy and satisfied.

After taking a couple orders from the patio outside and chatting—or trying to—with the customers, I returned inside with a tray full of dirty dishes. Fouchard was behind the counter, every inch of him powerful and virile with a smile that crinkled the skin around his brown eyes and made me shiver from head to toe. Cristina arrived at the counter at the same time as I did, her tray also laden with crockery and leftover food. We both set the trays down on the counter and leaned over it for a quick breather.

"That was the weirdest conversation ever," I said, wiping my hands on a napkin. "That guy with the mustache from the eighties kept telling me this was the first time he had been able to go out since he got constipated."

Fouchard, who had just taken a sip from a glass of iced water, spat it out in an apt imitation of a geyser, and Cristina bent over roaring with laughter.

I was puzzled. "What? What's so funny about being constipated?"

My friend and employee gripped my shoulder, still laughing. "You idiot. You really have to learn Portuguese," she said, choked by her own laughter. "*Constipado,* not constipated."

"Tomatoes, tomahtoes," I said, still at a loss. "Same thing."

My boyfriend wiped his eyes with the back of his hand before saying, "No, Aiden, not even close. *Constipado* means with a cold, not having pipework trouble."

I stared at him, my mouth slack while I processed the new information. Then I burst out laughing too. "Shit. I do need to learn the language." I spoke and understood a bit. Very little. I could take orders without major incidents and I could chat briefly about the weather and soccer scores. Otherwise it was all Greek to me—well, Portuguese, which amounted to the same where I was concerned. I'd been too busy to put too much energy into it, first enjoying the male sights of the place and later enjoying my own cranky man.

"You didn't suggest he take a laxative, did you?" Cristina asked, laughter still punctuating her voice.

I bit my lip and squinted. "I may have told him he should drink some prune juice—at least I think that's what I said. *Sumo de punhos.*"

More out of control laughter. What had I said now?

Cristina explained, "That means fist juice. Prune is *ameixa seca.*" I would have never guessed that. "The poor guy must have been really confused."

We didn't close until after nine, and even then, there were people loitering around the patio, sitting on my chairs and enjoying a nice cool night. No matter how hot it had been during the day, the ocean breeze always brought in some respite in the evening. Cristina drove home, and Fouchard and I walked hand in hand toward the *paradão,* a wide concrete walking path that ran for miles along the shore. We had made it our nightly routine to walk along the beach, maybe sit at a beachside café and have a beer or two, or head to the same bench where we had exchanged our first kiss. As my love for the big man grew, so did my cheesiness. It was rather embarrassing.

We were already on our way back after shame-lessly making out on *our* bench when I heard a whizzing sound that I immediately recognized as not-so-friendly fire. I didn't have time to warn Fouchard, so I did the only thing I could: I jumped in front of the flaming bolt of energy aiming at my boyfriend. It caught me at the top right of my chest, right beneath my shoulder, and knocked me off my feet. Losing my balance, I flew—my feet actually leaving the ground—onto the hard and normally welcoming chest of my merrow. It was not so welcoming this time, for I had been thrown against him with an unnaturally powerful force, and when my head hit the hardness of his muscles, it felt as if it exploded. He stumbled backward, and we both fell, he on his back and me on him.

I wanted to talk, but the air had been knocked out of me. My shoulder was on fire—literally. Flames and smoke erupted from it as if from a volcano. Pain was quickly beginning to make its way to my conscious-ness, but I didn't have time for it. We had to get out of there. I tried to straighten, but it was as if lead had lodged itself on my shoulder and I was anchored to Fouchard, who was also struggling to sit up.

From behind the haze that was gathering over my eyes, I felt my boyfriend's hands probing my shoulder. "Fuck, you're burning." Fouchard slipped out from beneath me and stripped off his shirt to snuff the fire out. "Speak to me, Aiden. Are you okay?"

No, I was not okay, but I was perfectly aware of the necessity to hightail it out of there before whatever hit me hit us again. "We have to go now." I was not sure I spoke loud enough for Naël to hear me, but I suddenly found myself being lifted into his strong arms and moving.

"Call 112 now!" That was the last thing I heard before darkness overcame me.

TWO

GREAT FINS OF FIRE

Nothing like being ejected from a volcano to put your life into perspective. Well, it *felt* as if I had been thrust out of a molten, fiery mess. When I came to, two things became quickly clear to me: I was not anywhere I recognized, and my shoulder burned like a mother. I winced and placed my hand to the flat side of my chest where the weapon had lodged itself, sure I would find a giant hole big enough to put my fist through. But my fingers found flesh and bone— excruciatingly sore flesh but still solid and whole.

"What the fuck just happened?" I yelled, looking around me in a panic. Where the hell was I? "Naël, where are you?" A new fear took hold of my heart; had the attacker managed to hurt my boyfriend too?

A strong, warm hand on my unhurt shoulder told me he was there beside me. "I'm here, Aiden. I'm okay." I tilted my chin up and looked behind me to find Fouchard standing, his eyebrows knitted in the middle and lips stretched into a thin line. "You're going to be all right."

"Where are we?" Another quick survey didn't tell me much about our location. I was lying on a narrow bed, my head comfortably resting on a pillow, a blanket over the lower half of my body.

"You're at my place, Aiden." I knew that voice. I tried to sit up, but Fouchard anchored me down.

"What's going on, Taz?"

"Naël brought you to me after the attack," she explained, coming into view. "He couldn't very well take you to a regular hospital. They would freak out when they saw how fast you heal. So he called me instead."

Fouchard came around a bit and sat on a chair next to me. "You fucking called the witch?" He shrugged, a tiny smile twitching on his lips.

"The witch has a name," Taz said, a hard edge to her voice that vanished almost immediately. "And it's not Sabrina or Samantha." She laughed at her own joke. If I hadn't been in such pain, I would have laughed too. Taz was the only person I knew who had the same taste in jokes as I did. "He did the right thing. You were obviously hit by some magical object, and he couldn't take you to a doctor. So you got the next best thing."

"What? A voodoo master with a taste for pop culture?" I exclaimed, happy to be distracted from the burning in my shoulder. "I'd rather face a quack."

"Tsk, tsk, Aiden Mercer," Taz said, tapping her foot. "I'm a witch with mad skills."

Fouchard muffled a chuckle, and I threw him an angry glance. "Don't encourage her. Well, witch, whatever you did to my wound is not working. It hurts like the dickens."

Taz poked a finger right on the crux of the pain, and I yelped. "You are such a baby. There is a good reason why women are the ones who have babies," she said, not too sympathetically. "If we left it to you guys, humanity would go extinct."

"Can you not add more pain to the injury, please? What's your problem?"

"You're fine," she said. "A little shaken, but the wound is already healing, and soon there will be nothing there but a faded scar to remind you of your close encounter with whatever that thing was."

"It was a *brahmachakram*," I said, the pain easing slightly, a prickle running over my skin like the feel of a thousand ants. My wound was healing fast.

Taz raised an eyebrow. "What the hell is that?" She perched on the edge of the bed as Fouchard slid another pillow under my head. "Sounds like a bad pop song from the '90s."

Fouchard was the one to answer, "A weapon stolen

from Brahma." I nodded in support of his claim. I managed to sit up slightly, my head swimming in the process.

"The Hindu god? Brahma?" Taz's eyebrows had arched so high above her eyes, they almost touched her hairline. "Impossible. He's a myth."

I snickered. "Same can be said about witches and the Fae," I said. "I know what I saw, and it was definitely a *brahmachkram*. Someone is trying to kill us, and he or she is not of this earth."

Taz bit her lower lip in thought. "All right, you stay here for as long as you need," she said after a moment. "I will go talk to our High Priestess about this. Be careful." She grabbed her hat and sunglasses from a nearby table and turned to go. She stopped and twisted halfway back to look at me. "And Aiden, try not to piss off any more gods, please."

I groaned, swallowing the cuss burning on my tongue. Fouchard grabbed my hand and brought it to his lips for a gentle kiss. As soon as his mouth touched my skin, every muscle in my body relaxed. "I thought I'd lost you there for a second," he whispered against my hand. "Don't ever do that to me again, you hear?" It was a low growl that vibrated through my skin.

"I don't plan to," I said, my heart aflutter from his touch. The pain was definitely fading quickly, now reduced to a slight burning sensation radiating from where the bolt of energy had hit me to the edges of my shoulder. "But can we just go home? It gives me the creeps to be in a witch's house." I looked around again. I frowned. "And in her bed. Yikes, get me out of here."

Fouchard shook his head. "You're still weakened. Just lie still and relax." He smiled that wicked one-sided smile of his. "I could try to squeeze in there with you."

That was something I could totally get behind. But the bed was very narrow. "Not sure that big, luscious body of yours can fit."

As to prove me wrong, my merman pulled the blanket aside and crawled in bed beside me, his awesome ass hanging out from the edge of the bed. "It's not a perfect fit, but then again, what is?" he said with a chuckle as he crossed his arm over my chest.

I kissed his strong nose, now just mere inches away from me, and laughed. "*We* are a perfect fit." We were. Running the risk of sounding like a cliché, we completed each other in ways I never thought possible.

I allowed myself to drift into sleep in his arms as he stroked my hair and peppered kisses on my face. I didn't know how long I slept, but when I woke up, daylight flooded the small room, haloing my lover's body. Fouchard still slept, his body awkwardly curled against mine, half on the bed, the other hanging precariously off the edge. The window right behind

Fouchard was devoid of curtains or blinds, and the sun had no trouble shining in through the glass. I watched my merman sleep, his hard features softened by the peace of slumber and his usually furrowed forehead smooth as if he had not a worry in the world. I had never thought I would love like this— fiercely and completely. But Fouchard, my sweet and sour merrow, proved me wrong. I could love after all, not just with my excitable nether parts but with my whole heart and soul. I could, and did, want to be someone's life, to be a couple forever. Before, the idea would have scared me, but now it filled me with wonder and joy—and lust, of course, but that went without saying.

"Stop looking at me that way. You're freaking me out." Fouchard didn't bother opening his eyes as he spoke. "I love you too, but when you stare at me like that, I feel like a fish kebab. You look hungry enough to eat me."

I burst out laughing. "Well, not too far from the truth. I do love the way you taste." His eyelids opened slowly to reveal his beautiful deep russet eyes, and my heart somersaulted in my chest. "In fact, can we go home so I can do just that?"

He made a big production of looking shocked. "Why, love, you're injured." I frowned at him, and he smiled. "How's the wound, by the way?"

Now that he mentioned it, there was no pain

anymore. I gingerly touched it with my fingers and turned my eyes in its direction, but there was nothing there other than a whitish, slightly elevated circular scar. It looked as if someone had grabbed a knife and carved a perfect circle on my shoulder.

"Holy shit. It's gone." It was still hard for me to believe I could heal that fast. I had always been a quick healer, but I had never suffered a major injury like this. To see a hole the size of what I had earlier close up and totally heal within hours was amazing and really preposterous when you thought about it.

Fouchard lifted himself on an elbow and examined the scar with the tips of his fingers, making me shiver all over. "Damn! If I didn't see it, I wouldn't believe it."

My T-shirt was in shreds, so I had to go home topless. My boyfriend, who wore his now ruined shirt, made a few jokes about it while he drove me to his house, even though a lot of guys walked around bare chested this time of the year. Once we got home, I dug up a shirt from the drawer Fouchard had given me in his room. I kept a few of my clothes there since I spent a lot of time at his place. Then I called Cristina, who would be wondering why I hadn't shown up for work that morning, and told her I'd be coming later.

By the time I went back to the living room, my wonderful merman had fixed me a cup of strong coffee and prepared a couple of sandwiches. As soon as I took a bite, I realized I was ravenous. I chewed my way through both sammies in no time, surprising even myself. I had never been a big eater.

"Fuck, I have never seen you eat with such gusto." Fouchard laughed, handing me the rest of his own sandwich, which I didn't hesitate to accept. "I guess the healing process takes a lot out of your energy supply."

I stopped midbite and stared at him, mouth still open. "Shit, you're right. I feel…" I searched for the right word to describe what I was feeling, not only in every muscle of my body but also in my head and in my bones. "Depleted. I feel depleted." A new thought occurred to me: food was not going to be enough to refill my energy store. "I need to go to the beach."

Fouchard raised an eyebrow, and his lip twitched. "Do you think this is the right time to go sunbathe? There is someone—a god, no less—out to get you, and you want to go to the beach?" Reaching out, he grazed his thumb over my lower lip, wiping away a dollop of mustard. I stared as he took the burnt-yellow-covered thumb and stuck it in his mouth, licking it clean. My naughty bits groaned awake.

My eyes were still on his mouth, that delicious and oh-so-proficient mouth of his. I swallowed the knot in my throat. "I need to feel the sand against my skin to recharge," I explained, stuttering a bit. "Whatever I am, I am connected to the earth elements. I need them to keep my energy levels going."

Fouchard was quiet for a moment, and I could almost hear his thoughts as he concocted another of his great ideas. "Let's go to the basement," he said, grabbing my hand and pulling me to my feet. "I know just the thing."

My legs were still not working fully, so I stumbled behind him, glad of his support as he led me down the stairs to his underground beach. At one point, I almost fell, so he scooped me up into his arms and carried me the rest of the way. It was freaking hot that he could carry me, a six-foot-two man with a decent muscle mass—if I say so myself—as if I weighed nothing more than a baby. *Be still my beating heart—and tingling nether regions.*

Once at his secret beach, he lowered me to the cool sand and gave me one of his wicked smiles. Without saying a word, he began stripping me of my clothes slowly, an insanely arousing plucking that had me on fire in no time. "As much as I want to make love to you right now, do you think it's the wise thing to do? I mean, I can't believe I'm saying this, but I'm not sure I have enough energy to make you fly." It pained me to say those words, but it was true. I just wasn't strong enough yet. Having sex right now would probably kill me.

"This is just foreplay, Aiden," Fouchard said in a

low, sexy voice. He didn't bother to pull my under-wear down; he grabbed it at the seams and ripped it apart, a rare—but effective—show of how strong he really was. "Lie on the sand."

I obeyed, still not quite grasping where all of this was going. The damp sand welcomed my backside in an embrace, and I actually sighed in relief, immediately feeling the waves of energy transmitting from the gritty grains to my skin and beyond. I closed my eyes, only to open them almost immediately, startled by the cool kiss of sand on my torso. Naël was scooping large amounts of sand gently over me, creating an earthy cocoon around my whole body. It was bliss.

"Thank you, Naël," I managed to say, my eyes closing and all my senses in tune with Mother Earth.

"I expect payment later," he said, planting a kiss on my lips. "I am hoping you use some of that newly gathered energy to take me to cloud nine," he said in a playful voice.

I groaned as the sound of his deep voice caressed me. "Baby, you have no idea how high I'm going to take you." And I meant it. It was going to be epic.

THREE
WORDS OF MASS DESTRUCTION

FOR THE NEXT WEEK, I WAS MORE PARANOID THAN A doomsday conspiracy theorist. I sunbathed on my small ocean-facing balcony and gave up my evening strolls along the *paredão*. That got old really fast. I might not be the bravest of men, but fuck if I was going to cower forever behind walls. I needed my fresh air, the feel of the sand under the soles of my feet, the cool caress of salty water, and the whispers of the ocean breeze in my ears.

"I'm going to the beach today," I announced to no one in particular as I stood in the middle of my empty coffee shop with a broom in my hands. Both Fouchard and Cristina looked up at me in surprise. We had all joined forces to do a more thorough cleaning of the place, since Bicas R Us was closed on Mondays.

"Fuck the gods and their weapons of mass destruction. I need some sun and sand."

Fouchard half smiled. "We could always repeat that epic night after the attack," he said suggestively.

Hell, that would be awesome, but as epic as the aftermath of my sand cocoon recharge had been, I wanted to feel the sun on my face, arms, legs, and even my toes. "Tempting, but I'm tired of being scared." I was. I had moved to Portugal to put some distance between me and those in DC who wished me harm. I couldn't live in constant fear that they would hurt me or worse. I was not going to let this god or whatever it was ruin the great life I had built for myself in the small country by the sea.

"I'll go with you," said Fouchard, promptly dropping the rag he was using to clean the counters. "You shouldn't be alone."

I raised a hand, my palm facing him and Cristina, who seemed about to yell at me. "No, I'm a big boy and I can do this without a babysitter." My boyfriend's face grew somber. "No, Naël. I know you just want to protect me, but I did fine my whole life without a bodyguard." Minus some cuts and scrapes, millions of bruises, a near drowning, and a couple of broken ribs. I always bounced back.

"Is that what you think I am? Your fucking bodyguard?"

Shit, I had gone and done it again; I had said the wrong thing to the one person I loved the most.

I rushed to him, laying my hands on his arms. "I'm sorry I said that. I didn't mean it that way." I didn't. Not really. "I'm just frustrated and annoyed that trouble followed me here too." Fouchard's mouth was set into a thin, tight line, and his eyes half closed. He was royally pissed. "You know I love you and nothing makes me happier than lying in the sand beside you—well, maybe lying in bed doing the nasty, but I digress." My attempt at levity fell flat. He didn't look amused, a short, deep growl the only sound coming from him. "Come on, baby. I love you. You know that, right?"

Fouchard turned his back on me, grabbed his car keys from the counter, and in two long strides, he was at the door. "Call me when you need a babysitter." And he left.

"What the hell, Aiden? Why would you say something that stupid?" Cristina slapped me across the back of my head none too gently as per her usual. "The man loves you something fierce, and you go and say something like that? *Mas que parvo, homem.* Dumb, seriously dumb, man."

Cristina walked away to the other end of the room, tsking under her breath, and I hit the kitchen door in anger—not the satisfying move I had hoped, since it flapped a few times instead of slamming. "Fuck me."

"Is that an invitation?"

Holy Mother of God, if it wasn't Taz, doing one of her freaky sudden appearances.

I gave her the look of death. It didn't work; she still smiled at me as if I had told her she was the most beautiful woman in the world. "Go stuff a sausage, witch." *Nice, Aiden, a really smart and mature comeback.* "What do you want now?"

She giggled softly, a sound that didn't seem to suit her at all. "Apparently I'm here to fuck you, if your invitation still stands."

I literally growled, an honest-to-God pissed-off dog growl. "Stop messing with me, witch. I'm not in the mood."

She looked around the store as if searching for something. "Where's your main squeeze?" I blinked and clenched my jaw. She opened her mouth in sudden realization. "Oh, trouble in paradise then."

"What are you doing here?" I enunciated each word separately in case she couldn't understand me. Cristina was still oblivious to her presence, which told me Taz had concocted some sort of glamor around us.

Taz pulled out a chair and sat down, crossing her long legs and rocking a stiletto-heel-shod foot back and forth. "I have some information for you." For a moment, I forgot the hurt in my merman's eyes and focused on what the witch was saying. "There is someone who may be able to help you."

A little spark of hope ignited inside my chest. "Really? Who?"

"There is an oracle that may be able to give you the answers you seek." An oracle? Like the slightly mad ones in Greek tragedies? "He lives with the Capuchos in Sintra." Of course he did. Why was Sintra such a damned magic-infested place? "I can arrange for you to go stay with them for a while."

Wait! What? "Stay with them? Why would I do that? I can just go there and ask the oracle the question." Sintra was only thirty minutes or less from where I lived, a gorgeous *serra*, a mountain with its own microclimate very much favored by every magical being in Portugal.

"It's not that simple." Of course not. "The oracle is a bit…" She hesitated, looking for the right word. "He's not all there, if you know what I mean."

What the hell? She wanted me to trust a loon? "If he's crazy, then why should I even ask him anything? Come on, Taz, I've had quite a week, and I'm not in the mood for jokes."

Taz waved a hand in the air, biting her lower lip. "He's not crazy," she said. "He's ancient, some say as old as time, and his mind often wanders off."

I ran the palm of my hand over my face, groaning. "And why would I listen to an older-than-dirt madman? What can he possibly know that will be of any help at all?" My life just kept getting crazier and crazier. After a whole lifetime of seeing magicals for what they were even through their glamors, I found out I was one of them. Then some lunatic god from Hindu mythology decided to kill me and my boyfriend, and now I was being asked to put myself in the metaphorical hands of an unhinged prophet. Just peachy; my life had made a turn to clinical insanity.

The witch picked some invisible fluff from her bare legs. "He knows things no one else does. After centuries of gathering information about the mystical world, his mind is bursting at the seams with vital data. Think of him as a supercomputer whose memory is so full, it slows down its processing. It can still do it; it just takes a lot longer and freezes for periods of time."

I let out a bitter chuckle. "What happens when he gets the dreaded blue screen?" I asked, the sarcastic bite back in my voice. "Do we reboot him?"

Taz didn't even bat a lash. "Yes, the Brothers do it all the time." Was she joking? With Taz, you never knew. "All I have to do is make a phone call to our High Priestess, and she will arrange for you to stay with the Capuchos for a little while."

"I still don't understand why I must stay there." Annoyance and frustration had filled my chest with toxic gases, threatening to explode at any time. "Why don't they just call me when the oracle is lucid enough to talk to me?"

Taz jumped to her feet, teetering on shaky heels for an instant. "Because the monks don't have phones and his lucid moments are short and far between. There is zero chance that even if they could call you, his mind would still be clear by the time you got there." She slid her sunglasses over her nose. "Well, do I call her or not?"

I sighed loudly and deeply, hanging my head in surrender. In a world of crazies, you either joined them or went crazy yourself. "All right, call her. I will go see the fucking madman."

She clicked her tongue. "Oracle, Aiden. You really need to be more respectful of your elders." She sounded like a mom chiding her son. "Be a good boy and learn how to address your superiors."

I was just about ready to tell her where to stick my superiors when she vanished with a soft pop. "I hate when she does that." I groaned.

Cristina turned to me. "What was that?" She hadn't seen or heard any of my exchange with the witch, of course. Not sure why Taz had chosen to hide from her, considering Cristina knew her and was well aware of the magical world around her. Being a human who had been allegedly kidnapped by the Fae as a child, she was unruffled by the world I had spent a lifetime trying to avoid.

"Taz was here." I watched as her eyes rounded to the shape of saucers and her brow wrinkled. "Don't ask. She wants me to do something I don't want to do."

My friend moved to another table. "Then don't do it." Yes, I wished it was that simple, but unfortunately nothing dealing with the magical world was ever easy.

"She *is* trying to help," I admitted, however reluctantly. It was almost physically painful for me to do so; I was so much more comfortable when despising all magicals. But I couldn't do that anymore, could I? I was in love with a merman, and Taz, despite her irritating penchant to pop in unannounced and suggest irritating things, had done nothing but help me since day one. I had to be fair and give credit where credit was due: not every magical creature was an asshole. "Have you ever heard of the Capuchos?"

She lifted her head, mildly interested. "The monks? Yes, their monastery is in Sintra." She scratched the back of her head. "I could never understand why they call it a convent when there were never any nuns there. Maybe they were an order of transsexual monks." *What?* Cristina's mind took her to unexpected places sometimes. She resumed her wiping. "Why? Are you planning a visit?"

"Kind of. Why did you use past tense?" I pulled a chair and sat down, suddenly exhausted. A trip to the beach was definitely in order.

Cristina strode to the counter and dropped the rag before turning to me. "Because they don't exist anymore. The *convent* has been deserted for a long time. It's a tourist attraction now."

That made no sense whatsoever. The witch had just talked to me about these monks as if they were still roaming the halls of the monastery. "Taz wants me to go talk to an oracle there," I said, feeling stupid for uttering those words out loud. "She seemed to think the monks are still there."

She frowned, lifted a hand to her head, and made little circles in the air with her amber finger. "Taz *é maluca*, crazy." She was probably not too far from the truth, but I suspected there was more to the story. "I like her." Of course, she would.

Cristina went to the kitchen to rinse off all the cleaning rags, and I sat in silence, ruminating over the events of the last hour—and that's when it hit me. I'd just had my first fight with my boyfriend. I didn't like the way it felt, the way his eyes had reflected how much he was hurt by my comments. I didn't like myself much at that moment. I had hurt the one person who loved me, possibly the *only* person in the whole wide world who truly loved me.

I picked up the phone and called him. The phone

rang for a long time, voicemail the only one picking up. I didn't want to leave a message. I wanted to talk to him, to hear his deep growling voice and to caress him with mine. But after many tries, I finally got the message: he wasn't going to pick up, he didn't want to talk to the prick who had hurt him. So I left a message. "Naël, please talk to me. I love you, and I'm so sorry I said what I said. I've been alone for too long and I'm not used…." My voice trailed off. What? What was I not used to? Being loved? Loving someone? Accepting that there was someone who could care for the person I myself found so hard to love? "Call me, Naël, please. I'm so sorry. I love you."

I wished I could retract my words and swallow them, make them dissolve inside me, but I couldn't. That was the thing about words—they often hurt more than anything else, because a bruise eventually fades away but the meaning behind a word takes residence in your memory, never to leave again. Words had power, and I had used them against the wrong person. What if Fouchard would never forgive me? Had I uttered the words that would destroy the love of my life?

FOUR
BREAKING UP IS HARD TO DO

After a million phone calls, give or take a few, Fouchard was still not picking up and my heart was breaking apart, or so it felt. I had never been in a real relationship or cared enough for anyone before, so I was lost as to what to do next. How did I fix it? Could it be fixed at all? I had done the cheesy thing and sent him a dozen roses, a singing telegram, a variety of old-fashioned snail-mail letters in the last two weeks. Nothing. Total radio silence. It was breaking me; the fight with my love was breaking the man Fouchard had pieced together from the scattered shards I was after years of loneliness.

"Why don't you try to talk to Vee?" Cristina suggested after a particularly rough day. I had moped around the coffee shop, being more of a nuisance than help, head in the dark clouds and eyes forever seeking my merman. "She's coming to spend some time with me tonight. You can come over and see her. She's been asking about you."

At least someone still cared enough to ask if I was alive or dead. I loved Vee, Fouchard's little mermaid sister and a force of nature in a tiny body. Vee and I had bonded before and definitely after I had rescued her from the hands of Pescado, the demented merman killer who had been hellbent on "cleansing" the magical bloodlines. She knew her brother better than anyone else. Maybe she knew what I could do to make him forgive me.

"Yes, I'll come by after closing," I said over the whistling sound of the espresso machine. "Save me some popcorn."

"Popcorn?" Cristina sounded outraged. "Popcorn is for wimps. Girls go for the big guns. We binge on chocolate and ice cream."

I laughed, amused by the intensity of her words. "Okay then, save me some chocolate. The dark kind." I winked at her, and she made a face at me. Hanging out with an eleven-year-old was rubbing off on her.

It was a slow day, an unusual occurrence this time of the year when the beaches were bursting at the seams with tourists and locals. But the day had dawned cloudy and windy, sending sand flying against beachgoers, tiny torpedoes that lived up to their origins as rocks. The first few brave—or maybe foolish

—bathers of the day had quickly run from the beach as umbrellas flew and the flying grains battered their skin. Only a handful of courageous souls remained, wrapped in towels, with hats on their heads as if expecting the weather to take a sudden turn for the better. Experience told me the wind was here to stay.

Even though money was not being made, I was enjoying the lull. I had brought a book and, after brewing a *bica*, I sat at one of the tables by the window, immersing myself in someone else's problems, a sad attempt at forgetting my own. Cristina was finishing up in the kitchen and then heading out. I had given her a half day off so she could go on a date with Silva. The very thought gave me stomach cramps. I still was having a lot of trouble dealing with the idea of her dating a warlock, but she was determined. Hopefully it was a lust thing, not a love affair; I'd hate to see my only friend's heart broken by an unscrupulous magical. Not that I knew for sure he was a cad, but he was a warlock, old as dirt and jaded. Enough said.

"Don't look now," I heard Cristina say. Absorbed in the story I was reading, I hadn't noticed her coming. I took my eyes from the book and looked at her. "The friendly neighborhood witch is coming."

I followed her gaze outdoors and was shocked to see Taz, in beach clothes and a sun hat with a huge brim, walking toward the shop. She always just appeared out of nowhere. I didn't think I had ever seen her actually walking into my coffee shop. Hell had frozen over.

"You can walk?" I exclaimed as soon as she came through the door. "Where's your broom?"

Taz removed her hat and sunglasses, her curly hair pinned up in a messy bun. "You really should have been a comedian, Aiden. It's a glorious day, so I wanted to walk instead."

I squinted in disbelief. "Gorgeous day? It's cloudy and windy," I said, stealing a glance outside. "What are you? Mary Poppins?"

She sat on the chair facing me and laid her hat on the small table, effectively covering it completely. "I absolutely adore wind," she said, not a note of sarcasm in her voice. "So do the banshees. I saw a few on my way here." *Lovely*. Taz looked at Cristina, who was gathering her belongings. "Oh hi, Cristina. Leaving so soon?"

Cristina smiled at her. "I have a date." She slipped one arm through the backpack's straps.

"Ooh, with the hunky warlock?" Women. Even witches couldn't resist the hint of romance. "He is so freaking hot. Lucky devil, you are."

"I'm not arguing," Cristina said, the innuendo in her words making me cringe. "Tó is delicious in so many ways." *Please, someone plug my ears*. Cristina glanced at me and laughed. "You're just jealous he's not gay, Aiden."

I opened my mouth and slapped the top of the table with both hands. "I may throw up," I said, pretending to gag. "I wouldn't touch that with a ten-foot pole."

Cristina laughed again and headed to the door. "I'm not talking about that kind of pole, Aiden." Naughty girl. "See you later then? Nine-ish?" I nodded, and she opened the front door. "Bye, Taz, I will tell Tó you said hi." And she left.

Taz was wearing a smile that turned a single corner of her lips upward. "You really don't like the High Warlock, do you?"

That much was obvious, so I didn't answer, choosing instead to shrug and change the subject. "Do you have news for me or just decided to come bug the mystery magical a bit more?" It goaded me knowing I was one of *them* but not knowing what species.

The witch cleared her throat. "As much as I love teasing you, my darling Aiden, I do indeed have news for you." It was about time. Two weeks without Fouchard by my side made it an excruciatingly long time. "We secured you a place with the monks at the convent."

"For when?" I wasn't looking forward to being away from my business for any amount of time, but a part of me thought that if maybe I was focusing on something else, I may be able to live without the agonizing memory of my fight with Fouchard. "And how long will it be?"

Taz snapped her fingers, and a *bica* popped into existence on the table before her. I winced and looked around, checking to see if any of my customers had seen it, but there was not a soul around. "There's no telling how long, Aiden. However long it takes," she said, and my stomach lurched. Holy Mother of God, what was I getting myself into this time? "As to when, they are expecting you this weekend." That soon? It left me with only one day to prepare. "Bring comfy clothes, blankets, sleeping bag, and books."

"They don't have a room for me?" I was not too fond of camping unless I had my boyfriend's hot body against me.

"They have a room but no linen. Or bed, not really." What kind of joint did these monks run? "Also no internet, electricity, or TV, and it does get cold, so bring some warm clothes too." Thank goodness I was a reader, or there would be a very good chance of me dying of boredom. "Can Fouchard take you there?"

My heart actually contracted in my chest at the sound of his name. God, I missed him. "He's not talking to me," I admitted and immediately regretted it. "It's just a lover's spat. We'll be fine, but in the meantime, I don't have a ride unless Cristina can take me."

Taz stood up and placed the hat back on her head. With large sunglasses and that humongous hat, she looked like a Hollywood star from yesteryear. "We'll figure something out." She picked up the small espresso cup and downed its contents in one gulp. "Sweetheart, take some free advice from me: kiss and make up with that man of yours. He's a rare one." For once, I actually agreed with her. She grabbed her big beach bag and left through the door like a normal human being.

I closed early and sat in the empty coffee shop for a couple hours just staring into space, thinking of a way to effectively apologize to Naël. Obviously I had been doing a seriously poor job, since he wouldn't even answer my calls.

At seven on the dot, I walked the few blocks to Cristina's apartment. Vee opened the door, and her freckled brown face lit up immediately. "Aiden," she squealed, jumping and hanging from my neck. "Where have you been?"

I took a few steps inside the apartment, wearing her as a necklace, and closed the door behind us. Cristina was in the kitchen scooping ice cream into large bowls. Cristina's apartment was tiny, basically a large room separated from the small kitchen by a high counter and a separate bedroom and bathroom. She waved at me with the scoop, and several chunks of ice cream flew around her. She cussed as I set my young friend down.

"You haven't shown up in weeks." Two weeks, two days, and three hours, to be precise, but who's counting? "Naël misses you. He has gone back to being a cranky old merman." Did he really miss me or was she just being nice? "Why haven't you called?"

I sat on the couch and she sat beside me. "I did, Vee, many times, but he won't call back." She cocked her head in a birdlike movement. "We had a fight, and he won't forgive me."

"That's silly," she said, her small lips puckered into a frown. "You guys love each other. What did you say to him?"

I opened my fucking mouth and vomited something stupid. I couldn't tell her that.

Cristina saved me from having to answer. "Ice cream for you too, Aiden?"

I nodded, acting a lot more enthusiastic than I felt. "I'm going away for a few days." I raised my eyes to my friend, hoping she could read between the lines. She knew about the monk thing. "I will be visiting an old friend." *You have no clue how old.* "Can you give your brother a message for me, Vee?"

Vee nodded, her wild, kinky curls bouncing. "Sure. What do you want me to tell him?"

I thought for a moment, not sure how to put it.

"Tell him I followed Taz's advice and I will be visiting my very, very old friend in Sintra." Hopefully he would be piqued enough to ask the witch what I meant by that. "That I love him and miss him something awful." One hundred percent true. "I haven't slept properly since our fight, and I am so sorry for hurting his feelings. Tell him I'm a—" I stopped just before uttering the word *dick*. "I'm an idiot, and I want him back. Can you tell him all that?"

"Of course, word for word. I have a very good memory," she said, her green eyes twinkling like stars and two fingers tapping her temple. "I will do my best, Aiden. I miss you too." She wrapped her arms around my neck again and kissed my cheek. "You're part of the family now, and I don't want to lose you." I didn't want to lose her either. I especially didn't want to lose her beautiful brother. Not because he was beautiful and strong and made my pants shrink with only a look, but because our souls were connected. Our hearts had been beating in unison for months now, and I couldn't lose that, the only thing in the world that I could call home.

FIVE

MONKS AND TOILET BOWLS

"Are you sure we're in the right place?" Cristina asked, sticking her head out of the driver-side window. We both stared at the thick wall of trees covering what was supposed to be the entrance to the Capuchos Convent. "Don't convents normally consist of at least one building?"

I nodded, not sure what to think. I had heard about this place but had never visited, mostly because —well, you guessed it, it was located in magic central, Sintra. Now that we were here, I couldn't find any sign of life anywhere.

"I thought that maybe you could see something that I couldn't," said Cristina, scratching her head. "Like a glamor or something."

I shook my head. "No glamor that I can see." Making a decision, I opened the door and stepped out of the car, stretching the kinks out of my back. "Might as well go check it out."

Cristina joined me, and we both headed to where the entrance to this convent should have been. Taz had called me earlier to tell me not to go until after closing and avoid the throngs of tourists that always swarmed the area. If this was indeed the place, it was empty of anything living, not a single person in sight.

"How do you get in?" Cristina said. "There's hardly any space between the trees and the bushes. Don't tourist attractions normally have a ticket booth of sorts and a gate?"

It was baffling, but as I reached out to touch one of the bushes, the branches trembled and moved apart to reveal a path beyond. "Fuck. Magic." I felt it in my body like ants crawling on me, goose bumps covering my skin. We both stared at the long path leading to a few stone steps and into a humble building, too far off for me to be able to see in detail.

Cristina held my arm. "Do you want me to come with you?" I did, but I knew she shouldn't. I was the one who had been invited, and magicals didn't take kindly to intruders.

I shook my head again. "No, you better go home. Let's get my bag from the car," I mumbled, pissed off at myself for feeling this anxious about a bunch of monks and a crazy oracle.

We collected my bag from the trunk of the car

and walked back to where the greenery had opened into a path. I kissed her cheek, and she gave me a hug, holding on to me longer than necessary. "Do you want me to call Naël?" she whispered in my ear.

I pulled myself away from her. "No. I have done everything I could to apologize. Now it's up to him, I guess." I gave her a quick hug again. "You take care of the coffee shop, and if you need help, call someone you trust. I don't know how long this is going to take."

Cristina looked at me, her lips trembling a bit as if not sure whether to smile or cry. "You be careful, Aiden." I gave her a nod and walked into the pathway. When I turned around to wave at my friend, the natural gate had closed behind me. "Be careful." Cristina's voice reached me, muffled and distant. I had no choice now but to walk to the building at the end of the path.

No one seemed to be around, and even the birds had stopped singing. There was indeed some kind of glamor over this place, a sort of shield that kept the outside world out of range. I had never seen or felt anything like it and was not too excited about it. I walked inside the building, a small space illuminated by candles in wall sconces. In front of me there was a door with a skull and crossbones leering down on me. Creepy. Not sure of what to do or where to go, I headed to an opening on the right from which I could see flickering light and hear a humming of sorts. I ducked my head to go through the squat doorway and found myself inside a small chapel with walls covered in white and blue tile and a simple empty niche on the rock wall.

I sighed loudly. The place was empty too. Where the hell were all these monks I was supposed to be meeting? The humming I had heard before was still vibrating in my ears, annoying and disconcerting since I couldn't find its source. *Damn magicals.* Nothing was ever straightforward with them. "Where are you? You invited me, the least you can do is show up." Did the monks even speak English? An irrational panic took over me. Hell, I didn't speak Portuguese, save a few words and phrases. I really needed to learn it.

"Patience, young one," a throaty voice said behind me. Startled, I turned around only to find more empty space. "Here we worship peace and the slow passage of time."

I swallowed but couldn't stop myself from saying, "News flash, whoever you are, time does not slow down for anyone, and I'm not getting any younger standing here waiting for you to show yourself."

The air wavered, and the hooded figure of a monk appeared. He was dressed in a brown habit with an equally brown scapular connected to a large cowl. A belt made of what looked like thick rope was tied loosely around the waist. Hidden under the hood, his face was hard to discern in the dimness of the chapel.

"Welcome to our sanctuary," the man said, his croaky voice spilling from the darkness of his cowl. "My name is Brother John, Aiden. I trust you had a safe, pleasant trip here."

It wasn't as if I had traveled from far away. I nodded, and the Brother took one hand from its hiding place within the folds of the scapular and pointed toward the door. "I will show you to your quarters."

I bit my tongue so I wouldn't ask him to remove the mysterious cowl from his head and followed him. I looked at his feet as we made our way through the main hall with its creepy death door. He walked slowly but steadily on sandal-shod feet that seemed to not quite touch the floor. I shook my head, trying to dismiss the fancies of my imagination. *He's just a man in an ugly, scratchy tunic.*

A man who could materialize out of nothing. Magic saturated the air. I could feel it, smell it, over-powering and heavily perfumed like a lily-packed funeral home. I stuffed my hands in my pockets to stop them from trembling. When had I become this cowardly?

The monk continued his ghostly journey into a church, a humble space that contrasted strongly with its luxurious marble altar. The monk stopped in front of the altar to genuflect briefly and bless himself before continuing toward a small exit door to the side. I didn't know what to think so I decided to enjoy the tour. Inside the small hallway between the church and the next space, a dark corridor slanted downward. Why were we going underground?

"I totally respect your reverence for the dead, but I am a bit squeamish around rotten flesh." I was doing my nervous-talking thing again, trying to fill the oppressive silence with something less threatening. "So I hope you're not taking me to the catacombs."

"We don't have any dead buried here," the monk said, not slowing down his pace down the tunnel. Darkness enveloped us as we proceeded deeper into the ground, the earthy smell of dirt, rocks, and mois-ture assailing my nostrils. "We're walking through the Brothers' cells. Please, keep silent while we cross them."

It was a narrow corridor that looked like it had been carved directly from the rocks. Squat and narrow doorways placed at intervals opened into equally small cells divested of any comforts or light other than a flickering candle. This was where these monks slept? My back hurt just thinking about sleeping on that rocky floor. After a moment or two, we were going uphill and toward a space that promised more light. As soon as we went over a large stone step, the air became fresher and lighter, and my lungs almost quivered in delight. At the top of the steps there was another doorway, this time normal-sized. Brother John opened the door and invited me in.

"This will be your lodgings while you're with us," he explained, his face still annoyingly hidden inside the cowl. He pointed down the dark corridor. "The cell has direct access to the small cloister and the latrine house." What? Latrine? That didn't sound very modern or terribly comfortable and hygienic.

I ducked slightly under the doorway and entered a small room bare of any decoration other than a small niche on the wall that housed the image of a saint. A rudimentary mattress covered most of the floor space. The room was far from comfortable, but at least it had a window that would offer natural light during the day. The walls were covered in something porous the color of light honey. Curious, I reached out and touched it. It was cork, a natural insulator widely used in Portugal.

"I trust you'll be comfortable here." Brother John turned to leave.

"Wait. Is that it? You are just going to leave me here for the night?" I asked in a panic. "When do I see the Oracle?"

The monk waved a hand in the air. "Patience. Tomorrow I will show you the rest of the convent and tell you about Brother Serafim," he said in an irritatingly calm voice. "Rest and let fate take the reins."

No, absolutely not. Fate was a fickle and cruel mistress, and I refused to trust her. "What if I need something during the night?" Like being rescued from a ghost or maybe even a zombie. The place was spooky enough.

"Just call me, and I will come." Was he going to sleep outside my room? Or did he have some kind of magic sense of hearing that allowed him to hear me call him from afar? He stepped outside the room. "Goodnight, and sleep with the angels." I would definitely not sleep with anything remotely dead.

I watched him close the door and leave me alone in that dreary space, the light of the candles projecting eerie shapes onto the walls and low ceiling. I don't think I moved at all for a while, too overwhelmed by the silence and darkness of the place. The candle burning on the windowsill offered little comfort, as the shadows it created stretched and wavered along the walls, ghostly figures that only added more anxiety to my already about to explode nervous system. I shook my head and lowered my backpack and sleeping bag to the mattress, trying to keep my body and mind busy and away from unsettling thoughts.

As I rolled out the sleeping bag over what passed for a bed, my thoughts roamed to my boyfriend, wherever he was. God, I missed him so much. Bile climbed my throat to cover my tongue. Would he ever forgive me for being such an asshole to him? How could I redeem myself if he wouldn't even talk to me? The sleeping bag I had was not the same one we had made love in for the first time, but it still brought back sweet and toe-curling memories. I placed the few bottles of water I had brought with me on the makeshift table, a single slab of rock jutting out from the wall, and threw a couple of books on the bed. Resigned to the fact I would have to spend the night in that dreary room, I stretched out on the sleeping bag, ready to read for a while.

I must have dozed off, but I woke up with the horrifying realization that I needed to go to the bathroom. The monk had mentioned latrines. What exactly did he mean by that? I tried to hold it in, but my bladder wouldn't listen to reason, so I got up and decided to risk a trip down the corridor to where the monk had pointed earlier.

The narrow corridor was lit by candles in sconces along the wall and ended in a room I expected to be the bathroom. When I emerged on the other side of the door, it became clear to me that the word "bathroom" was not quite adequate for what I was looking at. The chamber was much larger than any of the ones I had seen on the way to my room. It looked as if it was round in shape and, just like the corridor, lit by a profusion of candles. On the facing wall to the right there was a weird structure that resembled a small house with a couple of wide troughs in front. On the left there was a wooden bench that ran the length of the wall. I approached, an uncomfortable feeling in my chest. That couldn't be the latrines, could it?

"Holy Mother of God," I exclaimed when I spotted the holes cut out from the bench seat. It *was* the latrines. I had to give it to the monks; this was definitely very organic and earth-friendly, toilets that were nothing but shitholes. Literally. At least it didn't smell too bad—maybe I should ask them for whatever they used as deodorizer. I thanked the heavens that I didn't have to go number two, since the idea of fitting my bare ass in those dark holes was daunting. Who knew what lurked beneath them? I did my business as fast as I could and rushed to my room.

The crazy Oracle better make it worth my staying in this weird, spooky house of toilet horrors.

SIX

A CONVENT TAIL

MY STOMACH HAD BEEN SINGING THE FEED-ME SONG for at least an hour. I couldn't say how long I'd slept but knew it hadn't been enough. Thankfully there were no mirrors in the room, so I didn't have to flinch at the unavoidable dark circles around my eyes. One of my foster moms used to say I looked like a raccoon with a hangover every time I didn't get my beauty sleep. My energy was at an all-time low, it seemed, so after chancing another quick trip to the bathroom from hell, I slipped through a small opening in the corridor into a small yard dominated by a large tree, bushes, and grass. I stretched under the tree, right over its roots, and dug my fingers into the soil, desperate to absorb some earthy energy. I felt better almost immediately and was carried away into slumber as my body, now recharged, shook off all the anxieties of the previous night.

A familiar voice tore me from the delicious dream I was having. "Aiden, you're not dead, are you?" Brother John stood beside me, his bulky body casting a wide shadow over me. I groaned in protest. "Oh good, you're still alive." Was the monk making jokes? "I was hoping you'd join us for breakfast."

At the hint of food in my immediate future, I wasted no time and jumped to my feet—a bit too fast. My head swam, and I braced myself against the trunk of the tree for support. "Head rush." I waited for the world to stop moving and settle before saying anything else. "Thank you, Brother. I'd love to have some breakfast."

Brother John was still hiding his face in the shadows of his cowl when he pointed in the direction of my room. "This way, Aiden. I expect you slept well." *Like hell I did.* "And that our lovely *sobreiro* was able to share some of its energy with you." So he knew about my weird connection with the elements. I wondered who had told him, considering that even Taz was not aware of it. At least, I didn't think she was.

I nodded and followed him past my room and into another narrow entrance just ahead. Brother John lowered his cowl, and I had my first view of what he really looked like. He didn't look like a monk—at least not the way books and movies depicted them. His skin was the color and texture of bark from the cork oak tree that grew profusely in my adopted country, with small sky-blue eyes and thick brown hair tied at the back of his head in a short ponytail. He smiled at me, and I couldn't help it—I smiled back. His face was as amiable as it was rough.

I walked in behind him and found myself faced with a handful of other monks, all dressed in the obligatory brown habit, sitting around a large slab of stone that served as a table.

"Please, sit with us." A younger man stood up and offered me a seat next to him. Prejudiced by years of Hollywood movies, I was in awe of how different they all looked. Some had beautiful faces with smooth and unblemished skin; others looked like prunes that had been in the sun for far too long. A few had long hair, while others were either bald or close to being bald. None had the look I had expected from a monk—you know, the bald spot at the back of their head, chubby, and homely.

I sat on the hard, cold stone bench and feasted my eyes on the delicious-looking array of food covering the rustic table. These monks may live in humble lodgings, but they obviously knew how to cook for and feed themselves well. Following the example of the others, I packed my wooden plate high with food and stuffed myself until I thought I may explode. After I finished eating, I needed to move to help with digestion, but I wasn't sure it would be acceptable to leave the table before the others. Thankfully, they all saved me from having to ask, because one by one they stood up, said their farewells, and departed from the refectory. Only Brother John was left.

"Is the Oracle ready to talk to me?" I asked, a little less anxious to get the hell out of there after that amazing meal but still unwilling to linger longer than I had to.

The monk shook his head. "Unfortunately, Brother Serafim is still in a meditative state." Translation: out of his freaking mind. "I invite you to enjoy the grounds. The convent is beautiful and one with nature. I noticed how you strengthen yourself with the elements." Sharp. I had been there for less than twelve hours, and he had already picked up on what had taken me years to notice. "Exploring this place should fill you with plenty of energy." Subtly, he guided me to the door.

"Is there anything I should know?"

"After nine, the wards we have over the convent shift," the monk explained. "The guests and some of the employees who are not magical will be able to see you but not us. I must ask you to place all your goods in the hidden compartment of your room so the visitors won't trip over them. You will still be able to see us, but I suggest you don't address us unless there isn't anyone else around or you will be deemed insane by the onlookers."

Not that that would be a first for me.

My host showed me around the grounds for a while and then guided me back to my room so I could hide my stuff before the opening. He was just about to leave when he turned around one last time to say, "Oh, and during the day there are modern bathrooms between the entrance to the monastery and the ticket booth close to the parking lot."

"I didn't see any parking lot when we came in. Or bathrooms." Brother John winked. Fuck, those were some serious glamors they had over the convent. *Color me impressed.* Even if I was not too fond of magic.

Delighted with the idea I wouldn't have to sit on what passed for toilets in the convent, I scampered off shortly after I squeezed my backpack into the hidden enclosure behind the image of the saint and left my bedroll still spread on the mattress, since no one would trip over that.

Brother John had not been lying. The grounds were beautiful, with lush vegetation and tons of nooks and crannies with interesting pieces of architecture. My favorite was by far the church building, which had been camouflaged by a giant rock. The whole place would be a paradise for any modern conservationist, with its organic structure. This convent was one with nature, and even though I loved modern comforts, it fit me like a glove—then again, I would never be able to live in a place where the toilets looked like some sort of gateway to hell. I would stick to my beachfront living instead.

Wandering around all day was a strange, other-worldly experience. Tourists soon began flooding in and filling the quiet spaces with careless chatter and movement. I circulated among them, listening and observing, and awed by the fact that the monks, all ten or so of them, walked side by side with the regulars without being seen. The monks were experts at avoiding close encounters with the tourists, ducking and dodging every time it was necessary. For a few hours I forgot why I was there and just enjoyed the surge of energy the place offered me.

By closing time I felt stronger, calmer, and more focused. Apparently the Convento dos Capuchos was a magnificently efficient charger for my batteries. Who would have thought?

After the tourists and the cleaning crew were gone, I watched as the greenery closed behind them, isolating the convent from the outside world once more. Silence hugged me like a warm blanket on a cold day. I sighed. The only thing missing was my merman. Was he still mad at me? Would he ever forgive me?

I ate another sumptuous meal with the monks and retired to my room, determined to sleep better. Brother John had hinted that I may be a little ripe, so I headed to the room of horrors with a towel I had brought and a piece of soap. The place was deserted as usual, but I knew where the washing basins were. One of the monks had explained that the troughs by the strange mini house that turned out to be a cistern were bathing tubs. One was used for small ablutions and the bigger one for full baths. I undressed, dropping all my clothes into a pile on the stone floor, and dipped my hand in the water.

"Fuck. It's cold." I should have known; everything in Sintra was always several degrees cooler than its surrounding areas. There was no avoiding it. Climbing over the high edge of the tub, I swung my legs inside, my skin instantly puckering into goose bumps as my legs went underwater. I took a deep breath and, like ripping off a Band-Aid, allowed myself to slide all the way in until my head was underwater.

"Fuck, fuck, fuck." The shock of the icy water on my body was intense but invigorating at the same time. I wasted no time and lathered myself as fast as I could, dunked my hair in again, and shook off the excess water like a dog. Shivering, I got out of the tub and towel-dried my hair, my upper body, and was just about to focus on my lower regions when a voice just about gave me a heart attack.

"I'll be glad to help you with that."

I turned around so fast, I saw stars. Of course it may have been because of what my eyes saw; my lovely merman was standing just behind me, tall and menacing as usual and hot as hell. The cold left me, and my exposed skin tingled with a comforting heat. Fouchard lifted the corner of his lips in a half smile.

"Well, do you need any help?"

I almost dropped the towel, but instead I took two hesitant steps toward him. "Are you really here?" This place was weird. I might have been hallucinating. "I'm not dreaming?"

Fouchard smiled full blast then, his white, perfectly aligned teeth glittering in the semidarkness. "Yes, it's me."

"You're not mad at me anymore?" I dared not dream for fear of more heartbreak. I yearned for his forgiveness like I craved oxygen or the heat of the sun. "Because I *am* sorry, Naël, I'm so very sorry. I was a dick, and you have the right to hate me. I didn't mean it the way it came out, I just—"

Taking a wide step in my direction, he enveloped me with his arms and shut me up with a fierce kiss. Even though I was naked, warmth ran through my body like an electric current. My hands, still holding the towel, were stuck between us as he squeezed me in his arms, his lips and tongue playing with mine. I moaned, and he pulled us apart.

"What are you doing here, Naël? Did the monks let you in?" Not that it was important; the main thing was he was indeed there within touching distance and setting me on fire as he always did. "Did you forgive me, or are you still pissed at me?"

Fouchard threw his head back, his deep, throaty laugh echoing in the bathhouse. "If you give me the chance, I will show you how much I forgive you." The wicked man had done it again. With not much more than words and a kiss, he had me hard as a rock. He lowered his eyes to my favorite body part and smiled. "Shall we retire to your room?"

Shit, he could explain how he had managed to infiltrate the convent later. I grabbed his hand and pulled him out of the hellish bathroom and all the way through the short corridor to my room. As soon as we were inside and the door was closed behind us, I dropped the wet towel and latched my lips on his again. It had only been a couple weeks, but it felt as if I hadn't tasted him in years.

"I missed you, Naël," I whispered into his mouth, my hands sneaking under his shirt to touch the hard ridges of the muscles on his back.

Fouchard shrugged his T-shirt off, and I shivered when my skin was in direct contact with his. "I missed you too, Aiden. Let's not fight anymore."

I attacked the zipper of his jeans with enthusiasm. "Promise me one thing, Naël," I said, making him tremble as I pulled down his pants, grazing my fingers against his skin. "Don't ever believe what comes out of my mouth when I'm upset. I usually don't mean it." I groaned, my hand wrapping around the length of him. "Fuck, Naël, you feel good."

Fouchard pushed me backward until I was pinned between him and the wall. In that position, the expression "stuck between a rock and a hard place" took on a totally different meaning. "You ain't seen nothing yet," he murmured, a promise in his voice.

"Show me then," I dared him, nibbling on his lower lip as he pressed my lower body against his. "Show me what you can do."

I had no doubt that he would.

It was probably blasphemous to do the dirty in a convent, but I was beyond caring. I hadn't seen Fouchard and had carried around the fear he wouldn't forgive me for more than two weeks. I was not yearning for my beautiful merrow; I was ravenous.

Fouchard grazed his teeth along the side of my neck as I tilted my head to the side to give him easier access. I had a hand cupped on the back of his neck, and the other wandered along his hard biceps and strong shoulders. I wanted to drink him in with my eyes, my hands, my mouth. He captured my lips with his one more time, running his tongue along the outline of my mouth and making me shiver. I suckled on his tongue, thirsty for his taste, that heady mixture of sunshine and ocean soaking and charging me as a bolt of energy. He moaned, and I deepened my kiss, my hands traveling to his firm butt. With my hands flattened against his ass, I pulled him closer, the front of our bodies fusing together, no space in between, two made one.

"I love you, Aiden," he whispered, peppering kisses on my face, my nose, the corners of my mouth.

He was as hard as me, but fuck if I was going to hurry. I wanted to make it last—a very unusual occurrence for me. I normally went for the sprint rather than the marathon. But with Fouchard, all my rules and habits had been broken, replaced by a need so intense it had slowed down time itself—just as it also sped it up. I guess that's what love was, a contradiction in terms, a paradox that obliterated everything else.

I pushed him roughly toward the bed. He fell back on the mattress, making me cringe a little. That bed was not soft. I hoped he wasn't hurt. His wicked smile confirmed he was fine—oh, so fine as he sprawled on the sleeping bag, his body language spelling an invitation. No, a dare. Not needing another invite, I stretched myself over him, shivering as each inch of my skin touched his, slowly and sensually. We both groaned at the same time as I began kissing him again —starting with his lips and slowly making my way down, lingering over his sexy pecs, down to his abs, and then to the part of him that could always send me into fits of ecstasy. I caressed him with my tongue, running it along his length from top to bottom and back again. His velvety skin tingled against my tongue and lips, sending waves of electricity to the rest of my body. I loved this man with every fiber of my body and soul.

"Stop teasing, Aiden," my boyfriend said, desire thick in his voice.

He arched his back to look at me, and our eyes locked. He made a sound, a deep, throaty growl that left me breathless. I intensified my ministrations, and he groaned again, placing a hand behind my head and pulling me closer. His pulsing quickened my desire, the urgency to make him see the stars and then make my own journey there. I slipped a hand behind him and squeezed his butt, my fingers edging between his cheeks, teasing.

A muffled whimper told me he was ready. "Do you have lube?" he asked, panting in that sexy way of his.

I smiled and rolled off the bed for a moment to rummage in my backpack. "Have we met?" I waved a tube of lubricant before returning to him. "I pride myself at being prepared for every situation."

Fouchard laughed out loud and grabbed the hand that held the tube. "You're an idiot." I had missed his sweet insults. "But a lovable one." He took the lube from my hand and lost no time slathering a generous amount on my arousal, almost bringing me to the brink. "Careful there, stud," he teased. "Don't want to spill that seed before you're inside me."

I feigned outrage, and placing my hands on his knees, I parted his legs as wide as they'd go. A thought crossed my mind as I devoured him with my eyes. "How do you make love when you're in your aqua form? Is there some strange fissure in your tail?" Was it terrible of me that the idea turned me on even more?

Fouchard smirked. "Not much sex when in aqua form," he answered, his eyes roaming my lower body, oozing hunger, a predator eying his prey—his very willing and excited prey. "To have sex, we prefer to be in our land form. Remember, we are not fish. In fact, we are more human than anything else."

"I don't care what you are," I whispered, my eyes hooded as I poured more lube on my fingers and began preparing him, drawing a low moan from his lips. "I love every inch of you, and I never, ever want to fight with you again."

Nothing could be more heavenly than the feeling of utter and complete union with the man I loved as I buried myself in him, bookending him with my arms and bracing myself on my hands. The pressure in my groin grew to impossible heights, and I whispered his name as I started rocking back and forth inside him, a wave-like movement that made me think of the ocean where my love came from and where he would always wander to. Making love to him was much like absorbing energy from the salty waters or the wet, warm sand: glorious and invigorating.

I exploded, my head thrown backward as my hips arched forward, tightening our connection. He was right behind me, a tone of ecstasy in his low growl. I felt his warm seed run down my abs to where we were still connected and mingle with mine. I exhaled loudly and collapsed on top of him.

"I love you, Naël," I whispered, my lips against the flat of his shoulder. "I love the way you make me feel."

I love the way you make me like myself, make me feel relevant and wanted. I wouldn't voice those feelings, but they were there nevertheless. Growing up in foster homes—some better than others—without a single memory of my early childhood or my parents had made me feel unwanted, empty, a floating piece of driftwood, aimless and useless. Fouchard changed all that, and I still often woke up thinking I had dreamed the whole thing, that my merman was nothing but a figment of my imagination.

Fouchard flipped me off him so we were now lying on our sides, facing each other. He kissed my forehead and then brushed his soft lips down my nose before kissing my mouth, a gentle, loving kiss that melted my heart. "I love you too, fool."

We fell asleep in each other's arms, unaware of the cold bite of the stone around us and the hardness of the mattress beneath us, our hearts beating in harmony, our bodies fused against each other. It was the best sleep I ever had.

SEVEN

MONKS, ORACLES, AND MERMEN, OH MY!

WHEN BROTHER JOHN CAME TO WAKE ME UP THE next morning, unceremoniously entering the room without a knock, he didn't even blink at the sight of two naked men wrapped tightly around each other. You would think that a celibate monk would at least have the decency to blush a bit, but I couldn't be sure these monks were celibate. After all, they were not your average brand of religious order.

I reluctantly untangled myself from my merrow's warm embrace and reached for a pair of pants. It was a little unnerving to stand stark naked in front of a monk. Fouchard stirred, still asleep, and moaned a few words. "Come back to bed, love. I'm not done with you yet."

I was split between laughing or blushing furiously,

so I did a bit of both, chuckling like a fool while my face burned.

"Sorry, Brother John," I said, slipping into my pants. "I hope you don't mind that my boyfriend came for a visit." I was still not sure how Naël had managed to breach all the wards and glamors placed on the convent grounds at night, but I was so glad he did.

The monk waved a hand and shook his head. "We knew he was here," he said.

I stared at him in surprise. These monks had some mad skills. "You could sense him?"

He laughed. "No, nothing magical. The wonders of modern technology." I must have looked utterly confused, because he explained further. "The surveillance cameras caught him hiding in the cloister and then sneaking into your sleeping cell."

The world I was a part of—whether I liked it or not—was indeed amazing. Where else would mysticism, magic, and technology blend this seamlessly?

"When you didn't kick him out or scream for help, we figured he was friendly." He had no idea how friendly Fouchard had been. Or maybe he did. These monks kept surprising me.

My boyfriend was slowly waking up, flopping onto his back and exposing that beautiful body of his to me and the monk. I shifted, trying to block the view.

Brother John had an amused twitch to his lips that totally clashed with his austere monkish look.

"You need me, Brother?" I asked, another sad attempt at distracting him.

"Yes, I came to tell you Brother Serafim is lucid today, and he will see you after breakfast," he said, dropping his cowl and revealing the other incongruence in his appearance—that small, hip man-bun that belonged on the head of a beach bum like me, not on a religious man. "Do you think you can wake up your man? He's welcome to join us to break bread." He turned to leave. "But make sure he's wearing clothes. Some of the brothers haven't seen that much skin in a long time."

Shit. They *were* celibate. I nodded and closed the door behind him.

"Naël, love, you need to wake up," I said, approaching the side of the makeshift bed. He didn't move. I went closer, my shins touching the edge of the mattress. "Naël, wakey-wakey," I said again, leaning slightly over him.

Without warning, Fouchard made a grab for my legs and pulled me on top of him. I yelped in surprise but was soon moaning into his mouth in a delicious morning kiss. "Why are you dressed?" he asked, catching my lower lip with his teeth. "I had planned a very naked and pleasurable morning with you."

I groaned in frustration. Of course the crazy

Oracle would choose this morning of all mornings to want to talk to me. "I can't. The Oracle is lucid and has summoned me." I grumbled and pulled myself away from him, my whole body fighting against it. "Who knows when he'll be half sane again. I got to go."

Fouchard crossed his arms and pouted in a spot-on mimicry of his young sister. I burst out laughing. "You just don't love me."

"Stop it," I said, throwing his discarded clothes at him. "Get dressed and come with me. Acting like your sister while naked is just too creepy even for me."

As if he was light as a feather, Fouchard jumped to his feet in a fluid, athletic move, and my friend Pinocchio made an appearance. Before sliding into his jeans, Fouchard bent down and planted a quick kiss on my lips again. "You're going to introduce me to the monks?"

"More like torture them," I mumbled. "They haven't had sex in a long time, and I'm going to dangle a nice piece of ass in front of their starved hormones. Not fair."

Fouchard was threading his head through the neck opening of his T-shirt. "Are you jealous?"

I tsked. "No, just concerned with your safety." Right. Concerned for a giant merman with the superior strength of a warrior.

With a loud chuckle, he crossed the narrow space

between us and crossed his arms behind me in a tight hug. "You're so cute when you're jealous." He kissed my nose, and I couldn't help it—I laughed. "Let's go make those celibate men green with envy."

The monks were all in the refectory already, and as soon as we walked in, they greeted us with smiles and offered both of us seats among them. I introduced my merman to the community and accepted their delicious food with delight. At some point during the meal, Fouchard became involved in conversation with a couple of the younger men, and I leaned back onto the wall to watch him. This was a new side of him I had never seen other than when we were alone; this was an affable, accessible Fouchard, not the cranky, menacing man he normally showed the world. He didn't seem to need his armor here among people who had no interest in life outside these walls. People who didn't judge or want anything from him, who didn't pose any threat to him or those he loved. I liked this younger-looking and more relaxed Fouchard just as much as I loved the cantankerous merman I knew. The Fouchard he normally reserved for me and his sister alone.

After breakfast, Brother John prodded me out of the refectory with the promise he'd take Fouchard on a tour of the grounds while I was conferring with the mad oracle—well, he left the mad part out, but it was implied.

We walked side by side out of the building and crossed the short space to another freestanding humble structure with only two small windows in the back. "What's this?" I asked, wondering what I was about to face; would Brother Serafim look like a normal person or would he have that loony look so common in Hollywood movies?

"The library," he replied, guiding me to the other side of the structure. "Brother Serafim likes to be surrounded by books, so we have moved his cell into this room where he can be among the things he loves most."

A bookworm oracle. I could totally identify with that. I liked him already.

A thought crossed my mind as we arrived at the front door. "How shall I address him?" His Holy Oracleness didn't sound right somehow.

The monk shrugged. "The Oracle is not one for formality, just call him by his name." That might feel a bit weird. I mean, he was supposed to have the deep, mysterious answers I had been looking for and who knew? Maybe he even had the answer to life itself. "He's named after a rank of angels. You can't go higher than that." He winked at me, that mischievous smile I was becoming used to dancing on his lips.

Both the monk and I had to duck slightly under the doorway to enter the library. We walked into a small space, bare of any furniture other than a small table with brochures. To our left there was another door that opened into a larger space outlined by shelves laden with books. In the middle of the room, sitting on a mattress much like mine, was an old man in the ubiquitous monk habit with snow-white hair that stood on end, as if someone had run a staticky balloon over his head. His bushy white eyebrows topped sharp eyes, so blue it looked as if the sky had taken residence there. I'd expected a solemn-looking man, but instead I got a smiling Einstein look-alike.

He invited me to sit on the floor in front of him. I obliged, frowning as the chill of the stone seeped through my pants. He chuckled. "Cold, yes? I'd offer you a cushion, but we all need to be reminded of our earthly body once in a while, and comfort makes us complacent." Nice of him, I guessed. I couldn't help noting that he apparently didn't need the same reminder, since he was sitting on the softer surface of the bed. "I understand you have questions for me."

Did I ever! "Brother Serafim, thank you for seeing me." I could be diplomatic and proper when needed. "My name is Aiden Mercer, and I am being hunted—well, at least I think it's me, not my boyfriend—and I'd like to know by whom and why."

The old man squinted his eyes, observing me. "You really should learn Portuguese." That was not what I expected him to say. "How are you supposed to live here and not understand the language?" I'd been doing fine so far. "You know, with your skills, you can learn very quickly."

"What skills?" It came out a bit too harsh, and I tried to soften it by smiling. "Almost everyone speaks English in Portugal. Even you."

The Oracle broke into raucous laughter. "But Aiden, I don't speak English at all. Neither do most of our monks." What? What the hell was he talking about? "You just hear us in English, but we are speaking Portuguese."

I shook my head, trying to dispel an incoming headache. "Sorry, what? You *are* speaking in English." I was sure. The man was totally bonkers, as I suspected.

"Aiden, my dear boy, we have wards over the convent, as you know," he explained, laughter still making him hiccup through his words. "Those wards allow anyone to hear what we say in whatever language they understand. You should have that man of yours teach you the lingo."

What in heaven's name had triggered this lecture about my lack of motivation to learn the local language? "I will do as you say; I'll ask Naël to teach me." There was no point in pissing him off, since I was the one seeking answers. "Can we go back to the reason for me being here?"

The Einstein look-alike wiped away invisible tears I had apparently caused with my hilarious life and trained his blue eyes on me. Damn, he was a master starer. He sat there for a good five minutes just gawking at me, not once blinking. It was unnerving, and I had to fight not to lower my gaze. When I arrived at the conclusion I had come to the convent in vain, he broke the connection and licked his lips.

"You are indeed the target for this killer," he began in a whisper that carried. "You have angered him, and he's bent on revenge."

Someone from my past? From my DC detective days? "Revenge for what? What does this man accuse me of?"

"He accuses you of being who you are, and he is not a man."

Well, shit. Could he be any vaguer? I was about to say something snarky when he started speaking again. "The simple fact of your existence threatens him, so he wants to eliminate the one thing he views as a major obstacle between him and power."

Oh, sweet Jesus, why did magicals and their cronies talk in riddles? Was that one of the requirements to be a magical creature? I imagined the application claim in their employment form stating, "I can turn everyday mundane things into a riddle that no one can understand."

"You need to cultivate patience, Aiden," the Oracle said, changing the subject once again. "Nothing good ever came from rushing into things."

I contemplated what might happen if I strangled the old madman and decided it wouldn't be a good idea, so I apologized. "Please, forgive me. Can you elaborate on the reason I am someone's hated life obstacle?"

Was there an amused smirk on his lips? "He wants to be the most powerful demigod, but you stand in the way."

Fuck. Brother Serafim seemed to be slipping into his meditative state again. "Demigod? What do you mean? I don't know any gods, demi or full."

The monk sighed deeply. "Aiden, you were born with some powers that are normally only bestowed upon the gods themselves." No way. No freaking way. "Have you ever wondered why you can't remember who your parents were or your earlier childhood?" Every miserable day of my life. It was hard to love yourself if you didn't know where you came from or who or what you were. "You know of Brahma, right?"

I nodded, still not knowing where this conversation was going. "Yes, he was a powerful Hindu god credited with creation of the world who lost credibility after he fell for the woman he had created to help him with his job. Legend says he became almost obscure and his powerful weapon, the *brahmachakram,* was stolen from him."

He smiled, pleased. "You've done your homework. Excellent." Condescending much? I was not stupid, despite appearances. "Yes, the weapon, an extremely powerful weapon that could create as much as destroy, was stolen from him by one of his sons, one of the children he had with Shatarupa. The problem was this child was not powerful enough to use it, for only someone of comparable power could yield it."

Still in the dark as to how all of this family rivalry had anything to do with me, I asked, "If that's true, how is it possible someone is using what I believe is the *brahmachakram* against me?"

The Oracle lifted a hand as if to shut me up. "Later, this weapon changed hands. A full-blooded son of Vishnu, Brahma's brother and god of destruction, stole the weapon from him. This child is powerful enough to use it if he so chooses."

My mouth fell open. Fouchard and I suspected that whoever was after me was some kind of god because of the weapon we had managed to identify while studying the many magic tomes in the High Priestess's library a few months ago. But a son of Vishnu? "You're saying this demigod is after me? Why? I don't even know him."

"Well, that's the kicker, my son. Unbeknown to religious historians is the fact that Lakshmi, Vishnu's, wife was just as powerful as the three brothers put together. She had the powers of forgiveness and regeneration, among others. She was the vessel of all that's good and victorious over evil."

Okay, I'll admit it, I was piqued by the story in a researcher-type of curiosity even if I was not connecting with it in any personal way. "They say that behind every powerful man is an even more powerful woman." Not sure why I said that, but I felt I needed to interject something.

"How very feminist of you, Aiden." Was he mocking me? "Yes, Lakshmi was extremely powerful because she could yield the forces of nature. She was exiled a couple of times for different reasons, but I suspect the real reason was the other gods saw her as a threat. During one of those exiles, Lakshmi met a mortal man and got pregnant."

You would think the gods had a good handle on contraception, but mythology was packed with stories of bad judgment and unwanted pregnancies.

"Let me guess; they loved each other and lived happily ever after." Now I was just being rude, but I grew impatient with the whole conversation, however interesting this whole god-talk might be.

The monk clicked his tongue in disapproval. "Lakshmi knew that if her husband or any of her in-laws found out about this child, they would kill it, no questions asked."

"Why? The baby was not a full-blood god, right?"

"No, but the man the goddess had fallen in love with was a powerful druid with a direct line to the gods and connected, as most druids are, to the elements. Their offspring would be just as or more powerful than any of the other full-blooded children of the gods. Lakshmi and her man knew they needed to hide this baby."

My heart must have stopped for a moment. Was he hinting at what I thought he was hinting at?

"Yes, Aiden. Lakshmi was your mother."

***

"No fucking way." I had a feeling Fouchard was even more shocked than I was with the news of my origins. Not in a million years would I have guessed I was the son of a goddess and a powerful druid. No wonder I needed the elements to recharge; no wonder I could heal at the speed of light. Cristina was going to have a field day with this one. She'd probably immediately find me a nickname like godling or mini god.

I did not feel like a god. In fact, I didn't feel like much of anything unless I was in the arms of my gorgeous boyfriend. He, and he alone, made me really feel, made me want more, made me happy.

"Pretty much my exact words," I said, raking my fingers through my short, messy hair. We were both seated in a niche in the beautiful and peaceful cloister in the back of the buildings. A stone bench under another *sobreiro* tree had offered us the perfect spot for our hushed conversation. The monks had somehow managed to close that area of the convent grounds to keep the visitors away and allow the two of us some privacy. "How is that even possible?"

"They left you at an orphanage so no one knew who you really were?" Fouchard hadn't been able to close his mouth yet, looking comically like a fish out of water. I would have pointed that out to him with a laugh if I wasn't just as stunned by the revelations of the last hour or so. "But weren't they afraid you'd be hurt or killed even? A helpless baby with no one to protect him, no one to love him."

Nothing I didn't know, but those words, that reality coming from his mouth instead of my mind, hit me like a bolt of lightning. I think a sob actually escaped my lips. Fouchard opened his eyes wide and drew me to him, sheltering me within his arms.

"I'm okay," I lied. "Just shaken up. I haven't had much time to process the whole thing yet."

His breath caressed my ear. "Of course you haven't. Shit, I don't know how I would react in your place." He kissed my cheek. "You're amazing, Aiden. So strong, so cool under pressure."

I made a choked sound, half chuckle, half sob. "I am no such thing, Naël, but I love that you think so." I leaned into him, inhaling his scent, allowing myself to see me through his eyes. "Mind you, being the offspring of such powerful parents might not be too good for my health. It seems as if one of my divine relatives is pretty anxious to scratch me off his list of threats."

"Why? It's not like you are going to ascend to wherever the gods live and take the throne—if such a thing even exists." His reasoning had a great big hole in it, however logical it sounded.

"The one who stole the *brahmachakram*, Vishnu's son, does not like the idea that someone potentially more powerful than him is out there," I explained. "Whispers of my adventures must have reached his ears, and he now knows who I really am. He knew it before I did, and he wants me dead."

Fouchard grazed his lips on my forehead. "Well, he'll have to go through me to do that." That's what I was afraid of. I wasn't scared of what this godly brat would do to me—okay, maybe I was a bit frightened—but the idea he could hurt my man froze me to the bone. "We'll figure it out. Together."

I relaxed against him, grateful for his words and his love. I had looked—hoped—for that feeling of belonging, of being loved for so long and had almost given up on it. Now I had it and I was going to hold on to it as fiercely as Scrat, the saber-toothed squirrel from *Ice Age*, held on to his acorn. I just hoped I was as resilient as the animated rodent.

"Now what? What do we do?" Fouchard asked,

pulling away and looking at me, his intense brown eyes searching mine.

"We go home." What else could I do? The Oracle had spoken, and there wasn't much I could do to prevent another attack. I had to be vigilant and hope I could see it coming so I could defend myself and any innocent bystanders—Fouchard, Cristina, even little Vee. "Brother John told me we could stay one more night and leave after breakfast tomorrow." One more night of feeling secure, of knowing my lover was safe and sound in my arms and under the protection of the monks.

My scorching-hot merrow winked and turned a corner of his lips into a smile. "Your bed may not be the most comfortable in the world, but I wouldn't mind another lovemaking session on it. Fuck, we can make love in the hellish bathroom for all I care." I laughed, imagining the looks of horror in the poor unsuspecting monks' faces as they walked in on us inside the bathing troughs amid the throes of passion.

"I think we'll stick to my room," I said, catching his lower lip with my teeth. "Let's just enjoy our last day here."

We lingered in the empty cloister for most of the day, enjoying the sunshine, the cool kiss of the moun-tain breeze, and the connection with the elements, which from then on would include Fouchard, since his kisses and touch energized me as much or more than any of the other earthly fundamental forces. We stepped out of our magical haven only long enough to eat and call Cristina to check on Vee.

"Haven't you love birds got enough of each other yet?" Cristina had asked Fouchard in her usual sarcastic way. Now that I knew I could hear from a distance without the need for any special gadgets, I didn't even bother with the speaker feature on the phone. "You'd think two whole days of make-up sex would have exhausted anyone."

"Vee better not be around to hear you, Cristina," Fouchard said with a hiss. The protective guardian was showing his hackles. "*Isto não é para ouvidos de criança.*" I raised my eyebrows at him. Shit, I really needed to learn the language. Fouchard obliged. "Not for children's ears."

"Relax, you big bad hunk of a merman." *Oh boy, here she goes.* "Vee is in the bathroom with a book. It will be at least another half hour before she gets out."

My hand, resting loosely on his arm, felt his muscles immediately relax. "Cristina would never talk like that in front of Vee," I said. She wouldn't. Cristina saved her inappropriate comments and sarcastic comebacks for adults only.

"Sorry, Cristina," Fouchard apologized with a long exhale. "I'm just—"

"Protective of your sister," my Portuguese friend finished for him. "I don't blame you after everything that's happened. I will keep her under my laser-eye surveillance and protection." After Vee's kidnapping a few months ago, my boyfriend's level of anxiety whenever Vee was not near him had risen to mammoth heights. "Besides, Tó has been here with us, and he has been growling at anyone who comes closer than a foot to her." I chuckled. "Don't laugh, Aiden, we may have lost some clientele because of that." Her words were stern, but her voice was not. I could guess at the smile behind her tone.

We told her we would be back the next day and said our goodbyes before retreating to our sheltered corner of the convent grounds. We sat on the edge of the fountain in the center of the cloister, and Fouchard pointed at a spot next to the granary, a rustic stone stairway leading into the woods behind the building. "Where does that go to?" he asked.

I had no idea. Brother John had not taken me farther than this cloister, but he had mentioned a legend involving a spot somewhere down that path and a Franciscan monk of some notoriety. "Want to go check it out?"

Together, hand in hand, we walked down the rough steps burrowing into the low green canopy of the woods. Eventually we came to an even narrower path that led down to what looked almost like a hole in the rocks. It was big enough to accommodate one and a half humans side by side in relative comfort.

Fouchard looked at me, his lips curved into a wicked smile and eyebrows rising suggestively. I shook my head. "No way, it's too tight."

"I like tight places." *Wicked man.* My insides immediately turned into molten rock.

"Naël, be reasonable," I said, unconvincingly even to my own ears. I might be resisting it, but I so wanted to. "It's too small of a space. We'll end up with ivy up our asses and dirt in our mouths."

Fouchard laughed, a low rumble that made me hard. "Not if there is something much more scrumptious filling that space already." I licked my lips and swallowed, my mouth watering at the thought.

He didn't give me much time to fight him. Taking hold of my hand, he pulled me toward the small half-enclosed space and pushed me against the rough stone wall. "We'll make this place ours." The monks would probably take exception to that, but I wasn't going to argue. His lips descended on mine in a crushing kiss as his hard body sandwiched me against the wall.

Panting, I escaped from his lips long enough to say, "You're just trying to distract me from my fucked-up life."

Fouchard growled softly. "Is it working?"

Silly question. When did his touch ever not work to distract me?

"Hell, yeah! You're doing an amazing job." When

I tried to wrap my arms around him, he grabbed and pinned both of my hands to the wall on either side of my head and covered my face and neck with kisses, his warm lips causing havoc in my nether regions. "I can't even remember my name."

His laughter vibrated on my neck as he settled on a particularly sensitive spot to flick his tongue over it. "Aiden, your name is Aiden," he whispered over my wet skin. "The most beautiful name on earth because it belongs to the man I love, who I'll always love."

My heart softened and oozed into a cheesy puddle, while my favorite body part hardened and twitched in anticipation.

"I thought merfolk lost their strength as they moved away from the ocean," I said, in awe of his powerful muscles holding me to the wall. I wasn't the strongest man at the gym—if I actually frequented such a place—but I was not a wimpy dude with no brawn either. Yet, he could subdue me so easily, it would have been frightening had I not trusted him with my life.

As to demonstrate how strong he was, he pulled my hands off the wall and flipped me around. "That's true," he whispered in my ear. My skin tingled as his face brushed mine in a subtle caress. "But I seem to gather strength from you, Aiden. I guess it's true what they say."

What do they say? I couldn't think straight. One of

his hands had slipped between my body and the rock against which I had my face plastered and worked its way under the waist of my sweats.

"Love is the most powerful thing in the world." My merrow closed his big hand around my arousal, and I moaned, so close to the edge I could see the stars already. "You make me stronger, so I will return the favor, sweetheart."

"Sweetheart?" I was so surprised by his words, I almost forgot what we were doing. That was the sexiest thing he could have uttered, the first time he'd ever used a term of endearment when addressing me during our lovemaking.

Fouchard's voice went lower and deeper than ever, desire coloring it as he pulled my pants and under-wear down to my ankles. "Don't you like it?"

Hell, I absolutely loved it. One little word that somehow brought a new layer to our intimacy. "No, I love it, Naël. Love it." The roughness of the rock against my face was the only thing still connecting me to the ground. Every other part of me, body and spirit, was soaring high above.

Tilting his head to the side so I could see him, my boyfriend stuck his index finger in his mouth and sucked on it for a moment, making me whimper in frustration and yearning. His gaze burrowed into mine, hot and promising, as he took the finger down and slid it inside me. I yelled out in pleasure. "Do you like that, sweetheart?"

I had lost the power of speech, my hands splayed on the wall and my butt shamelessly sticking out as Fouchard worked his magic on me. I mumbled some gibberish and bit my tongue. The stars were just behind my eyes, ready to explode into supernovas. My merrow didn't relent, sliding his closed hand up and down the length of me, his finger still teasing my backside, and I couldn't hold it anymore. I shattered into a million pieces, the whole Milky Way dropping inside me in a glittering, intense explosion. Fouchard turned me around, glued his body to mine, and held me as I shook from head to toe in complete and wonderful release.

"Whatever happens, Aiden, I'm here for you."

Still flying high from his loving, an overflowing heart, and the strangeness of all that had transpired the last few days, I broke down and cried.

"I'm here with you, sweetheart. Always and forever."

I believed him, and that knowledge made me whole again.

EIGHT

SILK TIE THERAPY

"FUCK IT." CRISTINA THREW HER HANDS UP IN THE air, the rag she had been using to clean the stubborn stain on the floor flying in an arc over her head.

"I'm shocked with the language used in this establishment," an unexpected voice said. Half in the store, his hand still holding the door open, Antonio Silva watched my foul-mouthed friend with a smile on his sexy lips.

Cristina jumped up from her kneeling position with an adolescent yelp and ran to hang from the tall police detective's neck. I rolled my eyes and let out a loud sigh. I would never understand what she saw in that man—okay, maybe I would. He was torridly sexy with his dark hair, olive skin, and dark, piercing eyes, but I didn't trust him. At all. I always had this nagging feeling he was hiding something.

"What did the floor do to you, *bonitona?*" the policeman said with a chuckle, depositing a lavish kiss on my friend's lips.

I pretend puked. Yes, Cristina was beautiful with her amber skin and wild, kinky hair but the term *bonitona*—gorgeous—coming from his mouth sounded like a travesty. "Dude, I just ate." Like a disgruntled teenager, I rolled my eyes again and went into the kitchen so I didn't have to witness the love fest going on in my coffee shop.

I swung the flapping door and walked in only to stop abruptly, my heart jumping up into my mouth. "Holy shit, Taz! Stop doing that. You're going to give me a heart attack."

Taz was leaning against the small work counter, studying her long red nails and looking utterly bored. "You're the son of a goddess. You can't have a heart attack."

I begged to differ. If the way my heart was beating right then was any indication, I so could die of a coronary.

"You haven't been spreading the news, I hope." Shortly after we came back from our visit to the monks, I had decided that it would be a good idea to let our allies know the truth. The witches, as annoying as they were, had been on my side from the get-go, so I counted them as friends, however grudgingly. That didn't mean I wanted the whole magical world to know. "I told you in confidence."

"Keep your panties on, holy man." *Not funny, Taz, not funny at all.* "No one else knows."

I leaned against the wall with the serving window, facing her. My heart was finally slowing down. I didn't used to be that jumpy, but these past few months had been trying, to say the least. It had been almost a month since the revelation about the origins of my birth, but I still had weird dreams about it. Not nightmares exactly, but strange, *Twilight Zone*-type dreams.

"What do you want now, witch?" I was still reluctant to think of her as a real friend—ally, maybe. Friend? Doubtful.

She frowned, feigning outrage. "Is that any way to talk to a bestie?"

"In your dreams, Taz. That position is already taken." I had to admire the witch. Nothing fazed her. My many—and sometimes cruel—barbs seem to slide off her like water on a raincoat. Nothing stuck. "Hurry up. I have customers to serve."

Taz looked over my shoulder into the main room and humphed. "The place is deserted unless you count those sloppy lovebirds as your customers." Her face contorted into a comical frown of disgust. "If he sticks his tongue any further down her throat, he'll suffocate her."

This time I felt nauseated for real. "Stop talking

about it, please. It's bad enough they're dating, but when they decide to make out in front of me…. Let's change the subject."

The witch's lips curved into an amused smile. "Poor little god-child. No stomach for the sexual appetites of others, I guess. I didn't take you for a prude."

"I'm not a prude, but that's my best friend he's slobbering all over," I protested, annoyed with myself for admitting it. "She's like a sister to me, and that cop is shady."

Taz pushed herself off the counter and took a few steps toward me. "Why? Because he's a warlock?" She placed a hand on my bicep and gave it a squeeze, uttering an exclamation. "Ooh, you've been working out." She squeezed my arm again. "Look at those muscles, honey. Ugh, why couldn't you be straight? I so would love to take that ride."

"Please, I'm already nauseated. Even if I was straight, you'd stand no chance at all." She was a beautiful woman. Her red hair was like a fiery crown on top of a perfect ivory face. I would never tell her that. "What do you want, Taz?"

"The High Priestess would like to talk to you and your lover." The mere mention of the witch who presided over all witches in Portugal brought back both amazing and terrible memories. The last time I'd seen her, Fouchard and I had had a deliciously sensual night in one of the rooms of her inn in Óbidos, unfortunately immediately followed by news of Vee's kidnapping.

"For what?" I knew I was just as much a part of the magical world as any of them, but I still wanted them to leave me alone. Why couldn't the magicals just let me be?

"That I don't know." She knew, I was sure of it. "But she said it was somewhat urgent."

Of course it was. "I'm not sure I have time to go to Óbidos." The small medieval walled town was still at least an hour drive from Carcavelos, the Lisbon suburb where I lived.

"She's at her Lisbon residence right now." Taz had lost interest in my bicep and was now rummaging through a basket of fruit as if looking for a treasure. "She stays at her castle home right here in the capital for most of the year. Do you have any peaches?"

I ignored her question. "What castle?" This woman had a thing for castles apparently.

"Why, Castelo de S. Jorge, of course." That couldn't be possible. Saint Jorge Castle was a Moorish fortification built on the highest hill overlooking the city of Lisbon and surrounded by its oldest neighborhood, Alfama. I had visited a couple of times until I realized the place was also crawling with magical creatures. There was nothing in that castle that remotely could be considered a residence. "I know what you're thinking, but her quarters are there nevertheless."

I had no wish to go visit the witch even though she was a class act and had helped us in the search for whoever had attacked us months ago. If I didn't talk to any of them, I could live in the illusion everything was well with the world, that there was no crazy mythological creature hunting me down, and that I was most likely the offspring of a teenage couple who couldn't handle the whole parenting thing.

"Tomorrow at three," Taz said, obviously not interested in what was going through my head. "Head to the restaurant and ask for Penelope Moreno. They'll show you the way."

Before I could protest, Taz turned around and left, throwing a few chosen words at the smooching couple on her way out. *Here we go again.*

"When did Taz get here?" Cristina asked me when I left the kitchen. I was tempted to tell her the witch had sneaked in when the cop was swallowing her whole, but I didn't. I shrugged instead.

"You never know when she will show up, do you?"

The place was pretty deserted today, probably because of a nasty punishing wind blowing in from the ocean. I needed to talk to Fouchard, to see and touch him to make sure he was still there. As if on cue my phone rang, and his deep voice sounded in my ear. "Are you busy?" he asked.

"I was just about to come over," I said, turning my back on the couple so the warlock wouldn't hear what I was saying. My voice shook. "I have news."

"What's wrong?" My boyfriend was getting better and better at deciphering the subtlest changes in the tone of my voice. "You sound stressed."

He wasn't wrong. Whatever the news was, history taught me nothing good came from the words "urgent" uttered from the mouths of magicals. Despite the silent self-affirming mantra I had going since Taz had said those words, my heart had found its way up my throat, and it was pounding as if I had run a marathon.

"Witches," I said as if that explained everything. "I need you." When had I become this dependent on my lover for relief of whatever ailed me? But he did indeed have a strange soothing power over me, and who was I to fight something that felt so right?

"Meet me at your place. I'm not far." I looked at the clock on the wall. It was still early morning. He must have taken Vee to one of her camps.

I asked Cristina to mind the store, and she was more than glad to do it. It was Silva's day off, and he immediately offered to stay with her. I bit my tongue so I wouldn't say something sarcastic about him and left. The wind was crazy, blowing everything and everyone off balance. All the restaurants in the town square had closed and tied their umbrellas, stacked their chairs, and brought any loose objects inside. As I walked past all the stores in the direction of my condo, I felt revitalized, alive as the wind buffeted me with its whip-like strokes. The more aware I was of myself, the more I realized that my body was like a giant battery that recharged anytime I came in contact with nature: the ocean, the sand, the wind, and the rain.

Fouchard was already in the condo. I had given him a key a few weeks ago, once I thought it wouldn't spook him away from our relationship. He had also given me a key to his place, so even though we were not living together, we had sort of consolidated our homes.

Sprawled on my couch was a very naked merman with only a long, thick silk tie covering his delicious intimate parts. As soon as my eyes fell on that gorgeous body of his, it was impossible to stop it. Instant wood.

"You're a little flushed," he said, a wicked smile settling on his lips. "Was it the wind or the sight of me?"

I licked my lips, stunned into silence and paralysis. He snorted, and my tongue flicked out again, like a lizard trying to catch a fly. "Holy Mother of God. What's the occasion?" Not that it was that unusual for him to surprise me with something like that.

He crossed one leg over his knee while playing

with the tie that had dropped between his legs, moving it just enough to make my mouth water but revealing nothing. "Do we need a special occasion?" *Wicked.* "With this wind, I figured you would need to release some of that extra energy." And a distraction. He knew me so well. My merrow knew exactly how nature affected me and could anticipate any change in my mood. Sometimes it was almost as if we were mentally connected, as if he could read my mind. "I can always get dressed and make some coffee."

I stepped forward, my hand outstretched to him. "No, don't." I sounded a bit desperate, I guessed, but I knew he didn't mind. My need for him gave him as much pleasure as his gave me. "Don't move."

His smile vanished, and his eyes closed halfway. He cocked his head slightly in a dare he knew I couldn't resist. I crossed the space between us in a second flat to land on my knees by his feet. I glanced up at the face I loved the most in this crazy world, and my heart began drumming as he uncrossed his legs so I could slide in between. His chest moved as fast as mine, up and down as our breathing became quick and shallow. Fouchard groaned softly when I placed my hands on his knees, his skin warm and soft under my palms. He had very little body hair. Something about merfolk DNA, he had told me once. His face was usually covered with a shadow of scruffy beard, but he had no hair on his arms, chest, or legs. I was okay with that, loving the expanse of his light brown skin that always seemed to glow as if he held light inside him.

"I thought you had news," he teased, his strangled voice betraying his desire.

I grunted, unwilling to get distracted by any kind of adulting. I wanted to focus on this scrumptious, beautiful man in front of me. Which of course was his plan all along. "Later."

"I thought I was the cranky one in this relation-ship," Fouchard said with a dry chuckle, shivering as I slid my hands up the front of his thighs.

"You still are, as long as you don't get between me and the enjoyment of your exquisite merman bod." Otherwise I would be seriously cranky, like growling, biting-your-head-off mad. "No more words."

Fouchard bit his lip, split between amusement and frustration. My hands had finally reached the edge of the tie and they shook in anticipation. I touched the blue silky fabric with two of my fingers and then captured it between them, stealing another glance at my boyfriend's face. He bit his lip harder and moaned almost imperceptibly, his breathing quickening further. But no words. He kept them in and allowed me to continue the trek of my fingers.

I threatened to pull the tie aside, but instead I slid the palm of my hand over it, enjoying the sharp intake of breath I coaxed out of him. He was as hard as me under that sliver of silk. I bent forward and kissed him over the fabric of the tie before latching my lips around his erection, the silk between him and my tongue growing hot and wet. He threw his head back onto the seat, and I let him go for a moment. I chuckled at his growl of frustration before blowing air against the wet fabric where my lips had just been. Fouchard didn't say a word, doggedly sticking to what I had asked him.

I pushed him back until he was lying on the couch, the wet tie now displaced, and his hard length exposed to my hungry eyes. If there was such a thing as an award for the speediest striptease, I would have won it. With my clothes in a messy pile on the floor behind me, I looked around for the bottle of lube but couldn't find it.

"No worries," Fouchard finally said. "I already took care of that." He was not lying; he was ready for me, and I was so freaking ready to be inside him it hurt.

I positioned myself on top of him, my arms holding my weight as I rubbed my hardness against his, moaning and shivering. His hand brushed my butt in a thrilling caress, his fingers grazing between the cheeks. I couldn't hold it any longer. I scooted down just enough so I could glide my length inside of him, and we were finally one. He yelled, I yelled, both so turned on I knew it wouldn't be long before we climaxed. Like the movement of the tides, I ebbed and flowed in and out, mimicking the same movement with the hand I had wrapped around him. When I reached my release, it was as if a cold ocean wave had washed over me, regenerating, energizing, cooling my lust fever. I collapsed on top of him, his semen hot on my hand, exhausted and yet full of energy. I rested there for a moment, my face on his chest, listening to the beating of his heart against my ear, the warmth of his body merging with mine. I loved being this close to my man, bodies and souls entwined. I loved my merrow.

Without lifting my head and not wanting to miss a single beat of his generous and brave heart, I whispered, "Thank you."

"For what?" he asked, his warm breath blowing my hair.

For so many things: his love, his company, his patience. "For knowing exactly what to do to pull me out of my anxiety whirlpool."

Naël laughed softly. "Want to talk about the witches?"

I raised my head enough to look at him, furrowing my brow. "Witches? What witches?"

NINE
PEACOCK TAILS

"Look at those peacocks." Fouchard pointed in the direction of two young men obviously strutting their stuff for a pretty girl who walked by.

I was a bit shocked by the comment. So unlike my boyfriend. "That's not a very nice thing to say about those guys, Naël."

Fouchard snorted, staring at me as if I had just grown two heads. "I was talking about the birds. You know, the actual peacocks." He pointed at a flock of the showoff birds as they walked around with their funny gait, their fanned tails fully open in a glorious mix of rich colors and patterns. "Not the guys."

That explained it. I chuckled and tugged on his hand. We had arrived at the castle more than an hour ago, but we were caught by the beauty of the monument, an originally Moorish castle that had been expanded and restructured somewhat by the medieval Portuguese kings. The building itself was beautiful, but the view was amazing. No matter where you walked along the outside walls of the structure, the city of Lisbon, with its red tiled roofs, wrought iron balconies, and colorful clothing fluttering from clotheslines, spread below like a colorful wave heading out to meet the Tagus and the ocean beyond. It was stunning, peaceful, and yet kinetic like an oil painting by Van Gogh. We had hung around for a while just soaking in the atmosphere, sitting at the patio café drinking a beer and admiring the view sprawled before us.

"We better go get this done." Whatever *this* was. I held Fouchard's hand in mine and pulled him closer to me as we strode toward the entrance of the restaurant where we were to meet the High Priestess, the stunning Penelope Moreno. We had met her once before, and I had been impressed by her serenity and magnanimity, unlike Taz who seemed to thrive on annoying me.

The restaurant was housed in the old royal quarters of the castle, a reconstruction of the original building that was destroyed during an earthquake. We walked under the green canopy and through the arched stone doorway into the dining area. The place was huge, with stone walls partially covered by panels of typical Portuguese blue and white tile.

As soon as we stepped under the high arched ceilings, a host came to welcome us. "*Quantas pessoas?*" He wanted to know how many seats we needed. The dark-haired man smiled at us as if we were his best friends and waited patiently for our response, throwing a surreptitious glance at our joined hands.

"We're here to see Dona Moreno." There was no point in pretending I could speak Portuguese. Cristina had been making a valiant effort at teaching me for the past couple weeks, but apparently I was a slow learner.

The man's smile widened. "Of course, you must be Mr. Mercer and Mr. Fouchard." His English was flawless, with just a hint of an accent. "Please, follow me. She's expecting you."

I should be surprised that a regular—because he was indeed no magical creature—knew Moreno so well, but then again I had lived my whole life seeing creatures that no one else saw and I had just discovered I was part druid, part freaking demigod. It took a lot to surprise me these days.

Fouchard gave me a tug, and we followed the host through the restaurant, navigating the maze of round tables and customers all the way to the back where an archway led to a stone staircase. "Her office is at the bottom, through the door at the end of the corridor," the man said, pointing down. "Just give me a call if you need any assistance."

I threw a worried glance at my boyfriend, who shrugged. "Well, this either leads to a magnificently magical room or possibly hell," he said with a crooked smile. "Win-win." He laughed at his own joke and led a very hesitant me down the staircase and into the dark landing at the bottom.

As it turned out, the darkness that seemed to loom over the bottom all but vanished once we came down the last step. Bright light illuminated the whole corridor suddenly, and I opened my mouth in wonder. "Whoa, that's some magic trick."

My merrow's burst of laughter startled me. "You idiot," he said, ever the complimentary one. "It's not magic. Those lights are on a sensor. Very twenty-first century, you know." He bumped his shoulder into mine playfully. "Magic trick, my ass." And what a lovely ass it was.

"It's not very kind or smart of you to laugh at your boyfriend who, by the way, could probably smite you with a single stare." What was the point of being a demigod if you couldn't use that fact to your advantage? He laughed even harder, and I had no choice but to join him. His laughter was simply contagious, and I loved that sound just as much as I loved the man producing it.

The door at the end of the hallway was closed, but as soon as we drew near, it clicked open. "Come on in, gentlemen."

We followed the slightly muffled female voice into the room behind the door. I had half expected a dungeon-type den or dark, manly office with leather chairs and a lot of dark wood, but instead we were greeted by a well-lit room. It was a well-decorated space with comfortable and colorful furniture and accents, welcoming and warm.

"Welcome, my friends." Penelope Moreno was sitting at a small, practical desk, her body half turned to us. "So nice to see you again. Please, come in and make yourselves comfortable." She slid to her feet, her bright green eyes twinkling in her perfectly oval face, and signaled toward the overstuffed couch and chair. "You're looking well, Mr. Mercer." Translation: you're looking great for someone who almost died. "Sit, sit."

Penelope took a seat on the armchair, and Fouchard and I got comfy on the couch facing it. "I understand you wanted to talk to me," I ventured, my mouth suddenly dry. Finding out I was some sort of deity and dating a merman had not assuaged my misgivings about magicals. "Is there a problem?" Fouchard squeezed my hand, soothing my nerves a tad.

"No problem, Aiden," the witch said, straightening a wrinkle in her pants. "At least, I don't think there is. But I must ask you for a favor." Uh-oh. In my experience, nothing good ever came of those words.

My concern must have shown on my face, because she chuckled softly and added, "Nothing bad, Aiden. Just something I think you'll be perfect at accomplishing, that's all. After all, it turns out you have a very special set of talents." She punctuated her words with a wink, and I flinched. No, no, no fucking way; did she know something about me that I didn't? Not that it would surprise me. I was a mystery only to myself, it seemed.

I raised my eyebrows in a gesture I hoped spelled my confusion in a dignified, grown-up way. "What talents would those be?" I tightened my hold on Fouchard's hand.

"You are the only one I know that can see things no one else can," she explained, and I relaxed. She wasn't speaking of any talent I didn't already know about. "You can see through glamors and wards while everyone else can't."

So far, no unwanted surprises. "True, but I still don't see how that can help you."

"There is a restaurant in Alfama where strange things have been reported." Uh-oh, I didn't like the sound of that. "Chairs moving, food being thrown across the room, lights turning off and on by themselves; this always happens after customers complain that the beer or wine they ordered suddenly vanished from the glass."

I hated to admit it, but I was interested. A ghost?

Unlikely; ghosts had better things to do than hang around an old town joint to terrorize its customers.

"It doesn't look good for the magical community that someone we suspect is a magical is having such fun messing with the regulars. It goes against all of our laws."

Right. It might end up revealing the existence of that secret strata of society. "What can I possibly do that you witches can't? You have magic on your side. I have nothing." Denial, of course, but I would keep on denying my magical side for as long as I could. "And I can't see dead people."

Penelope chuckled. "You're so funny, Aiden." I was? My hand resting on Fouchard's thigh shook, and I realized he was quietly laughing too. "One day you'll admit to how powerful you are." Today wasn't the day. "We are asking you to go there and identify whoever is doing this so we can discipline him or her appropriately."

I bristled a bit at her request. "You want me to be a snitch?" God, I sounded like a fourth grader even to my own ears.

Fouchard kept silent, obviously not wanting to interfere with what he considered my business. I loved him for that, but at that moment I wished he would come to my rescue. Telling on others was not something I relished doing. It hadn't served me right in the past—in fact, it had often resulted in a boatload of pain.

"Call it what you want, Aiden, but you'd be doing your own community a huge favor." I shook my head, stubbornly holding on to my refusal to be a rat of sorts. "Think of it this way: we will owe you." Oh, she was good. She knew exactly what buttons to push. Having magicals in my debt was a very attractive prospect. "A debt that you can cash in anytime, in any way you want."

I turned my face to my boyfriend, who bit his lip. "For fuck's sake, Naël, just say what you want to say before you explode."

He let out a whoosh of breath and licked his lips. "I think you should do it," he said. "Not only would they owe you a favor, but it would look good for you— an excellent way of winning your way into the hearts of your people."

"They're not my—" I stopped myself just in time. Old habits died hard, and I had spent a lifetime not wanting to have anything to do with the group of creatures I now knew I belonged to. I hung my head for a moment, collecting my thoughts. "All right, I'll do it." The high priestess clapped her hands. "But you have to promise me this won't come back to bite me or Naël in the ass." I was the only one allowed to do that.

Penelope stood up and extended an elegant hand

toward me. "It's a promise. Let's shake on it." The fact that a handshake served the purpose of closing a deal with a witch tickled my funny bone, but as soon as our hands touched, I knew this was not just a plain handshake. A charge of something akin to electricity ran between our hands and climbed up my arm, shoulder, neck, and settled in my brain. It tickled rather than hurt, but it startled me enough I jumped. "No worries. It's a magic bond between us. Sort of like a contract without the paper."

Contract, my butt. I would much rather be bound by a legally signed document than be magically obligated to fulfill the conditions of this one. It was done though, and there was no way out of it. I would go to the fucking restaurant and find out who the drunken poltergeist was.

"Any particular days this whatever-it-is seems to happen, or will any day do?" I asked, resentment plainly evident in my tone.

Penelope combed her shiny dark hair with her fingers. Her hair had grown since I had last seen her, but it was still cut into a short bob that framed her face. She was one classy lady, I had to admit. "He— she—seems to be there every Tuesday evening. Sometimes on other nights, but mostly Tuesdays."

"Maybe that's his day off from whatever ghosts do for a job." That gave me a couple of days to plan my approach. Should I be subtle and cool or go in with all guns blazing? Not that I had any guns, of course, but metaphorically speaking. "Then what? Do I report to you, send the info with Taz, or something else?"

"You report directly to me, please." Her assertiveness came through in her words. "Thank you, Aiden, for helping us."

"Don't thank me yet," I said, standing up, closely followed by Fouchard. "We may be better off not knowing."

We said our goodbyes and left. The restaurant above was still as busy as before, and the sun still shone outside as the afternoon led into evening. We lingered in the castle grounds for a while longer, soaking in the sunshine and the amazing view. We came across another flock of peacocks, proud and vain as they displayed their deep-colored tails to the humbler females.

Fouchard laughed and pulled me against his side. "You're the polar opposite of those birds," he said, planting a kiss by my ear.

"Oh, you mean I'm ugly as sin then." A tingle covered the spot where he had kissed me, and my body came alive as it always did when I was with him.

My merrow snorted. "No, idiot. The peacocks feel the need to advertise their male power with stunning displays of color, but you, my love, hide your power behind a mask of the ordinary when you are in fact extraordinary. It's a very attractive quality, you know?" He purred by my ear, and my whole body lost some of its solidity. "Very sexy indeed."

I surveyed the area around me and, finding it empty of other people, I opened my palm on his chest and pushed him roughly toward a nearby wall. "Sexy, yeah?" I said, flattening myself against him, seeking his lips with mine. "Let me tell you what I'm going to do to you as soon as we get home." And I crushed my mouth on his, devouring the sunny deliciousness of my merman boyfriend.

TEN
DREAMS, VISIONS, AND PREMONITIONS

MY BODY SHATTERED INTO A MILLION PIECES AS IF each muscle, each sinew, every inch of me first imploded and then released all the gathered energy in one overwhelming explosion of the senses. It was glorious.

Fouchard slid off me and kneeled on the sand beside me, his intense brown eyes scouring me from head to toe. "You look beautiful when you're breathless like this," he whispered, his voice a tender caress.

"Do you really have to go?" I buried my fingers in the cool sand, my muscles still twitching from the intensity of my climax.

"I do. Neptune wants to talk to me." He smiled. "When our king calls, we go. No questions asked."

A sigh escaped my lips, a not-so-subtle protest against his impending departure.

Fouchard, still on his knees, ran a hand over the center of my body, from the base of my neck to my most precious parts, lingering there just long enough to make me whimper. "You're wicked," I mumbled with a groan. "You're going to leave me all hard and needy."

He laughed. "You're always hard and needy." True. He bent over me and kissed me long and hard, his tongue dancing with mine until he abruptly broke the connection and jumped to his feet, his glorious body already showing signs of mutating into his aqua form. "I love you, Aiden. Wait for me, and I will show you how much. Again." He winked and ran to the edge of the water, diving into the ocean just as his beautiful tail materialized. I rose on my elbows to watch him swim away as he flicked his iridescent blue tail on the surface of the ocean. I'd never get tired of that, watching my stunning mate gracefully meld with the dark blue water, an organic and exquisite union that left me breathless every time.

I was left to figure out what to do with myself while I waited for Fouchard to come back from his meeting with Neptune. I chuckled, recalling my shock at finding out that there was such a creature as Neptune, king of everything fishy. Of course, it was not the Neptune of myth. My merrow had explained that every king of the oceans took on the name once in charge. Obviously merfolk were not thinking of how freaking confusing those history lessons would be for the younger generation. I could just imagine the conversation in the classroom: *"King Neptune started a new law—"*

"Excuse me, prof. Which Neptune would that be? The one that legalized kelp-smoking or the one who brought the legal marriage age down to fourteen?"

I rolled to my belly and laughed out loud.

"Do you ever wear clothes?" Taz's unexpected appearance scared me shitless. I jumped to my feet, forgetting I was butt naked. She made an appreciative sound. "Not that I'm complaining though. Damn, you're hot! Are you really sure you don't feel even a tiny twinge of curiosity of how it'd feel with a female? Because I'd be a willing test subject."

I mumbled something totally obscene and searched the sand around me for my clothes. Taz ambled over—why in heaven's name was she wearing high heels in the sand?—and handed me my pants with a wink. I snatched them from her hands and stumbled into them, balancing on one leg at a time.

"Do you ever knock? This is private property. You can't just mosey in here anytime you want." When had Fouchard invited her in? Witches, like the traditional vampires, couldn't enter a private home unless invited first by the owner.

"Technically this underground beach is part of nature, and as a witch I'm connected to it," she said with infuriating logic. "You should know this with your druid blood and all."

I zipped my pants and scowled at her. "Thanks for reminding me of my freakish beginnings." I wasn't even sure why I resented my ancestry that much. Most people would probably be happy to find out they had some magic powers. I wasn't most people.

"Anytime, Aiden." Nothing fazed the damn witch, which made me admire her, however grudgingly. "I don't blame you for wanting to idly wait for your delicious lover, but maybe we could have a cup of coffee together and talk. You could invite me upstairs."

No way in hell.

I guessed I could use a cup of java or two. It would be a while until Fouchard came back. His meetings with the fish king were always long and tedious, or so he told me. "Let's walk to the beach café."

The witch vanished, only to show up by my side once I had exited my mate's house. "What a gorgeous day," she exclaimed as if we were out on a date or something. She hooked her arm in mine, and I threw her an are-you-kidding-me look. "Snap out of it, Aiden. We're friends, and you know it. Who else will get your silly pop references?"

True, she was the only person I knew who was as bad as me at making obscure references that no one else understood. But we were not friends. Maybe friendly, but definitely not buddies. At least I didn't think so.

"What do you want now, Taz? Every time you show up, something is about to happen—and not necessarily something good either." I conveniently ignored the time she had been the only friendly face when I had to face the depraved Alabyran in his den or the time she had given me some much-needed protective herbs.

"Do I need to have an agenda to come visit a friend? You've been alone for far too long, Aiden."

That struck a chord. I hadn't been alone, so to speak, since I never had any trouble finding a warm body to share my bed, but I had been lonely, isolated from the world at large, too scared of trusting the wrong people. When you didn't remember your past, you became wary of everybody and everything, not knowing who or what to trust. That had been me for most of my adult life—and probably before that—but no longer. I had Fouchard, Cristina, and even young Vee. Could Taz be another friend, another person I actually trusted and wanted around? *Too early to tell, I think.*

"Better alone than annoyed." It was meant to come out hard, but instead a note of amusement softened the blow. I hated to admit it even to myself, but I enjoyed the repartee between me and the witch. Sometimes.

I stole a glance at her. Taz had an open smile on her lips, the red hair piled up on top of her head in a messy bun shining like a ruby in the sun. The freckles across her ivory nose made her look younger than what she surely was. "I know that deep down inside you love me," she said with a snicker.

"I don't know, Taz. It's so deep, Indiana Jones would have a hard time digging it up." As I expected, she burst out laughing, a rowdy, out of control sound that captivated even me.

We sat at a small table in an outdoors beach café and ordered two coffees. Even though it was hot, I had never been a soda or lemonade type of person. Coffee, on the other hand, always brought me a measure of joy and comfort. We stared into the horizon where the blue ocean met the lighter blue sky, both quiet for a while, savoring the hot drinks and the cool ocean breeze against our skin.

"No hat today, Taz?" I finally said, tearing my eyes from the ocean where my love was now meeting with his sovereign. "You'll end up with more freckles."

"I like my freckles, thank you very much." As if to prove it, she stuck her nose up in the air and closed her eyes against the glare of the sun. "But I did forget my sunglasses, and it's killing me. Having green eyes in such a sunny country can be painful."

I sympathized, having blue eyes myself. If I forgot my sunglasses, it would be a squinting fest all day.

Fouchard, with his brown eyes, didn't have such a hard time in the sun. "Come on, Taz, we both know you came to tell me something," I finally said, looking at her profile. She opened her eyes and turned them to me. "Or ask me to do something."

She sighed dramatically. "See? We're so close now that you can guess what's in my mind." I snorted. "Yes, I do have something to tell you. Actually it's a warning, a vision I had last night."

Taz was a part-time Tarot card reader under the name of Madame Solara. It cracked me up that someone with real magic powers would make her living pretending to be a carnival seer.

"I thought that was all a front for your job." She was the real McCoy, so I could mock her as often as I wanted, but I knew her visions rang true most of the time. My stomach clenched. "What was the vision about?"

She leaned in and lowered her voice to just above a whisper. "Fouchard is in danger." She might as well have knocked me out with a brick. My breath caught in my throat, and sweat immediately beaded on my forehead. "I don't know how or why, but something bad is coming his way."

My mouth had gone drier than the Sahara. "What the hell are you talking about, Taz? You can't just drop a bomb like that on my lap and then say you have no details." I shouldn't be angry at her, but my body had gone rigid with fear, and I needed to lash out.

"I'm sorry, Aiden, but I really don't have anything else to give you," she said, her voice unusually subdued. "These visions are not very specific; they're more feelings than something concrete. But he's in some kind of danger."

To curb the anger and panic growing inside me, I took several deep breaths before speaking again. "He just went to talk to his king. Do you think it has something to do with that?"

Taz shrugged, her lower lip caught between her teeth. "I don't know. Maybe, maybe not."

In one single move, I jumped to my feet, accidentally hitting the table and sending the cups tumbling across the top. Quick on her feet, Taz managed to stop them from falling off the table.

"Fuck you witches with all your riddles and premonitions." Several heads turned our way, but from the fog of my misplaced wrath I saw Taz waving her fingers in the air. She was glamoring us against onlookers. I knew I was being unfair. Taz had done nothing but help me and Fouchard, however annoying she might be. "For once, one time only, I wish you could actually do or say something helpful."

The witch stood up and walked around the small table to stand beside me, a comforting hand on my shoulder. I shrugged it away and tried to catch my runaway breath. "Aiden, I know you're worried, and I don't blame you," she said, no longer the petulant, flippant character she always seemed to be. "You should be worried, but you need to keep your wits. Panic never helps." I took two long inhales, feeling as if I had somehow exhaled every ounce of air in my lungs when she sucker-punched me with her words. "I will do whatever I can to help you. You want me to shadow Fouchard when you're at work for the next few days, I'll do that. He will never know I'm there. I'll do whatever; just tell me what you want."

I might have been overwhelmed by the panic her words had conjured but even so, I could tell she was sincere; she truly wanted to help. With another long exhale, I allowed all that anger to flow out of me and looked her in the eyes. "I'm sorry, Taz, it's not your fault, and I shouldn't have—"

She interrupted me. "Don't even think of apologizing. What are friends for if not to be there when you need to vent?" Could we really be friends? Was that even possible? "Come on, I will walk back with you. You do what you think is best, but I think maybe you should tell him what I told you. That way he'll be on the lookout and won't be caught unaware."

Still breathing too shallowly and with my heart trotting inside my chest, I followed her down the sidewalk toward my boyfriend's house. I couldn't organize my thoughts, as they all jumbled inside my head, a massive tangle of incomplete, unsettling fragments of ideas and feelings. Taz held on to my arm and kept quiet for most of the way. What was I going to do? I couldn't be with him 24/7, nor would he accept that if I could. He was perfectly capable of defending himself, an ex-Navy SEAL who had been trained for armed conflict. But this was most likely connected to whoever the crazy god was who was trying to eliminate me. Who had the power and strength to fight against a god? Shit, we were going to need all the help we could get.

"Yes, follow him everywhere he goes if he's not with me," I said, giving in to the pressure. "But please don't tell him. He will have both our heads for dinner."

ELEVEN

WINE, BEER, AND FLYING BOTTLES

"Why can't I come?" Vee's strident voice scratched at my eardrums. God, that girl could break glass with a scream. "You haven't taken me anywhere this summer, Naël. It's not fair." In true form, she crossed her arms over her chest, stuck her lower lip out in a threatening pout, and tapped her foot on the tile floor. Fouchard was in big trouble. He may be a big man but he didn't have strong enough defenses against his pissed-off sister.

My poor boyfriend ran a palm across his face, took a deep breath, and stared at Victoria Fouchard, his formidable—however small—baby sister with trepidation in his eyes. I thought about hugging him, a feeble offer of comfort against what he was facing, but then I gave up on the idea; such an action would only make me the second target for the young mermaid's wrath. I may be in love with Fouchard but I wasn't that stupid.

"For heaven's sake, Vee, you've been having a blast at your camp, so don't tell me you've been left behind." *Ooh, weak retort, my love, too weak.* Vee's bright green eyes lit up like flames, piercing and dangerous. I pitied the person who would love her in the future and would be the butt of her ire. "Sweetie, you are going to a land camp where you have made a ton of friends, and you are also attending the mermaids' camp in between. You said you wanted to learn more about your kin, so it's perfect."

His comments just made her fume even more. I could have sworn I saw smoke wafting from her ears. "I am having fun at the camps, but I want to spend some time with you and Aiden. I don't even know what you guys do when I am not around."

And she'd never find out if I had anything to do with it. Fouchard and I spent a lot of our free time doing things totally inappropriate for a child's eyes.

She stomped one foot hard enough that it shook a cocktail table nearby. "I want to go to this *fado* place. I've never been to one."

Fouchard took another deep breath. "That's because those places are drinking spots for adults, not kids like you." Not to mention we were on a mission to find out who our not-so-friendly poltergeist was, and our visit could easily turn dangerous.

"Not true. My friend Adriana told me they are just restaurants where people sing the *fado*." She never relented and was always so sure her information was correct. I stopped my chuckle before anyone could hear it.

My boyfriend squinted in an expression that could only mean one thing: he had reached his limit and was on the verge of either giving up or exploding. Knowing the reason why we were going to the typical Portuguese bar/restaurant, I was betting on the latter.

"You are not going, Vee, and that's that. This is an adult-only place." His voice was deceptively calm, but I could hear the bubbling anger behind it. "I will make time to take you out with us one day this week, I promise, but it will not be to this place. Do I make myself clear?"

I considered leaving the room, but that would only veer the girl's attention to me, and again, I wasn't that dumb. Instead I sat as still as I could, my eyes the only thing moving. Vee humphed and mumbled something unintelligible but didn't explode like I'd thought she would. Maybe she realized she had pushed as far as she could.

After a moment of silence, she finally said, "You promise?" The angry, petulant voice of a moment ago was replaced by a child's wistful one. "I miss you guys."

Fouchard's anger dissipated from his eyes as he

opened his arms to her. "Of course, sis. I miss hanging out with you too."

The young girl ran into her brother's hug, where she snuggled for a while before turning to me and saying, "Come on, Aiden, you're part of this family. Group hug."

Touched beyond words, I stepped into the hug, a little hesitantly at first but then giving myself whole-heartedly to that feeling of belonging, of being wanted.

We both drove the young mermaid to her camp later that morning and then lingered around my coffee shop, helping Cristina with the many customers swarming the place. It was a glorious day outside, hot but kissed by a cool ocean breeze that made being outdoors a pleasure, a fact that didn't go unnoticed by everyone in town. The warlock cop showed up some-time after lunch but didn't stay for long, which was fine by me—it was all I could do not to throw up every time he stuck his tongue down my friend's throat.

"You really have to get over your dislike for Silva, you know," my merrow whispered as we watched the detective strut his way out of the store. "He's your best friend's boyfriend. I think you owe Cristina that much."

"He's a freaking warlock, Fouchard," I said, as if

that totally justified my attitude. "They are not to be trusted."

Fouchard blinked, an amused smile curling the corners of his lips. "Really? Why is that?"

I had no idea. He was too handsome, a policeman with resources none of us had, and he had been taking too much of my best friend's time. *Damn it!* I guess I was a bit jealous, and that was ridiculous. Thankfully a new customer waved me over and I was able to avoid answering. I couldn't believe I was actually jealous of the attention Cristina was giving this guy. She had always had her own separate life from me, but she'd never been this attached, this interested in someone. The idea I could be losing my one and only friend was a bit scary, I supposed. Fouchard was right; I had to snap out of it.

By the time we shooed our last customer out the door, it was already way past dinnertime and twilight was descending upon us. I was tired, and all I really wanted to do was go home with my boyfriend and take a shower or maybe even a long, hot bath with him. Despite my exhaustion, my body immediately responded to the image I had conjured. *Whoa. Down, boy.* We had something else to do first.

Not bothering to change clothes, we said goodbye to Cristina, who kindly offered to clean up and close, and we got in Fouchard's car and headed to Lisbon.

This bar/restaurant was called Adega do Mar, which roughly translated to Ocean Wine Bar—yes, Portuguese didn't always translate well into English, I was quickly discovering as I staggered through language lessons with Cristina and Fouchard—and was located in a medieval Moorish neighborhood. Alfama was built on one of the seven hills of Lisbon and was a typical example of Moorish urban architecture, with narrow meandering streets where no cars could fit and small whitewashed houses crowded together in a disorganized but charming pattern. Some of the cramped alleys between houses still displayed slanted buildings that touched each other at the top, the effects of the major earthquake that had basically destroyed the rest of the city in 1755. Garments hung from clotheslines stretched between buildings or hanging from small wrought iron balconies, adding further color to the old neighborhood.

We parked the car in the first space we found and climbed the winding streets to where this *adega* was. Even before we entered through its blue wooden door, the mournful sounds of *fado* reached us, a soothing however sad arpeggio of Portuguese guitar accompanied by the emotional, throaty voice of a female singer. This traditional and popular type of music was a reminder of this tiny nation's Northern African origins and influence.

I threaded my fingers through Fouchard's,

momentarily enchanted by the soulful tune, before we walked in. As tradition dictated, the room was dark, illuminated mostly by the candles sprinkled on all the tables and a few dim sconces on the walls. People sat around the rectangular rustic tables, mesmerized by the song, with wine or beer glasses in their hands. It never failed to surprise me how attentively the audience listened to the singers and the musicians, who often were just people from the audience. I had a theory that the Portuguese had invented the open mic night way before it reached the US but no way of proving it.

A host helped us find a seat in a corner of the small *adega* and took our order for some *tapas* and a couple of beers. We sat side by side, our hips and thighs touching, the whole romantic atmosphere from the half-melted candles to the fresh carnations decorating the tabletops turning me into a molten mess of lustful feelings. Could the stupid poltergeist just show up already so I could go home and get it on with my merman?

Fouchard slid a warm hand over the top of my thigh, and I actually gasped. His touch was the real magic, not this other voodoo. "Do you see it?" he asked in a whisper, his breath tingling on my skin.

I shook my head, swallowing the knot of desire that grew in my throat. I hadn't seen anything, but I needed to focus, and his hand caressing my thigh was not helping. "No. And if you don't stop that, I never will, since all I want to do is throw you on top of this table and show you how much I need you."

The musicians went silent at that moment, turning my private comment into a public one. Everybody in the place turned their eyes to me, and I blushed like a virgin bride. Caught with my pants down, so to speak, I did the only thing I could: I began actively looking for our ghost while totally ignoring the curious looks I had attracted with my passionate confession. I heard Fouchard snicker beside me. *Bastard*.

As if on cue, a plate flew off one of the tables and shattered on the wood floor, closely followed by a chair being pulled out from underneath the table by invisible hands. A few of the customers gasped; others screamed and immediately got up to leave. Soon the place would be empty. This could not be healthy for the business. I trained my eyes in the direction of the disturbance, and I saw him. Loud and clear. He was a short, dark-haired man with no outstanding features, nothing that would make him exceptional or even noticeable. For such a loud poltergeist, this one was just a Joe Schmo. He caught my eye and frowned, paralyzed for a minute before picking up a bottle and hurling it in my direction.

With feline swiftness and precision, Fouchard jumped to his feet and intercepted the glass bottle before it hit me. "What the hell? I thought this thing didn't attack people directly," he exclaimed, staring at the bottle in shock.

"This one apparently doesn't like me," I said, already striding toward the turd, who was now studying my moves intently. "I'm coming for you, dick."

I heard Fouchard's heavy steps behind me, and for a moment I forgot to be worried about his safety and felt relieved to have him as my backup.

The not-so-ghostly man tried to snatch another bottle, but I got to him first. I grabbed him by the collar of his unusual shirt and pulled him closer to me. "What's your problem, idiot?" I snarled, my voice rising above my usual volume. "What have I done to you, stupid? Did I fuck one of your boyfriends?" Memories of a similar scene in DC when a very nasty troll confronted me for the same reason invaded my mind; except then I had been the one being held by the collar. I apparently had a gift to piss off people without even trying.

"Let me go, Mercer." He knew my name. How was that for a twist? I had no clue who he was. He had brown skin and thick, shiny black hair pulled into a tiny ridiculous man bun on the top of his head. Now that we were up close and personal, I realized he was wearing something similar to traditional Indian clothes and had a nose ring connected to an earring by a thin gold chain. "Don't want to smite you in here."

His breath was ripe with stale beer. He obviously had been drinking. Heavily. Despite his diminutive size, he was strong. Had he not been so intoxicated, I was sure he would have already subdued me. "Who the hell are you? And what do you want?"

My attacker and would-be poltergeist burped loudly, a pungent burst of air that could probably kill a dragon. I coughed and controlled the urge to puke. "I'm your worst nightmare." Okay, so this guy was a fan of the old *Rambo* movies. "I will hunt you down and I will kill you." *Wrong quote, dude.* Liam Neeson would be pissed for being misquoted. "I'm going to skin you alive and use your hide for a coat." Fuck, this was quickly getting stupid, and I was nowhere close to knowing who he was.

"Name?" I asked, my voice dangerously quiet and calm. Maybe I would finally get to find out what other weird powers I had. Could I maybe just incinerate this creep with a single look?

He hiccupped and snorted, his head slumping toward mine. He was about to pass out. I shook him awake.

"Baburaj. My name is Bab-buraj," he said with an inebriated smile that looked more like a grimace. "I'm a demigod, and I am here to end your pathetic life."

I dropped him, surprised, and he slid down to the

floor in a heap of flesh and bones. This was the god who had been chasing me and had almost killed me not that long ago? Bob what? What kind of a name was that for a Hindu demigod? And who was he calling pathetic? Talk about the pot calling the kettle black.

I turned to Fouchard and pointed at the sniveling idiot by my feet, forgetting my boyfriend couldn't see him. "Meet Bob, my would-be assassin." Unfortunately I had underestimated his powers, because even drunk as a skunk, Bob just vanished into thin air. "And there he goes."

It was going to be a long week.

TWELVE

COFFEE, PASTRIES, AND EMBARRASSING CONVERSATION

"Holy shit, Aiden." Cristina stood by me, expertly balancing a tray full of dirty dishes in one hand. "Can you snap out of it? You look like the Grinch."

I couldn't snap out of it. This dark cloud hung over me like the Grim Reaper waiting for me to die. Except I was not the one in danger—at least not any more than usual. Fouchard, my lovely and cranky boyfriend, was the one in danger, at least according to Taz. Though I had always taken everything witches told me with a large grain of salt, this time I believed it. Taz might be a pain in my ass but I knew she was trustworthy. It had taken me a long time to admit it to myself, but I did count her as a friend now—not that I would ever tell her—a friend I knew I could trust to be there whenever I needed her.

"If your precious warlock cop was in danger, would you be all smiles and rainbows?" The fact that Fouchard had refused to let me go with him while he drove Vee to camp didn't help me feel any better. What if something happened on the way there and I wasn't around? Of course, my merman was so much more powerful physically than I was and had his own magical powers, but not knowing where the danger was coming from was eating me alive.

"Tó can handle himself," she replied, shifting the tray to the other hand. "But yes, I'd be worried too. However, *meu amigo*, sitting here sulking is not going to help, is it?" My recent lessons in Portuguese had finally begun to sink into my thick brain, and I was understanding the lingo a lot better these days. I smiled at her calling me her friend, and her lovely face opened into a grin. "*Melhor, muito melhor*. So much better. Maybe you could help me a bit, boss. I'm a little overwhelmed here."

In my distress, I had neglected to notice the sheer multitude of people now sitting around the tables of my coffee establishment. I stood up, freeing up much-needed table space, and headed outside to take orders.

Since Taz had told me about her vision, I hadn't been able to sleep much or relax in any shape or form unless I was wrapped around my man, knowing he was safe and sound next to me. It had been almost a week now, and nothing had happened since our close encounter with the most ridiculous demigod in the history of mythology, Bob the Drunkard. He hadn't shown up since that night he tried to kill me, but I knew it was coming. He was probably just licking his dignity wounds—if he had any dignity left in him.

Fouchard was worried for a different reason; his meeting with Neptune had yielded unsettling news about a poacher who was preying on merfolk for their tails. Apparently this new human obsession with everything mermaid had brought the old danger back after being dormant for almost a whole generation. What a couple we were: me worried about him, him worried about me and Vee, and me feeling guilty I was so worried about this threat to his life that I hadn't even given much thought to the very real fact that merfolk were dying in the hands of these unscrupulous hunters.

"Glad to see you moving around, Mr. Mercer." The deep, slightly mocking voice of my boyfriend had the effect of a hot shower, soothing all my nerves. I looked up at him, and my heart did that weird tap dance it always did when he was around. "Can I help with anything?"

I smiled, amused—and a little turned-on—by his pretense at not knowing me intimately. "How kind of you to offer, Mr. Fouchard, but I wouldn't want to impose on a customer." I could play the game. "Why don't you go sit down, and I'll come to take your order in a minute."

Fouchard licked his lips and moved around me toward the door, his hand surreptitiously brushing across my butt cheeks. I muffled a gasp. *Bastard.* Good thing I was wearing an apron that hid my reaction to his sneaky move.

I finished taking the orders in the esplanade and followed my merrow indoors. He was hanging by the counter, drinking a *bica* and chatting with Cristina.

"Nice, getting cozy behind my back," I joked, leaning against Fouchard. My body just seemed to belong there, as if it had been carved out from his, one of that two-piece puzzle. "Can't trust you two."

Cristina snorted, and Fouchard's arm went around my waist to pull me closer. "There's no one else for me, sweetheart," he whispered for my ears only, and I melted. His warm lips grazed my earlobe, causing a shiver to run through me from head to toe. It was lovely to be loved like this, as unexpected as it had been for me, the lone foster child without a past. "Love you."

As much as I wanted to stand there, tucked against my boyfriend's side, shooting the breeze, I had a whole café packed with beachgoers who demanded service. Both Cristina and I spent the rest of the day serving tables and putting sandwiches together while Fouchard did his best to both help and fluster me with his smoldering glances and wordless promises of delights. I couldn't wait to close the store and go home with him.

The crowds started to dwindle away as the afternoon went on, and by early evening the place was practically empty, allowing the three of us more time to actually talk. We sat around one of the tables in the back, speaking in hushed tones not because we were afraid someone would overhear us, but out of sheer exhaustion—it had been a very long day.

"Thank you, Naël," I said, reaching for his hand on the tabletop. He laced his fingers around mine and gave my hand a comforting squeeze. "I don't know what we would do without your help."

"I knew you'd need my business expertise from the moment I met you." He said it with a deadpan expression, but I could hear the amusement underneath the cockiness. I gave him a not-so-nice hand squeeze. He laughed. "But I must admit, despite your lack of business savvy, Bicas R Us is thriving, even if very few people can pronounce the name of your shop correctly." It was true. Most locals pronounced it as Bicas Err Ooss which always made me smile, especially at the hard, guttural pronunciation of the R in the middle.

I leaned over to him and kissed his lips. "Well, Mr. Cranky, thank you anyway," I said.

"Yes, thank you, Naël. It's been crazy lately,"

Cristina said, wiping her brow with a napkin. With the doors opening and closing nonstop all day, the air conditioner was having a hard time keeping up. "Maybe we should give some thought to hiring extra help, Aiden."

"I would be glad to help—with the right incentives of course." Taz appeared out of thin air beside us, her legs daintily crossed and a huge hat covering her red hair. "I could be persuaded by free pastries."

Cristina put a hand to her chest, yelping. "Shit, Taz, you scared the crap out of me."

I shook my head, a resigned frown on my face. "You really have to stop doing that, witch," I told her, not expecting her to actually do it. "There is such a thing as walking in through the door."

She waved a hand above her head. "And what's the fun in that?" It would most likely shave some years off of our lives. Every time she did her appearing act, it scared off a few precious minutes. "A woman has to have some fun in life. Right, Cristina?"

Cristina snorted. "Sorry, Taz. I'm with Aiden on this one. I don't know how much more my heart can take." She got to her feet. "Want something to drink?"

While my friend left to go get the witch a coffee, Taz removed her wide-brimmed hat and squinted at the two of us. "You look awful," she exclaimed with her usual aplomb and lack of filter. "You smell ripe too."

Fouchard laughed, and I groaned. "Thank you for your sharp observations, Taz," I said, letting go of my boyfriend's hand. "We have been working our asses off all day in the heat, so yes, we're probably a bit sweaty. But thank you for pointing it out."

"Well, it just doesn't look good for a coffee shop owner to look so disheveled, that's all." She tucked a few wild strands of hair back into her french braid. "I'm looking out for your interests."

Right, and I am a raging womanizer. "As much as I love having you scare the shit out of all of us, what exactly are you doing here?"

She ran a finger over her lips as if smoothing her bright red lipstick and trained her piercing eyes on me. "Just checking on my friends, that's all." Her eyes told me a different story; she was still worried about her vision and what it may mean. I swallowed hard at the implication. "Any unusual happenings lately, Naël?"

I turned my anxious eyes to my merman, who didn't seem to have a care in the world, his hands behind his head in a pose that made his strong, well-defined arm muscles flex and pop. Any other time I'd have been turned into hardwood, but I was too worried about what Taz seemed to believe was about to happen. "If you are alluding to your vision, my friend, no; nothing weird has happened," he said. "It was only a dream, Taz. I'm in no more danger than I've ever been."

"Only fools discount visions as bad dreams," Taz said, leaning forward on the table. "I'd sleep better at night knowing you are keeping a watchful eye on things."

"He insists on driving by himself to take and pick up Vee from camp," I blurted out like a ten-year-old tattling on a sibling. Fouchard threw me a half amused, half pissed-off glance. "Sorry, Naël, but after what happened to Vee and me, I can't stop worrying. I'd be a lot more relaxed if you let me tag along on those trips."

Fouchard brought his arms down and covered my hands with his. "Nothing bad is going to happen," he said in a hushed tone. "I'm a big boy, in case you haven't noticed. I can take care of myself."

Cristina returned with a tray packed with coffee and pastries. We all looked at her, momentarily distracted from our conversation. "What? These are all leftovers that will go to waste. I can't drop them off at the shelter tonight."

She set the tray down, and we all attacked the sweet confections—more out of frustration and stress than real hunger, even though I hadn't had anything to eat since breakfast.

"I know you are perfectly capable, Naël, but I worry." Fuck. I worried all the time. That was one side effect of being in love I was not too crazy about. "I can't help it."

Fouchard smiled, and my heart calmed down. "I know, Aiden, and I love you for it," he said, his thumb rubbing the top of my hand. "But I need you to stop it." I was about to protest when he leaned closer and whispered, "If you don't stop it, I will have to rethink what I was planning to do to you tonight." My cheeks —both upper and lower—burnt in excitement and anticipation. I had no clue what the plan entailed, but his tone promised something I would like. A lot.

"Be kind, Naël, and put the poor guy out of his misery. Let him coddle you a bit for his own peace of mind." Cristina came to the rescue, her lips covered in sugar from one of the *Bolas de Berlim*, a giant ball of sweet fried dough. "It's a give and take. You give him this, he will probably give you head tonight."

I choked and spat out the bite of pastry I had been happily munching on.

Fouchard and Taz guffawed in unison, as if they were the best friends in the world. "Look what you did, Cristina; my poor boyfriend just about choked to death because of you." He patted my back as if he was trying to burp me.

Cristina puckered her lips, feigning innocence. "At least he's not choking on your—"

Still coughing, I propelled myself over the table to cover her mouth before she blurted out the last word.

She protested against my hand, and I shook my head, refusing to let go. This was not a conversation to have with friends. I may be a man-whore—or had been one—but there were things that were not to be discussed outside the couple.

Fouchard grabbed my wrist and pried my hand from her lips. "Let her breathe, Aiden," he said, still chuckling. I did. Reluctantly.

Cristina shook her head and licked her lips. The sugar previously on them was now covering my fingers. "All I was going to say was…." I threw her a warning glance as I wiped my hand on a napkin. "All I was about to say was that at least he's not choking on your lips." She winked and smirked, fully aware she had gotten me. She had also successfully distracted me from my worries for a moment.

I looked up at the sky in exaggerated exasperation. "God give me patience. Who needs enemies with friends like these?"

THIRTEEN

PREMONITIONS, POACHERS, AND FEARS

FOR SOME UNKNOWN REASON, MY MIND KEPT wandering off to Brother Serafim, the Einstein-look-alike oracle who had given me the unsettling and unbelievable news about my parents. I hadn't thought about it much, my mind too busy with worry for Fouchard, but that day the Oracle's words kept playing around in my mind like a broken record. *Lakshmi was your mother*. But who was my father? I had forgotten to ask for his name or, more importantly, if he was still alive.

"Ground control to Major Mercer." Cristina's generous bosom was hanging a bit too revealingly over the counter as she tried to bring me back from my reveries. "Man. You are in la-la land today, aren't you?"

Shaking my head to dispel those thoughts, I

straightened and waved in her direction. "Girl, can you get those under control?" I pointed at her boobs, and she laughed. "This is not that kind of joint."

"Well, I don't know whether to feel flattered or disturbed that you of all people have noticed my girls," Cristina said, a wicked smile on her lips as she fixed herself. I humphed, and she laughed. "This stupid shirt seems a bit intimidated by them."

"TMI, *amiga*, TMI." I quipped, turning around to check the room. The place was not busy that morning. The day had dawned overcast and windy again, and not too many locals had ventured to the beach. Fouchard—still stubbornly refusing to accept my offer of company on his way back and forth from Vee's camp—had promised to come and hang out for a while. A quick glance at the wall clock confirmed he was running late, which immediately made my pulse quicken and my throat tighten in worry. "Damn it, Naël, you should have been here already."

My phone vibrated in my jeans pocket. It was my merrow. I quickly answered. "Where are you? What happened?"

Fouchard's lovely voice was colored with amusement. "Whoa, sweetheart. I'm fine. I had to make a stop on the way," he said. "I'll be there in fifteen." I let out a loud exhale. "Stop worrying, Aiden. Please."

How could I? How could I just ignore such an ominous vision? A year ago, I'd have ignored it, not being too trusting of witches or any other magical, but now I knew better than to dismiss certain things. Not knowing what or where this danger was coming from was driving me crazy. There was no guarantee I'd be able to protect my giant of a boyfriend, but it appeased my nerves to be near him.

As promised, Fouchard was walking through the door of my coffee shop fifteen minutes later, that forbidding expression of his opened into a wide grin. "I got it," he said, nonsensically. Cristina and I raised our eyebrows at the same time. "The party planner I wanted for Vee's birthday party."

Shit, I had forgotten that her birthday was quickly approaching. "Is that why you're late?"

He enveloped me in a bear hug and kissed my forehead. His unusual, almost bubbly mood was hard to resist. I chuckled against his shirt.

"Now I'm jealous and feeling a little left out of this love fest," Cristina said with a fake pout. Fouchard and I waved her in, and she quickly joined our hug. "This is better. I feel so loved right now." Her cheerfulness was contagious, and we all burst out laughing.

Since there wasn't much to do and a walk on the *paradão* didn't seem like a viable idea, we sat and talked. Antonio Silva showed up in the early afternoon and sat with us, joining our conversation uninvited.

Be nice, Aiden. You promised. I didn't need my boyfriend's pointed glances to remember our conversation of a few days ago. I would do my best not to want to murder the cop.

"Any news about the poacher?" Fouchard asked Silva, his hand over mine in warning.

"Nothing as yet," the warlock said, his dark eyes following Cristina around the room. The image of a lion watching a young impala popped into my head. I narrowed my eyes, a little knot of protective anger gathering in my throat. "But the body count is rising. Two more merrows were found dead and stripped of their tail skin." A violent shiver ran through me. I'd been so worried about Fouchard and the prophecy that I had almost forgotten about the terrible wave of murders ravaging the merfolk population. "It was a brutal crime. Forensics seem to show that they were skinned alive and then killed."

I blinked at my boyfriend. Why would they do that if the only thing they wanted was the skins?

Fouchard explained, "When a merrow dies, the shine of their tails dies along with the body. The tails become grayish and dull and they don't fetch the same kind of money a fresh, shiny tail will."

That was— I didn't even have a word to describe such an act. It was bad enough to kill before stealing their tails, but this? Who were these criminals?

"We have men on every beach on this coast, but

we don't have enough manpower to place undercover agents on ships and leisure vessels," Silva continued. "What does Neptune have to say about this, Fouchard?"

Fouchard shrugged. "What can he say? He has soldiers everywhere he considers vulnerable places, but with merfolk living both in the sea and on land, it is virtually impossible to guarantee their safety." Cristina was standing behind Silva's chair and biting her nails as if she hadn't eaten in years. "He's advising everyone to be on the lookout and not to travel alone if possible." I gave him a pointed look, and he shrugged again. "Aiden, I'm not just any merman. I have military training and can take care of myself."

Cristina came around and sat on the cop's lap. "That is absolutely horrible. What can I do?"

Silva let out a single chuckle. "You can give thanks you're not a mermaid."

"But Vee is," Cristina protested, her face turning red with outrage. "What if something happens to her?"

Fouchard leaned over the table and touched her arm. "She's okay. They are well watched in both camps and not allowed to leave with anyone but their guardians, and after that, I have her under my supervision all the time." His assurances seemed to soothe her, at least a bit, but now I was doubly worried—for

Fouchard and Vee. Damn it. Just couldn't catch a break.

A phone vibrated the table, and we all looked at our own phones, not sure which was ringing. It was Fouchard's. I took advantage of the break in the conversation to go grab a cold beer from the fridge and make myself a sandwich. Worrying made me extremely hungry. By the time I returned, my boyfriend was standing as if ready to go. "Where are you going?"

"Just got a message from Neptune," he said, grabbing my glass and taking a sip of my beer. "Gotta go. He says it's urgent."

"I can go with you," I offered without much hope he'd accept. I wouldn't mind waiting at his house while he conferred with the Big Fish, knowing there would be love to be made on that underground beach of his.

He gulped down the golden liquid and wiped the foam from his luscious lips. "No, that's okay. Meet me at my house after you close, okay?" He gave me a quick kiss on the lips. "I will call you when I'm back." And he left.

The business was so slow, I left Cristina for a while to go reenergize a bit. The wind was wild and punishing outside, perfect for such a recharge. I walked in the *paradão*, slapped crazy by the moving air and the sand it carried until my skin was red and I felt renewed. It was almost closing time when I began walking back to the store.

It came out of nowhere; something inside me jammed. It was as if whatever mechanism made my heart pump blood to the rest of my body had gotten stuck. It became hard to breathe, and my chest hurt. For a moment I thought I was having a heart attack. With a jolt, I realized I was having a premonition. A fucking premonition. Since when did I have those? I was not a witch or a seer.

Unlike what I always thought a premonition was like, this was not a clear picture of what was about to happen but more of a feeling, one that left me in total terror. The witch's vision had come to pass. Something terrible had just happened to the man I loved.

I didn't know how I got there, but one minute I was standing at the end of the *paradão* with my hand clenched over my chest, and the next I was crossing the threshold into my coffee shop. "Cristina, have you heard from Fouchard?" I yelled from the door.

Cristina turned around from the table she was cleaning. "No, why?" The confused expression on her face quickly mutated to worry. "What happened? You look like you've seen a ghost."

I grabbed the closest chair and sat, afraid my wobbly legs would collapse beneath me. "He's in trouble. Something happened."

Cristina didn't ask how I knew or how I could be

so sure. She crossed the distance between us and hugged me. "Have you called him?"

No, I hadn't. I was so sure something was wrong that I didn't even think of doing it. I grabbed my phone and fumbled with my shaking fingers to punch in the number. The phone rang until it finally went to voicemail. My merman was not picking up. There was no way Neptune would have kept him this late. Even before I broke the connection, another call came through.

"Vee? Are you okay?" Maybe Fouchard had forgotten his phone and was calling from his sister's.

"Where's Naël? I've been waiting forever for him to come pick me up." The girl's voice reflected what I was feeling. Somehow she also knew. "Something must have happened, Aiden. He wouldn't make me wait this long."

"We'll come and get you right now," I said, staring at Cristina, who was already grabbing her car keys and her bag. "Hold tight, we'll be there in a few."

"Aiden." Vee's voice sounded younger than usual, tiny and thin. "What if something terrible happened to him?"

I swallowed the giant knot in my throat. "He's fine," I lied to her and myself. "Who would have the guts to mess with your brother? He's big and scary."

Cristina's car was parked illegally in the back. Camp was only ten minutes away, down the coast a bit, somewhere between my house and Fouchard's. Cristina didn't mess around and put the pedal to the metal. Vee was waiting for us at the door, looking like a lost puppy. As soon as she saw us, she got to her feet and waved at us, her chin quivering and eyes suspiciously shiny.

I jumped out of the car even before it had totally stopped and ran to her. She didn't hesitate and threw herself into my arms, sobbing. "Aiden, something bad happened. I just know it." Could she have had a premonition of sorts too? Or was her bond with her brother so strong, she could feel when something was not right?

I ran a hand over her curly hair. "How do you know that? He went to talk to Neptune, so he's probably just running late." God, I hoped that's what was going on and not something much more sinister. "You're coming home with me, and we'll try to figure out what happened, okay?"

Cristina had the passenger door open and was looking at us with deep worry in her eyes. I turned to the camp monitor who had been kind enough to stay late with Vee and thanked her before leading a still-sobbing mermaid to the car.

Vee settled in the back seat while I sidled into the front seat, half turned back to look at her.

"He always calls if he's running late. Always," she

said, hiccupping between words. "I just know some-thing bad happened."

The crushing feeling on my chest told me the same, but I wasn't ready to let go of hope. "How do you contact Neptune? Do you have his phone number?" She shook her head, tears streaking her beautiful freckled face. I still had the phone numbers of the three mermaids I had met while investigating the serial killer who had nearly killed Vee. I searched my contacts and dialed.

"Hello, Mary." I still so wanted to call her Ariel, but this was not time for jokes. "Remember me, Aiden Mercer?"

"Hi, Mr. Mercer, what's going on?" It looked like Mary was not one for small talk. "Is something wrong?"

I sighed. "That's what I'm trying to find out," I told her, my eyes never leaving the girl in the back seat. Cristina had started the car, and we were driving back to my place. Now that there was a child in the car, my friend drove a lot slower and more responsibly. "Fouchard had a meeting with Neptune earlier today, but we haven't heard from him since and he never picked up his little sister from camp. Is there any way you can check with your king and find out if Fouchard is still there? We're worried sick."

"Hold the line while I call my friend Serena. She's Neptune's daughter."

Even though I had been dating a merman for the past few months, it was still weird to hear about how merfolk lived very similar lives to humans. I heard a soft click and then silence for a few minutes. All three of us exchanged worried looks, not daring to say a word. Another click announced Mary's return. "Hey, Mr. Mercer, Serena checked with her dad and he said he never met with Fouchard. He met with him a few days ago, but not today."

An arctic cold descended upon me, freezing my bones. For a moment, I stopped breathing. *No, not my Naël.*

FOURTEEN

TRACKING A MERMAN

"I have no other information, Aiden, I'm sorry." The tall warlock shook his head, for once looking and sounding sincere. "We're looking into it, but we don't even know where it happened."

In the last couple hours, my lungs had to learn how to breathe again, to break through that elephantine weight that had settled on my chest. We still had no clue where my boyfriend was, and it was killing me. For once I wished I was acquainted with all my god-like gifts; I might have one that would help me hunt down whoever had taken my beautiful merrow and rescue him. Silva was the next best thing, not something that filled me with hope and confidence.

"The phone." Vee's little voice rose above all others, and we all went quiet and stared at her. "Track his phone."

Silva sighed. "We did already. It's been turned off."

"Not that one," she said, lifting her red-rimmed eyes to me. "The weird one he bought after my kidnapping, one with a tracking chip like the one I have under my skin."

That was the first time I heard of this. Despite the situation, I felt a pang of doubt; why hadn't he shared this with me?

"He didn't tell you, Aiden, because he didn't want you to worry," she continued. "I found out by accident. It doesn't work as a real phone, more like a tracker."

Silva sat down next to her on the couch. We were all milling around my living room, trying to come up with something, anything that would help us find my love.

"Honey, even if he has it with him and it's on, a tracker can't be tracked. It only follows signals, not the opposite."

Vee shook her head. "No, it is trackable," she insisted. "He was so paranoid about what happened to me and then with all this talk about a premonition, Aiden's attacker, the poacher… he just wanted to cover all the bases." She gave me a sad little smile. "He meant to ask you to wear one too."

Fouchard was just as worried about all this as I

was, but his protective side didn't want me to know how much. Fool. Sweet, lovable fool. "Whoever has him probably found it."

She shook her head again. "Not likely," she said. "He told me that he had learned from his military training to hide something small like that. He must have it hidden somewhere safe." She handed me her phone. "He downloaded the tracking app on my phone. 'If you ever need me and can't get a hold of me, you can find out where I'm at,' he told me. You have to activate the GPS on the app."

I grabbed the phone in a trance. Could it be this simple? And why hadn't Vee told us this as soon as we figured something had happened to him? *She's a kid, Aiden. She was scared and couldn't think straight.* I asked her anyway, "Why didn't you try to track him when you were waiting for him at the camp?"

A cloud went over her pretty eyes and I instantly felt like a cad for bringing it up. "I was on the phone with one of my mermaid friends," she said, her lips trembling slightly. "We were so busy making plans for my birthday, I didn't even notice how late it was until one of the monitors came out to check on me." I brushed my hand over her wild hair. "Are you going to do it or not?" The Vee who I knew was back.

I did as she told me and pressed the activate icon. The phone sang a weird beeping song, and a GPS-like screen lit up. On the bottom there was a text box and a line of instructions that read *Type something.* I obliged. *This is Aiden. Where are you, Naël?* No response. Frustrated that the damned gizmo wanted to play games at a time like this, I almost threw it across the room just as another beep reached my ears.

Why the hell did it take you so long? it read. What the hell? Was the gadget making jokes? Then another message came through, one that almost made my heart stop. *You better hurry here. I'm not sure when these lunatics will come back.*

"It's him. He's sending me messages," I exclaimed, sounding like an excited schoolboy. "He's alive."

As the others all gathered around me to take a peek, Vee digging her way through the wall of adult bodies, I sent him another message. *Where are you? Are you okay?*

Seconds that felt like a hundred years passed before he answered. *I'm fine. Check the fucking GPS. It should have my location.* I moved my eyes to study the map on the screen, but another message came through. *I hope Vee is not reading this message.*

Idiot! Being the father figure even now. If it weren't for the worry that had settled like a rock at the bottom of my stomach, I'd have laughed.

The little man stick figure on the screen was not moving but was not too far from my house, just up the coast a bit past Cascais where the Tagus River finally totally melded with the ocean and the waves were wild and dangerous. I typed, *Got the location. On our way.*

Don't bring Vee. Too dangerous. The message didn't leave space for discussion, and Vee's face turned that purple hue it often did when she was mad. She was going to blow up.

Cristina was faster than I was and immediately draped an arm across the girl's skinny shoulders to pull her against her side. "We are going to let the big scary men do their manly thing, and we will just bake some cookies so your brother has something sweet to munch on when he comes back." Vee was about to protest when my friend bent down and whispered, "Men's egos are very fragile. We have to pretend we're weak so they don't shatter."

I suppressed a chuckle with my hand and Cristina winked at me.

One look at Vee told me the ruse had worked; she had straightened her back, her coloring back to normal, and her lips curling in that conspiratorial expression she adopted whenever she thought she was pulling one over her brother.

"You strong macho men go rescue Fouchard while

we stay here and comfort each other." Cristina was so deadpan, I had a hard time not laughing despite the situation. Cristina, the least meek woman I knew, pretending to be one was hilarious. I stored the information to share with my man when he was back home, safe and sound. He'd get a kick out of it.

My stomach clenched, and I repeated the mantra I had been whispering to myself: *he'll be back soon, he'll be fine.*

We didn't lose any time. Silva offered to drive, and I didn't argue, holding on to the phone for dear life. Thankfully the early evening traffic had dwindled to almost nothing, and we were able to make great time. Once in a while, Fouchard would send me a short message telling me he was still okay but that he would be really pissed if the kidnappers got to him before we did. My lips couldn't decide whether to smile in amusement or frown in worry.

Silva parked the car under a tree on the side of the lonely coastal road, and we walked the rest of the way to where the beeping GPS was guiding us. There was no stairway or even a path down the side of the hill we had to tackle, so the progress was painfully slow. Between the steepness and the loose rocks, plus the fact it was a dark cloudy night, our trek was difficult and dangerous. I slipped a couple times, and by the time we arrived at the bottom, where the cliff flattened into a sort of shelf, I was bleeding from scratches on my arms and legs. I vaguely acknowledged the quick healing taking place, leaving only the blood as evidence of any previous wounds while I ran inside the ramshackle hut built against the side of the cliff.

It was dark inside, but I could discern a slumped figure in a corner. "Naël?" I threw myself on my knees, wincing as I hit the rocky floor. "Are you okay?"

"Finally. I thought I was going to die here waiting for my knight in shining armor to come and save me." He was fine, his usual bite still intact. "My hands are tied." How had he messaged me? As soon as I reached out to untie him, I realized he had handcuffs on instead of zip ties, which allowed him to hold and type on a phone but not much else. "Silva, is that you?" he asked when the cop entered the hut behind me. "Oh man, you're going to love this."

"Silva, can you unlock the handcuffs?" The warlock crossed the space between us and waved his fingers at the silver cuffs. They popped open, freeing Fouchard's hands. My mouth fell open. I had never seen him perform any magic, and I'd been beginning to wonder whether he could or if maybe he was shooting blanks, so to speak.

"Let's get out of here," Fouchard said, shuffling to his feet. We didn't have to be told twice. I slipped an arm under his armpit and headed out of the hut.

Fouchard stumbled and almost fell. "Sorry, guys, you have to help me a bit more. I may have a broken leg."

I saw red, hot bright blood red.

"Don't get your knickers in a bunch, Aiden. It wasn't the damned idiots who brought me here. I tried to climb the fucking bluff with my hands tied, and needless to say, I fell."

It didn't make me feel any better or any more forgiving toward whoever these guys were. Silva came around to the other side and offered his shoulder for support. How in heaven's name were we going to climb the freaking crag with a giant of a man in tow? The same cliff we'd had so much trouble negotiating on our way down?

Silva was wondering the same. "There must be an easier way out," he said. "Did you come down the cliff on your own, Fouchard?"

Fouchard shook his head. "No, they knocked me out. I was unconscious." Another thing I would have to square out with the bastards.

"There is no way they would have brought you down that cliff," Silva said, looking around us.

The night had darkened further, if that was even possible. It was hard to see the drop from the shelf we were standing on, much less see anything else around us. The ocean crashing into the rocks below us and the sound of our breathing filled the silence of the night. I could teleport to the top but couldn't bring anyone with me. What a useless talent then, if I couldn't use it to protect those I loved. But it did help when Vee had been kidnapped by that serial killer a few months ago, I reminded myself.

"I'm going to risk it," Silva said, and both Fouchard and I stared at him, confused. What was he talking about? He waved his fingers in the air again, and the whole area became drenched in an eerie, soft glow that allowed us to see the ground and the cliff. It would also be visible to the kidnappers if they were close enough. "Aiden, quick, check the area for an easier path."

It didn't take long to find a path of sorts going up the side of the cliff right behind the hut. It had been built with rocks and pieces of driftwood and it was narrow, too narrow for three grown men to climb side by side, but better than what we thought we had to do. "Silva, you stay behind us just in case," I said, already heading to it, a limping Fouchard hanging from my shoulder.

Silva scoffed. "In case you both fall? Thank you, Aiden, I knew you didn't like me, but I didn't realize how much until just now. If you guys fall, I'll be dust."

Fouchard laughed. "Well, Silva, you are a cop after all. To serve and protect and all that shit, right?" I laughed against his side, placing my other hand on my boyfriend's hard abs for further support as we started our climb.

The warlock humphed, but didn't say anything, stationing himself right behind us. The climb was arduous, but we made good progress, and Silva was able to limit the magic glow to a smaller area so it wouldn't be as visible elsewhere. Fouchard stood on his own, but I could tell he was hurting, as low groans escaped his lips once in a while. After what felt like years, we crested the cliff and were able to get in the car and drive away.

I sat in the back with Fouchard, who I now could see clearly enough. I cringed at the way he looked, battered and bleeding. He had a big gash on his forehead, and my fingers found blood-caked hair on the top of his scalp as I examined him. "What the hell did they do?"

"They hit me with something to knock me out," Fouchard said, his voice faint and ragged. He was exhausted. "It's fine. I've had worse."

"Stop acting like a big tough marine," I exclaimed, frustrated and worried. "Lean on me and rest. It's not fine, and I'm going to kill the fuckers who did this to you."

A weak chuckle escaped his lips. "Now, there's my knight-in-shining armor," he said, sliding on the seat until his head was resting on my shoulder and his hand on my knee. "I love you, sweetheart."

Silva, who had been quiet since we got in the car, turned around for a moment, his hands tight on the steering wheel. "You said I was going to love this, Fouchard. What did you mean by that?"

His voice was so soft, we could barely make out the words when he said, "Oh yeah, one of the poachers is a cop. I thought you'd get a kick out of that."

FIFTEEN

COFFEE AND PLANS

"No, no, no. I won't hear of it." I stomped away from Fouchard and Cristina with my fingers stuck in my ears. I was fully aware I was acting like a child, but I couldn't care less. My boyfriend's safety was at stake, and I wouldn't take any risks. "You will go into hiding until these poachers have been apprehended."

Fouchard groaned loudly, his patience obviously stretched to the limits by my stubbornness. "Don't be ridiculous, Aiden. Where exactly are you going to hide me that they can't find? Better to face this problem head-on." He stood up and stormed in my direction to hold me by the shoulders and turn me around to face him. "Besides, I have Vee to think about, Aiden. I can't possibly go into hiding and leave her open to the poachers."

I narrowed my eyes, getting more annoyed by the

minute. My man was just making excuses. "You were the one who told us the poachers are only interested in older males." A tiny quiver of his lip was all that showed I had hit the target. "She will be perfectly safe with Cristina and me." Well, maybe not me with my demigod stalker at my heels, but Cristina was just a mortal with nothing any of the magicals wanted— with the possible exception of Silva, of course, but that was a want of a different kind.

Fouchard had told us upon his release that when he came to in the hut, he pretended he was still unconscious so he could listen in to the kidnappers' conversation. The two men had not only revealed that one of them was indeed a police officer but also the fact that they were not interested in risking getting caught for killing and skinning younger or female merfolk. Apparently their tails started in faded colors as youngsters and then grew brighter and more extravagant and distinct as they grow older. Females, much like the peahens at the castle, sported much humbler colors while the males developed into true works of art—the kind of color patterns that brought in a fortune on the black market.

"I still wouldn't feel comfortable," Fouchard protested, giving me one of his rock-melting glares. He didn't intimidate me anymore. "They could change their minds suddenly, and then what?"

Cristina stepped in. "I hate to say this, but I think

Aiden is right." Hated to say I was right? I probably should rethink who my friends were. "Now that we know one of them is a cop, Tó will be able to figure out who he is. Once he's caught, then things can go back to normal—or what goes for normal in your freakish world." She chuckled nervously, her eyes bouncing back from me to Fouchard. "You're not going to have a blow up about this, are you? Remember how hard it was on both of you guys the last time you fought."

For some reason, those words helped me relax just enough to make a joke. "Well, it was not all bad," I said, my eyes roaming to my boyfriend's intense dark eyes. "The make-up sex was epic."

All three of us burst out laughing, tension melting away with each chuckle. Fouchard linked his hands behind my back and pulled me closer to kiss me. "No need to fight to have a repeat session though," he whispered over my thirsty lips before taking them with his.

"*Merda*, and there they go again," Cristina said, feigning outrage. "You guys are the most oversexed couple I have ever known."

Still gasping for air as our lips parted, I stared at her and squinted. Fouchard's body was still glued to mine, and I could feel how our conversation was affecting him.

"All right, I admit," Cristina said, sliding to her

feet, "you are also one of the cutest couples I have ever met." She sashayed over and hugged both of us. "I love you guys. After all you've been through, you deserve a good roll in the hay every so often. Time to shake it off and open the shop." She walked away to go unlock the door to the patio where a couple of customers had already claimed a table.

"It will be just a few days," I said, still holding him as if for dear life. "I will ask Taz to ask the monks if you can hide there."

Bending down, he brought his mouth down on mine in a brief kiss. "I will do it only if you come with me." Oh, I wanted that. Very much. But it was the peak of summer, and Cristina couldn't do all the work by herself. "I know what you're thinking, but you can come after you close and stay the night, right? It's not far."

I nodded enthusiastically. I loved that plan. "Vee will stay with Cristina, and maybe Taz can lend a hand too." I hadn't seen her in a few days, but I knew where to find her. She had a kitschy palm reading salon in town where she was known as Ms. Solara and made money pretending to be what she really was: a witch. I was sure she wouldn't mind watching and protecting Vee. "It will be like a little getaway."

Fouchard snorted. "Yeah, complete with poachers wanting to skin me alive."

I shivered. Not something I liked thinking about.

We were not sure why they had kept Fouchard in the hut instead of killing him right away, but whatever the reason was, I was very grateful for it.

"Okay, get in touch with the witch before I change my mind."

In my hurry to get to the phone, I pushed him away a bit too roughly, and he teetered for a moment, his leg still having trouble holding his full weight. "Shit! Sorry, Naël. Are you okay?" His leg was not broken as we originally thought, but he had a bad ankle sprain. The stubborn idiot refused to use his crutches, and I had to threaten him with a future of zero sex to make him wear the boot that morning.

"I'm fine," he said, his wince belying his words. "Go call Taz."

Taz was more than willing to speak to the powers that be and request for us to stay at the convent for a few days. In true Taz style, she showed up at the coffee shop a couple hours later, wearing a bright pareo in oranges and reds tied around her slender waist, a cropped white tank top, and another straw hat that looked like a UFO. She waltzed into the store out of empty space to stand by the counter, her cherry-red lips puckered as if about to kiss someone and twirling her large sunglasses on one finger.

"Can you please stop doing that? You're going to spook my customers," I said, more out of habit than real concern. I knew she was glamored and that no one in the store had seen her.

"Don't get your panties all in a twist, sister." She plopped herself on a chair and removed her large hat to reveal red hair tucked into a large, fluffy bun. "The High Priestess has gotten you permission to stay with the monks for as long as you need."

That was good news, even though it meant I would only see my merman at night after work, but he would be safe and sound. "Thank you, Taz." I could be gracious when I wanted to.

"The Brothers will also be able to treat your leg, Naël," she continued, making a great production of checking out Fouchard's muscled calf and ankle. I threw her a fulminating glance, but she ignored it. "And as for you, my cranky friend, the Oracle may also be able to shed extra light onto your would-be assassin." Or my origins. I was still so stunned by the revelation of my last visit to the Convento dos Capuchos that I hadn't had much time to think about all its implications. For example, what happened to my parents? I mean, if my mother was a divinity, wouldn't she be immortal? What about my druid father? Was he still alive? What happened to him?

Maybe I can meet my own parents. Wouldn't that be something? I shook my head, dismissing my fanciful thoughts, and focused on the job at hand, which was running a business. Fouchard hadn't been able to help out much since the rescue because of his leg, but he still spent most of the time at the store, reminding me he'd be there at the end of the day with his open and welcoming arms, the space I craved to be in every second of the day.

Between serving customers and preparing food, we set it all up for the next day. We would drive up later in the evening and settle for the night. I had been the one driving Vee to camp every morning and picking her up every evening in Fouchard's car, and I would be driving it back and forth from the convent. My boyfriend was uncharacteristically quiet and resigned about all of this, and I wondered whether he was just a bit scared as well. Fouchard was not the kind of man who would admit to something like that, the tough military side of him fighting with the sensitive, caring man I knew lay just underneath that facade. I knew the whole kidnapping had shaken him, as much as he pretended it didn't. For the past few nights he had trembled and whimpered against me while he slept in my arms, undoubtedly tormented with nightmares of what may have been if we hadn't found and rescued him. Anger boiled inside me every time I thought about it, and an almost electric buzzing ran along my body, threatening to burst through my muscle and skin. I wondered what would happen if I allowed that angry energy to escape.

"And you won't let her go with anyone, even

friends." Fouchard went through his long list of concerns with Cristina, who listened patiently, nodding and smiling encouragingly.

Silva met us at the store before closing with an update on the progress of the investigation—which amounted to almost nothing—while assuring Fouchard he would keep extra eyes on Vee. "She will be safe, man. I promise you." Despite my dislike for the warlock cop, I believed and trusted him on this. He had nothing to gain if something was to happen to the young mermaid and everything to lose, his reputation as an officer of the law notwithstanding. "Don't tell her, but I even have a female officer posing as a camp monitor so we can keep an eye on her from the inside."

"What about when she goes to mermaid camp?" Vee had been so excited to participate in this twice a week evening camp, Fouchard hadn't had the heart to tell her she couldn't go once the poacher danger became known and mermen began popping up dead and skinned along the coast.

"As strange as it sounds, I don't think she's in much danger there," Silva said, his arm propped on Cristina's slender shoulders. "She's surrounded by other merfolk who are all on red alert." Fouchard opened his mouth to protest, but the warlock lifted his hand between them. "However, I will have someone there too. A couple of our officers are merfolk. You don't have one thing to worry about."

I clasped my hand on his waist and pulled him to me. "See? All you have to worry about now is relaxing and think of better and more exciting ways of pleasing me when I come to you at night." I was only half joking. This reputed man whore had quit that life to totally focus on one man only but still spent a lot of his time fantasizing about sex. Except now I didn't obsess about how *I* felt but rather how I made *him* feel; I wanted to be the best lover that gorgeous, cranky merman had or would ever have. Making him feel good was a priority in my admittedly oversexed mind.

While everyone else burst out laughing, Fouchard barely cracked a smile. Worry was eating him from the inside out. "I feel I'm being the worst brother ever, Aiden," he had confessed to me the previous night. "What kind of man goes into hiding to save his skin and leaves his little sister vulnerable to danger?"

"Naël, she has all this people watching out for her," I told him, tugging on his waist. "In this case, you are more vulnerable than she is. These poachers are looking for adult males, not mermaids whose tails have barely any color."

Taz stepped forward. "The witches have put a glamor around Vee," she said. "It's sort of like an alarm. If anyone wishing her ill crosses it, it will burst into a loud siren-like sound that anyone within a mile can hear." I raised my eyebrows at her. This was the first time we were hearing about this. "Just an extra precaution. I wouldn't want anything to happen to your sister."

Fouchard groaned and shifted on his feet, wincing as he put weight on the injured foot. "Thank you all, guys," he said, leaning on me for support. "I really appreciate this, and I will pay you back in kind someday. I can't tell you what this means to me."

"Group hug!" Taz yelled, startling all of us. She took a look at Fouchard's face and shook her head. "Okay, virtual hug then."

Laughter rolled through the store, and some customers joined in even though they had no idea what it was all about. Our group dispersed then. Silva kissed Cristina and left, Taz just vanished like the Cheshire cat, and Cristina went back to the business of the coffee shop. I helped my grumpy boyfriend to a chair and sat beside him, our thighs touching and hands clasped over his knee. "You know you don't have to be the tough guy all the time, right?" I told him in a whisper.

He turned his face to me, his lips still set in a straight, rigid line. "Can't fight who I am, Aiden," he said, his thumb caressing my hand. "Never let them see you cry and all that."

"I'm not *them*, Naël," I replied. "I will never think less of you if you break down and cry."

He pulled on my hand and tilted his face toward mine until our lips were a whisper apart. "I know, sweetheart, I know." Our lips met, and for a moment I forgot there were customers around us, cruel poachers on the loose, and a demigod who wanted me dead. There was only my boyfriend and me locked in a kiss—magic of another kind.

SIXTEEN

SEXUAL HEALING

THE SKY, A VAST SEA OF BLACK SPRINKLED WITH diamonds, stretched above us as we sat side by side on the stone bench in the small cloister between the guest cell and the bathroom. The night hugged the convent in a silence broken only by the swooshing of the breeze through the trees and the hooting of the owls, an atmosphere that lulled us into a sense of false serenity, a feeling of safety and comfort. We knew that out there, there were at least two poachers after Fouchard and other mermen and a drunken demigod with a chip on his shoulder who was very motivated to eliminate me, but in that moment, we had nothing to worry about. It was just us and the sky above, a tiny corner of the universe that belonged to me and my boyfriend, a moment in time that required nothing but our presence.

"This is beautiful," Fouchard whispered.

While he stared at the stars, I was watching him, studying the perfect line of his jaw, the dark stubble covering his chin and his face, the luscious full lips that I could never get enough of. "*You* are beautiful, Naël." I brushed my hand on his cheek, his bristly facial hair a rough caress on my fingers. "You are the most beautiful creature in the world. What are you doing hanging out with me?"

He turned to me, narrowing his eyes. "What do you mean? I'm with you because I love you."

"But I'm just an idiot who has spent his whole life chasing the next lay and denying who deep down inside I knew I was—an unloved, unwanted child who didn't know where he'd come from and had no idea where he was headed." I had thought this many times but had never said it out loud. Doing so made it real, and I had always known the truth could be my undoing.

Fouchard grabbed my hands and squeezed them in his. "You are not an idiot, and you are not unloved. I love you. Vee and Cristina love you. Hell, Taz loves you."

My heart melted at his words. "But you said it yourself, I have no idea how to run my business, and I'm lazy, much preferring to bum around at the beach than do hard work of any kind." It'd been a long while since he had uttered those words, but they had hit a raw spot then, and the feeling they stirred still lingered today.

He brought my hands to his lips and kissed my knuckles with such tenderness, tears pooled in my eyes. "I was just teasing you. You know that, right?" It was a plea. "Kind of distracting myself from the fact I couldn't get you out of my mind." I knew that, I did, but my insecurities came back to bite me in many different ways. His words were one of them. "You are doing an amazing job with Bicas R Us and you only stop working when you need to recharge. I just have weird mating rituals." We laughed softly, his chuckles mixing with mine until we couldn't tell them apart.

With the stars as our only companions, we lingered there for a while, mostly in silence, listening to the song of our hearts beating in unison. After a while the air cooled down so much, we were both shivering, and we decided to retire to our cell. The room hadn't improved since my last visit. Bare of almost anything, it was cozy nevertheless, small and lit by the soft glow of candles. We had dropped our backpacks on the rough stone floor by the thin mattress that served as a bed and unrolled a couple of sleeping bags over it to soften it just enough so it didn't feel as if we were sleeping straight on the cold rock. From the only window in the room the moon seemed to wink at us, inviting us for a good night's sleep.

As soon as we closed the door behind us, Fouchard threaded his fingers into the belt loops of my jeans and pulled me against him. I guessed the good night's sleep wouldn't come until later. I was okay with that.

"Whoa there, merman. I'm not sure I appreciate this manhandling." I was a great liar. "Take it easy, Naël, I'm fragile."

Fouchard laughed, his mouth against the side of my neck. "Right, you're like a little china doll." He grazed his teeth on my skin before nipping at it. A shiver went through me as his tongue swept over the spot he had bitten. "Let's try out that theory, shall we?'

Without any warning, he grabbed the bottom of my T-shirt and pulled it over my head in one smooth move. I moaned in anticipation as his hands slid down my neck, shoulders, and chest until they found the zipper of my jeans. "Do you need help with that, big guy? It takes some finesse that you obviously don't have in those fingers of yours."

He let out a sound that was something between a groan and a snort. "I can handle it just fine, sweetheart." And to prove it, he got me out of my jeans and underwear in record time. "See?" he mumbled, his lips busy splattering kisses on my shoulder.

"What about you? You going to stand there fully clothed, or are you joining in?" I said, fully aware I wasn't making much sense, but desire had taken over all my senses. He pulled away just long enough to demonstrate how quickly he could join me in my nakedness even with a bad leg. He stood before me as bare as a tree in the winter, and I shivered in delight. "You're stunning, Naël."

He grunted, grabbed me by the shoulders, and spun me until I was facing the wall. "I love you, Aiden. God, I love you so much." He pushed me until I was literally squeezed between the cold rock and his hard body. His lips descended to the crook of my neck and lingered there for a while, kissing, nipping, licking until I became intimate with the wall.

I wanted to turn around and kiss him too, but he was on a mission, and who was I to deny the man I loved the pleasure of pleasuring me? I splayed my hands on the wall, bracing myself away from it just enough I didn't scratch or squash my favorite body part, and surrendered to his sweet ministrations.

Fouchard trailed his mouth along my back, brushing his lips over my spine, one inch at a time in an excruciating caress. His hands slid down the sides of my body to settle on my waist, pulling my hips against his. He was as hard as I was, but not yet ready apparently. He continued his sweet torture, down, down until his lips grazed my butt cheeks. A loud moan escaped my lips. Holy shit, I was going to explode against the damned wall if he kept on. His hands followed his lips, kneading, caressing, teasing me out of my sanity. He crouched behind me and ran his fingers up and down my legs, curling his hands around my thighs and then cupping my buttocks as he slowly stood up.

In my pleasure-induced trance, I thought I heard a squishing sound. I sneaked a quick glance behind me, wondering why my boyfriend's hands were not on me anymore. He had reached for a bottle of lube and was squeezing a generous amount on one hand before dropping the bottle unceremoniously to the ground. "Sweetheart, I'm going to make you feel so good, you'll never again think that I meant any of the hurtful things I told you when we first met." I leaned against him, relishing his body heat. Whoever thought a merman would be cold like a fish had been drastically wrong. "I think you're amazing. Don't ever forget that."

With staggering slowness, Fouchard ran a lubed hand over my sensitive skin from the tail bone down and slid a finger inside me. I yelled, oblivious to the fact the monks would most likely hear me in the complete silence of the night. *Control yourself, Aiden. Too early. Not yet.* He worked his finger in and out, first slowly and gently but gaining momentum and ardor as we both got closer and closer to the edge.

"I don't know how much longer I can hold, Naël," I mumbled, my forehead flat against the stone wall, my fingers trying to dig their way through it. "It feels —" I bit my lip, trying to control and stop the wave of pressure my body wanted to release.

Fouchard pulled his finger out, and I whimpered in disappointment. But I need not have bothered, because he soon replaced it with another of his body parts, one I was very fond of. Hard as I tried, I couldn't stop my yelp of surprise and pleasure as he buried himself inside me, pushing me even harder against the wall. That was going to leave a bruise tomorrow, but at that moment, I couldn't care less. I wanted him to stay where he was, deep inside my body, one with mine.

Surprising me again, my merman braced his hands on my waist and pulled me away from the wall, and we awkwardly fell to our knees on the makeshift bed, me on all fours and him still inside me, rocking against my ass, his hand now sliding around my hip to clutch my arousal. "Fuck, Naël," I yelled, over-whelmed by the rising pressure in my lower body.

"I'm doing it, sweetheart, I'm doing it." My laughter turned into a stream of moans as pleasure once again rode my body from top to bottom. "Tell me if you've had enough yet."

Was he kidding? I would never get enough from him. Never. But as he slid his hand along my length, up and down and then up again, my body finally gave in and all that wonderful and agonizing pressure released as my seed spilled. A muffled groan against my back told me Fouchard had also reached his climax. I collapsed on the bed with my boyfriend on top of me, still connected, still shaking from the thrill of our lovemaking. We turned on our sides, Fouchard spooning me, both breathless and sated.

"Holy shit, Naël," I muttered. "What came over you? That was amazing."

A kiss on my shoulder made me shudder. "Are you saying it hasn't been good up to today?"

I snorted. "It's always mind-blowing, sexy merrow," I said, bringing one of his hands to my lips. "Always. But today it was—you know, I don't think they've invented an adjective for it yet."

Fouchard chuckled against my skin. "Wanna go again later?"

Did I ever. Shuffling, I turned to face him, our noses an inch apart. "Yes, as soon as you're ready." I would be in a few more minutes. Demigod genes had some advantages, it seemed.

"It may be a few hours, Aiden," he said, catching my lower lip with his teeth and gently pulling on it. "I am just a merman, and my strength wanes a bit when I'm far from the ocean."

I savored his lips and his tongue in a long kiss. "Take your time, Naël, you've earned it." He sighed, and his breathing evened out as if he was drifting off to sleep. "Next time maybe we should try a sixty-nine," I whispered, not sure he would hear me.

"Whatever number you want, I'm your man, sweetheart," he said, his voice groggy with sleep. "I'm your man."

He was indeed. My sweet and sexy merman. It was decided; I was going to catch and kill the sons of bitches who had tried to skin my man alive. No questions asked.

SEVENTEEN
THE BIG REVEAL

"Brother Serafim would like to see you," the young monk said, hiding his hands inside the wide sleeves of his habit. I wondered where Brother John was. "He says he has something important to tell you."

The first time I came to see the Oracle, he made me wait before talking to me, now he was in a hurry? Still, he had given me some very important information the last time, so who was to say he wasn't going to do it again. I couldn't afford to ignore his summons.

"Okay, but can I get dressed first?" I was standing naked, half hidden by the open door and feeling very self-conscious of the fact that the young man wouldn't raise his eyes from the floor.

The monk nodded, his eyes still glued to the stone beneath him. "Of course, Mr. Mercer. You and your

—" He gulped before continuing, "Boyfriend should have breakfast first too."

I thanked him and closed the door. Fouchard was still fast asleep, his gloriously naked body sprawled on the mattress. I kneeled beside him and watched his bare chest rise and fall in time with his quiet breathing. He looked so peaceful, so serene, so free of the night terrors he'd had since his kidnapping.

Slipping beside him, I pecked at his lips and brushed my thumb over his nose. "Wakey wakey, sleeping beauty." He wiggled his nose and swatted my hand away. I touched his lips with my finger again. His eyes popped open. "Breakfast time, love."

Fouchard blinked several times, lifting his head from the bunched-up T-shirt he was using as a pillow. "Don't want breakfast," he mumbled, closing his eyes again. "I need my sleep."

"No, no, lover. You have to get up and eat," I protested, flattening one hand over his strong chest. "After the lovemaking session last night, we need food. Let's go." I grabbed his arm to pull him up, but with a sudden tug, he pulled me off-balance instead, and I fell across his lovely body.

"You could always get back in here with me and put the sixty-nine theory to the test." He wiggled his eyebrows in a comical imitation of Groucho Marx. We had theorized that because I wasn't that much shorter than he was, that position was a total doer, but we were exhausted and had fallen asleep before attempting it.

I clumsily crawled over him, chuckling. "Tonight for sure, but the Oracle wants to talk to me," I explained. "And the brothers have breakfast ready for us."

He mumbled some obscenity under his breath, but turned on his side and sat, rubbing his eyes. "At least breakfast is great in this shitty hotel." He stood up, stretched, and yawned loudly, his fabulous body giving me second thoughts about my visit to the Oracle. With my shirt halfway down my chest, I couldn't resist and slapped his hot ass.

"Whoa, sweetheart, don't push it or you'll never make it out of this room," he said, a wicked smile reaching his piercing eyes.

It took us longer than it should have to get properly dressed and make our way to the refectory, where the monks were already sitting around the slab of white rock that served as a table. The food had not been touched, and I felt instantly guilty we had made them wait.

"Sorry," I murmured, a hot wave crawling up my neck to my face. "We had a wardrobe mishap." Such bullshit. I doubted if these solitary and chaste monks would know what that was. When I finally found the balls to look up at them, I was shocked to see mischievous smiles dancing on all their faces. Chaste, my ass.

These monks knew exactly what we had been doing in that room.

We both slid into our seats on the long bench running the whole length of the table and waited. We didn't have to wait long; the monks attacked the food like starved lions, and for a moment I was afraid that if I so much as attempted to grab some food from the wooden trenchers in the center of the table, one of them would bite my hand off. The food was delicious and hearty as usual, hitting all the right spots and making me want to crawl back in bed for the first nap of the day. But I had a madman waiting for me, or the Einstein oracle as I had come to think of him, so I left my merman to his own devices and followed the young man from this morning to Brother Serafim's quarters in the library.

The Oracle hadn't changed position since the last time, it seemed, still sitting on the edge of his mattress with a beatific expression on his face that clashed violently with his white hair standing on end. "Welcome back, my son," he said, looking as pleased as he claimed to be. "Have a seat."

I looked around, hoping that this time they had placed a cushion for my butt's comfort, and I was disappointed—but not surprised—that there was none. I slithered down to the cold floor and wiggled my derriere on the hard stone until I found a reasonably comfortable position. "Thank you, brother. I understand you have something you want to tell me."

"Yes, I do," he said, waving a hand at the young monk who was still hovering by the door. "Bring us some wine." Wine? That early in the morning? Was that how he achieved his "higher consciousness," by drinking himself into a trance? The monk hurried out the door and came back almost immediately with an unlabeled bottle of red wine and two cups made of thick glass. He poured the wine and then handed it to both of us. I didn't want to offend the Oracle, but drinking wine in general was not my thing and definitely not before nine in the morning. "Drink the wine, son. It's good for blood circulation."

Reluctantly, I took the cup to my lips and sipped it as if the wine held poison. It was a robust wine, and even I, who was not a wine connoisseur at all, could taste the sweet grapes in it.

"Thank you, brother, but may I ask why you called me here? Unfortunately I have to run to go open my store." Cristina would do it, but I didn't want to linger longer than necessary in the company of this kind but rather lunatic monk.

"The last time you were here——" He paused to take a giant gulp of the wine, then continued with a red wine mustache stain on his upper lip. "——I told you about your parentage, if you recall." Shit, how could I forget? Being told your mother is a goddess of sorts is not exactly your run-of-the-mill conversation. "I neglected to tell you a rather important detail."

What? I leaned forward, anxiously waiting to hear what he had to say, but he said nothing, sipping on his wine and staring into the distance with empty eyes. What the fuck was he doing? Had he gone into that mad corner of his mind he seemed to live in most of the time?

"Brother Serafim?" I was tempted to reach out and shove him just a smidgen, but when I lifted my arm, he snapped out of whatever that was and smiled at me—one of those wine-imbued smiles that preceded total intoxication. "You were saying?"

"Yes," he said, and then paused again, his bushy eyebrows drawn together. "You've been learning Portuguese." It was not a question. I nodded, not interested in discussing my linguistic adventure of late and antsy to find out what he had forgotten to tell me. "I'm glad. One should always learn the language of the place you call home." Wise words indeed, except they were not the ones I wanted to hear at that moment. I nodded again, a bit more emphatically.

"Nevertheless—" Oh my God! Was he going to drag this conversation on for eternity? The image of a sloth came to my mind, and I would have laughed if I hadn't been so annoyed. "Yes, I forgot to tell you that your father is still alive."

I'll be dipped in bacon fat! He *forgot* to tell me that?

My father, the allegedly powerful druid who had mated with a goddess and produced a one-of-a-kind child—one I still to the day had trouble believing was me. "He's alive?"

"You should have your ears checked, young man. You keep repeating what I said." He wagged a finger at me and then fell into that semi-coma state where his face sagged and his eyes went blank. I waited for him to say anything else, but after five minutes of sitting there staring at him, I gave up and left the library. Maybe he would tell me more tomorrow morning. Or maybe I would never hear from him again.

I was on automatic pilot as I crossed the courtyard in the direction of the building where Fouchard was, now that breakfast was long gone. He was standing outside, leaning gingerly on his right leg. His left leg was still messed up, and his refusal to use crutches to help him walk without putting any stress on the ankle often resulted in swelling and more pain. He was a sight for my sore eyes, tall and very male. A shiver ran through me, and for a moment the information the oracle had just dropped on me dissipated like smoke. He lifted his face to me, his hooded eyes meeting mine from a distance, and I had to restrain myself from running to him like in one of those slow-motion scenes in romantic movies. I had turned into such a freaking cheese, but I didn't care. It was worth it, just to feel what I had never felt my whole life: unconditional and all-encompassing love.

Fouchard enveloped me with his long arms. "How did it go? Did he really have something important to tell you?"

I allowed myself to melt against his strong chest, my ear over his heart. His heartbeat was a soothing lullaby, and I realized I needed it; the news had hit me a lot harder than I had thought at first. "Fuck yeah," I said, the whole import of Brother Serafim's revelation crashing down on me. "My father is alive."

Pulling me away from him, Fouchard looked me in the eye, his arms still solidly anchored on my shoulders. "What? Your father? Where? How?"

I laughed nervously. "Dude, that's a lot of questions," I joked, swallowing the large lump of anxiety that grew in my throat. "Yes, my father is alive, but the damned Oracle went back to la-la land before he could tell me anything else."

My boyfriend dropped a kiss on my forehead and drew me in for another hug. "Are you okay? That's a bombshell if I ever heard one." I was not sure how to feel yet. I guessed I was a bit paralyzed by the news. "If you need me to distract you, I'm always available."

I chuckled against his chest. Leave it to him to make me laugh at a time like this. One of the many reasons I loved him.

"As tempting as that is, I do have to get going," I said, reluctantly pushing away from his warm body. "Cristina will have me skewered with those eyes of hers if I don't get there soon to help her." I looked up at him and brushed a hand over his cheek. "You need a shave," I said, delighting in the scratchy feel of his day-old beard. "Be nice and smooth for when I come back tonight."

Fouchard guffawed and winked at me. "Have special plans, do you?"

I threw him what I thought was my most dazzling smile and said, "We have a sixty-nine theory to put to the test."

EIGHTEEN

BOB, INSULTS, AND SHRAPNEL

"And he didn't tell you where to find him?" Cristina's eyes were wide, resembling two perfect circles. Her hand was suspended halfway to her mouth, the cereal dripping from the spoon. "What's wrong with that monk?"

I snorted, making circles in the crumb-filled saucer with my fork. "Is that a rhetorical question? The man is cuckoo for Cocoa Puffs, plain and simple. I'm sure he will eventually tell me, but in his own time. And considering his time runs a lot differently from ours, it may be years before he does."

Now that I knew my father was alive, I had all kinds of questions I hadn't dared ask before. Who was he, and was he okay with leaving me to fend in a world that I didn't quite belong to? Was he fine with allowing me to grow up resenting my own kind and living a great part of my life in denial of who and what I was? Damn, was he even interested in meeting me now that the cat was out of the bag about who I really was?

"You want to find out, right?" Cristina said, a drop of milk running down from the corner of her lips. "I would love to find out who my father was, even if he's just a loser that couldn't handle knowing he was going to be a father." Her mother had killed herself shortly after Cristina's birth, postpartum depression getting the best of her, and had left my friend in the hands of the system. We had that in common, having grown up in one foster home after another, passed around like a hot potato. To this day she fantasized about having been kidnapped and brought up by the fairies. Unlike me, she had been fortunate enough to find a couple that fell in love with her and adopted her when she was on the cusp of her teens. I had been left to make it on my own after I came of age. Not a time I liked reminiscing about; a time fraught with pain, anger, and frustration. A time of extreme loneliness.

I shook my head, suddenly wanting to steer away from this conversation. "How's Vee? I'll pick her up today before heading to Sintra." Vee was having the time of her life hanging out with Cristina, who she idolized as an older sister. True to his word, Silva had set up a network of undercover cops to watch the girl pretty much every minute of the day and had Cristina's place under nightly surveillance. They were safer than Fort Knox.

"We're having a spa day tomorrow, since the store is closed." My friend collected her bowl and spoon and took it to the kitchen to rinse them off. The rush for breakfast was over, and the lunch crowds had not begun pouring in yet, so we sat together to talk for a while. Outside, the sun shone, a bright white disk in the cloudless blue skies as the late morning hush enveloped the town square. Soon the place would be crawling with morning beachgoers searching for a bite to eat and late sleepers who came to enjoy the ocean in the afternoon, but for now all was quiet, a timeless feel settling over everything, as if caught in a photograph. "Don't tell your boyfriend, but we talked to the camp managers and we got her out for the day. She's so excited."

I was not sure that was a good idea. "Isn't it dangerous?"

Cristina shook her head, sending her messy, kinky curls flying around her. "Tó will be with us most of the day."

I straightened on the chair. "What? In the spa?" I was not one hundred percent certain the policeman would be focused on safety in the company of my friend. "Isn't that for women only?"

Pursing her lips in mock outrage, Cristina said,

"Well, Aiden, how disappointing. You of all people shouldn't be so sexist." *Really?* "For your information, it's a unisex spa, but he will be providing surveillance, not enjoying what the place has to offer."

I exhaled in relief. In my mind I could see the warlock salivating over my sexy friend while she walked around the spa half-naked. A distracted cop was not an asset. "So, he'll be outside all the time."

Cristina, finished with the dishes, came over and slapped the back of my head. "*Parvo.*" Yeah, I was a fool most of the time, but how could I not worry about the safety of the two girls in my life? Without any family and not that many friends, I had become fiercely protective of those I did have. "Yes, he'll be outside with another officer so they can cover both exits." All right, maybe Silva was more of a professional than I gave him credit for. "We'll be safe and sound. You can enjoy your time with the hot merman without feeling guilty." Images of what we had done the night before and what we planned to do later found their way to my naughty bits, and as shameless as I normally was, having those feelings in front of my friend made me blush like a virgin on her wedding day. "Oh, my God, Aiden, you just thought about sex, didn't you? Eww, that's both hot and disgusting."

Laughing, I stood up and stretched, stealing a look outside to where people were beginning to pop out of the blue. We'd might as well get ready for the lunch rush. "Even you would blush if you could see what's in my head right now," I said teasingly. I knew her well; she most likely wouldn't.

The first customer of the afternoon walked in and sat by the large window. He looked familiar, small and stocky with raven black hair bunched on the top of his head into a bun—well, not quite a bun, more like a spritz of hair sticking every which way. *Bob!* My alleged archenemy was in my coffee shop.

Raising my arm in front of her, I stopped Cristina from taking his order. "That's my attacker," I told her, not trying to keep it down. I wanted him to hear it, to know I was not fooled by the jeans and the T-shirt he was wearing instead of the traditional Indian gear he had been sporting the first—and last—time I'd seen him. "I'll take care of him." I hoped my words sounded like a threat. The truth was, I was still learning about my strength, my so-called gifts, so I had no idea of what I could do to rough him up other than the very mortal punch to the nose.

He threw me a glance and smirked. "You remember me then." Duh. How would I forget the man—god—who was determined to kill me? "Good. I want you to remember my face when you're dying."

Despite the threat, I couldn't help but snort. It was hard to take this guy seriously. "Stop it. You sound like Syndrome from *The Incredibles*," I said, chuckles escaping my lips in between words. "If you want me to take you seriously, you have to drop the tough act, because it's not working for you, dude."

His light brown face exploded into a deep red while his lips thinned to a single line. "I suggest you take me seriously, because I am a direct descendant of Brahma, the Creator. You should think twice before you mock me."

I spied Cristina watching from behind the counter, her fingers in her mouth, chewing on her nails as if munching on movie theater popcorn. I returned my eyes to my incredibly un-scary foe. "You mean, Brahma the Forgotten? No one worships him anymore and for a good reason: he was an idiot who was more interested in the pleasures of the flesh than the matters of the soul."

Bob humphed and slammed a fist on the table. "Brahma is the most powerful of the triumvirate, and he has produced equally powerful offspring," he uttered, a statement he had obviously rehearsed and repeated many times.

He might not look like much, but I had seen and felt firsthand how powerful he was. Antagonizing him was probably not the wise thing to do, but who had ever said I was wise? "And which sniveling powerless spawn of his produced you? Did he have sex with a pig?" I heard Cristina gasp, a sure sign I was being extremely stupid.

Bob, the not-so-friendly god, sprung to his feet,

almost tipping over the table. "You better watch it, mutt. You're one to talk, the product of an unholy mating." His spittle found its mark on my face, and I wiped it with the back of my hand, too furious to feel disgusted.

"What's so unholy about my mother and father's mating? Is it because they were so powerful individually that you are fucking scared of how formidable their son might be?" Not that I believed that, but something in me—anger, frustration, whatever it was—had taken control of my mouth.

Tightening his hands into fists, the demigod shot me with imaginary arrows, his eyes seeming to pop out of their sockets. "Don't flatter yourself," he spat. "Your mother mated with a druid. A druid," he repeated as if it was abhorrent. "A lowly druid."

I took a step toward him, not quite sure what I was about to do. "Stop saying that as if it's a dirty word," I yelled. "What's so wrong about a druid?"

He cackled. "Druids are mere pawns of the gods, created to serve, not to mingle with divinity." He lowered his voice to a threatening mutter. "He and your mother broke every rule in the book."

"You mean like the rules your granddaddy broke over and over again every time he fucked Shatarupa? A glorified sex doll he created himself?" I had no clue how I remembered all of this from when Fouchard and I did our research in Óbidos, but it flew out of my mouth as if I had always known it. "You mean those rules?"

I had just hit the red button apparently. Bob lifted his fists to chest height and growled. The little man threw a ball of fire toward me, and I only had time to protect my head with both my arms. The ball of pure energy bounced off my forearms and ricocheted in Cristina's direction. I yelled out a word of warning, but Cristina didn't get out of the way in time; the fireball hit the counter close to where she had been standing and sent shrapnel flying toward my friend, who let out a scream both of pain and surprise.

By the time I turned to the ridiculous god, he was gone, leaving only a wave of smoke behind him as if he had been on fire. I ran to my friend, who had collapsed behind the counter, and as soon as I cleared the corner, I knew she was hurt. Badly. Her face, shirt, and arms glistened with the dark red of her blood. I threw myself onto my knees beside her just as I heard a clamor of voices entering the store. The explosion had been heard by every regular nearby.

"Cristina, sweetheart, can you hear me?" I gently prodded her face with my fingers, studying the damage done. It was hard to tell because of the blood covering it all, but I thought I felt jagged pieces of metal and wood sticking out here and there from her skin. "Call 112 now!" I yelled at whoever was behind me, not bothering to check who it was. Afraid of hurting her, I just stared at my unconscious friend through my rising tears.

"So sorry, Cristina, it's all my fault. Oh God, what have I done?" Not the first time my anger clouded my judgment, but this time I wasn't the one paying for it. This time I had gotten someone else hurt because of it. Someone I loved with all my heart.

NINETEEN

TEARS OF A CLOWN

Life went on. People rushed around me, heading wherever they were going, some talking, some silent, some laughing, some crying. I sat on the uncomfortable plastic seat, half bent over my lap, bracing my forearms on my upper thighs with a mind full of things and yet empty. There were so many thoughts and emotions running through my brain that I couldn't make sense of any of them. It was like watching two overlapping scenes in a movie set to high speed—I saw colors, shapes, but nothing I could understand. My chest was so full, I'd thought at some point I'd explode as the ambulance made its way through the busy streets of Carcavelos toward the hospital in Cascais, the siren screeching in front of me. I couldn't remember when I'd last driven a car that fast, but there I was behind the wheel of Cristina's car, speeding behind the ambulance where my friend lay hurt and unconscious. I couldn't really remember where I had parked or how I found my way into the lobby of the ER where the staff made me wait for news I both needed and feared. Cristina had not regained consciousness as the EMTs checked her vitals, examined her wounds, and then carried her away on a stretcher.

My coffee shop was left unlocked as the police crawled all over it, looking for evidence of whatever had exploded there. They wouldn't find anything, of course. The *brahmachakram* didn't leave any traceable evidence, but I couldn't tell them that. In fact, I was not even sure I had talked at all since the EMTs arrival. I couldn't care less about the destroyed counter and cake display, or the scorch marks along the wall behind it, or even the quickly healing wounds in my arms; I cared only about my friend, bloody and pale on the floor, life escaping her through the holes the shrapnel had carved in her.

I hadn't cared when Silva arrived like a strong ocean wind and grabbed me by the back of my T-shirt to pull me away from my kneeling position by her body. Or when he punched me square in the face, angry at me for bringing this upon Cristina—I deserved it; I wanted him to hurt me like my foe had hurt her. He didn't rough me up enough, bursting into tears and falling to his knees by his girlfriend. He followed the stretcher being carried to the ambulance with shiny eyes and a tear-streaked face but had to stay behind to make sure the regular police didn't sniff the magic in the air. I waved an EMT away when she tried to care for my cracked lip and swollen eye before picking up Cristina's car keys and taking off after the ambulance. My body would heal on its own; Cristina's wouldn't.

The hours passed, and the news was always the same: Cristina was still in the ICU being treated for all kinds of traumas and loss of blood. I was not sure I had moved out of that seat, not even to use the bathroom, and it wasn't until I heard Silva's enraged voice that I lifted my eyes from the floor. The tall dark warlock had fire in his eyes as he marched in my direction, fists tight by his sides. For a moment I hoped he'd hit me again; maybe then I could feel something other than a dull pain, the only thing filling the emptiness in my chest. But he'd had time to cool down, and the professional cop was in control, however belied by the tightness of his jaw or the poison in his voice.

"How is she?" he growled. "Any news?"

I shook my head. "They won't tell me anything." Was that my voice? Trembling and thin, barely audible.

The warlock studied me, his eyes burrowing into mine. His lips, stuck in a thin line when he first arrived, softened along with his eyes. His shoulders relaxed, and he sighed. "Sorry I beat you up."

No, don't be sorry. Do it again.

"I deserved it," I squeaked out, the desert of my mouth making it hard to speak. "I wasn't thinking—I didn't think he would—" Words failed me. I wanted to crawl down inside a hole and never come out again.

Silva gripped my shoulder and gave it a friendly squeeze. "No, it wasn't your fault, Mercer," he said, his attempt at a smile failing miserably. "I shouldn't have done that. Totally unprofessional and uncalled for. I know you would never put Cristina in danger on purpose."

We stood there for a few minutes, his hand on my slumped shoulder, that awful painful emptiness growing inside me.

It was Silva who broke the spell. "Listen, I will go see what I can find out," he said. "They will have to report it to me as the detective in charge. You must go pick up Vee." Right, because Cristina was lying unconscious and wounded in a hospital bed. I nodded, not sure I'd be able to drive to the camp. "You can do this, Mercer. Vee needs you. Fouchard needs you."

I knew he was right, but that didn't make it any

easier to leave the hospital without any news from my friend. I wished I could just fly to where Vee would be waiting for Cristina, excited about the spa day she had been promised. I closed my eyes, and when I opened them, I was at the gate of the small estate that housed the summer camp for extraordinary girls. I had left the car at the hospital, I acknowledged distantly. We would have to call an Uber to drive back.

"Aiden," Vee yelled and started racing toward me, leaving the girls she had been talking to behind. "What are you doing here?" She threw herself in my arms with her usual enthusiasm and squeezed me into a hug. Then she pulled away and looked around me. "Where's Cristina?"

I hadn't shed a tear since it happened, but for some reason her simple question shattered me, and tears erupted from my eyes, running down my cheeks, rivulets of sorrow I could no longer hold back. The young mermaid's eyes widened, and for a moment she seemed frozen. "Aiden? What happened?"

Sobs escaped my throat, an out of control stampede of emotion I had been unconsciously holding in for hours. "She's hurt, Vee. She's very hurt."

Vee wrapped her arms around my waist and drew me to her in another hug. "It'll be okay, Aiden. She'll be all right." Who was the child? Who was the adult? It didn't matter; I crossed my arms behind her and allowed all the pain to pour out of me, one tear at a time.

On the way back to the hospital, we hung on to one another in the back seat of the Uber, offering each other whatever comfort we could. Had I not been so distraught myself, I would have been in awe of how strong, how collected the young mermaid was in face of the situation. Fouchard had brought up a strong woman.

Fouchard! He'd be waiting for me within the next hour or so. As soon as we arrived at the hospital and settled in the waiting room, I pulled my cell phone out of my pocket and punched his number.

"Aiden? What's wrong?" His deep, husky voice washed over me like a soothing wave. I wished he was there with me, but I didn't want to put him in danger either. "Are you on your way here?"

"No, I'm not going to make it up there tonight, Naël," I said, a sob making me hiccup. "Cristina—" I couldn't finish the sentence, anger, pain, and guilt suffocating me.

Vee grabbed the phone off my hands. "Cristina is in the hospital," she told her brother in a shaky voice. "The freaking demigod who's after Aiden got her. Bad." She listened for a while, nodding. "Aiden is in bad shape. Maybe you should come."

I snatched the phone back from her hands and

yelled onto the receiver, "No, you stay where you are. Too dangerous." I looked pleadingly at Vee. "You have to think of your sister. She needs you, and putting yourself in danger is selfish." I needed him too and wanted to keep him far from the danger that loomed over all male merrows. "Please, promise me you won't come."

"Aiden, calm down, sweetheart." Fouchard kept his voice level and calm, and my panic dwindled to a manageable size. "I promise not to come tonight, but you have to promise me you calm down and stop blaming yourself for what happened. That's what you're doing, right?" He knew me well. "You take care of my sister and come see me tomorrow, okay?"

I nodded, forgetting he couldn't see me. "I miss you," I whispered into the phone, my voice still choked by sobs. "I love you."

"I love you too, Aiden." My heart warmed imme-diately, and tears stopped flooding my eyes. "Cristina will be okay. Have faith." I stupidly nodded again. "Tell Vee I love her."

Vee was staring at me with concern in her face. She seemed as if she had grown up in the last hour, a strong, capable young woman surfacing from beneath the child she still was. Guilt filled me again, this time for having fallen to pieces instead of taking care of her. "Are you okay, Aiden?"

A doctor, hands in his pockets, approached and we both straightened. "Any news?" I asked him. He ran his fingers through his white hair and repositioned his glasses before speaking. Silva walked right behind him, his somber face a punch to my stomach. "What's wrong?"

"Your friend's heart function has been compromised," the doctor said in impeccable English. "We haven't been able to stabilize her. All scans show that she seems to have a severe laceration in one of the heart chambers and also a concussion. We're going to attempt surgery, but I will be honest; realistically, she might not survive this."

Recalling the promise I had made to Fouchard about taking care of Vee, I suppressed a sob. "When are you operating?" Vee sought my hand, and I squeezed hers, not sure whether for her or my own comfort. Most likely both.

"They are prepping the room right now."

"Can I see her? Please, I need to see her before she goes into surgery." I didn't recognize my own voice—desperate, humble, despondent. "Please."

The doctor was about to say no when Silva interfered. "I will take Vee to grab something from the cafeteria while you visit," he said, throwing the doctor a look that left no margin for discussion. The older man opened his mouth to protest, but his face went suddenly slack and his eyes distant. The warlock had put him under some kind of spell. "Go, Aiden. The spell will only last for a short time." He didn't say it, but it was implied; he was giving me the chance to say goodbye to my best friend.

The enchanted doctor led me to her room and left me there. She looked so pale, so vulnerable with tubes sticking out of her nose and arms. Her facial wounds had been patched and covered in bandages—so were the ones in her arms—but her breathing was ragged and shallow. I was going to lose my friend. I didn't even bother with a chair. I stepped closer until my thighs touched the bed and placed both hands over her chest, lightly, afraid the pressure would make her bleed further. Then I closed my eyes tightly, her irregular heartbeat vibrating against my hands.

"I'm so sorry, Cristina, I wasn't thinking, goading the damned demigod that way," I cried, tears spilling out again. "It's all my fault. God, I wish I could heal you like I heal myself. What's the point of being a magical if all your gifts are useless to help those you love? Please, Cristina, don't leave me. You've been my only family for the past couple years, and I love you. Please, don't die."

I could have imagined it, but I felt a prickling of energy beneath my fingers. I opened my eyes, wet with tears. I had to blink a few times to be able to see clearly but when I did, I was still not sure what I was looking at; there were sparks of energy shooting from my fingers to Cristina's chest. I wasn't touching her anymore, but we were still connected by those ribbons of flaring light. A flush of color spread across her face, and her mouth opened suddenly in a sharp intake of air. What was I doing to her? I tried to disconnect us, but it was as if my hands had a mind of their own. My heart galloped in my chest, first in panic and then in excitement and hope. Cristina's heartbeat had stabilized, the spikes and valleys on the heart monitor screen evenly spaced, and her breathing had softened and slowed down. Was it possible? Could I have healed her accidentally by just wishing to do so? Similar things had happened before when I had wished to be somewhere fast or be on the other side of some major obstacle and simply *was*. Was that how my so-called magical gifts worked? As if I had some kind of genie in a bottle, except the bottle was me.

I didn't care about how or why; all I wanted to know was if it was true, if my friend was going to survive this. The waves between us faded away, and I was able to call the nurse, who wasted no time checking her vitals.

The nurse, a middle-aged woman with hair as dark as the night, looked perplexed as she checked the monitor a few times, at one point turning it on and off as if thinking the machine needed a restart. She checked Cristina's blood pressure and listened to her heart. "*Não entendo isto,*" she mumbled, shaking her head.

"What do you mean?" I asked. The fact she couldn't understand what was going on made me nervous. "What's wrong?"

She raised her dark eyes to me. "I will call the doctor," she said in heavily accented English. She left in a hurry, the soles of her shoes clickety-clacking on the hard white floor.

I was frozen in place, not sure whether to be happy or scared, my eyes glued to my friend, who now seemed to sleep peacefully in her hospital bed. The doctor didn't take long. With the enchantment obviously dispelled, he frowned when he saw me standing there but didn't say anything, waving me out of the room and proceeding to examine Cristina instead. I ignored him. After a quick examination, he scratched his head. "This is weird."

I looked at him expectantly. "What is?"

"I have to run some more scans, but she seems to be doing... better." His words were cautious, but they were like a balm to my aching heart; she was going to be all right, I just knew it. She was going to survive this. "Please, leave the room. I will let you know what I find as soon as I can."

I obliged, feeling lighter, and went to join Silva and Vee in the cafeteria. When I walked in the large and crowded room, they both turned to me, a question in their eyes. I nodded and smiled, not able to talk through the huge knot in my throat. *Shit, I'm going to cry again.*

At least this time they'd be tears of joy!

TWENTY

FRIENDS AND LOVERS

IT WAS WEIRD TO BE IN CRISTINA'S HOUSE WITHOUT her. After much discussion, we decided it was too risky to take Vee to my place, since Bob probably knew my address by now. Silva drove behind us, determined to check out the premises before he went home to rest. It had been a long and hard day for all of us. Even the handsome dark warlock showed signs of exhaustion.

"Where did you get the black eye?" Vee asked, her seat reclined halfway down.

I'd forgotten about the after-effects of Silva's wrath, but a quick glance at the rearview mirror told me that they weren't fading away as usual. "Long story," I said. Even talking was tiresome. "Silva kind of agreed that I was to blame for what happened to his girlfriend." My attempt at levity fell flat. All I wanted was to lie down and sleep for a few years. My energy was so depleted, I was a bit nervous about driving home. What if I fell asleep at the wheel?

Vee touched my arm. "It was not your fault, Aiden. No one blames you." Sweet girl. *I* blamed myself and would always, but it was sweet of her to say that. I managed a sad excuse for a smile and kept my blurry eyes on the road.

I almost held my breath up to the point when I turned into the street where Cristina lived. My arms and legs felt as if they were coated in lead, and I was having a hard time keeping my eyes open. Silva went ahead of us to check the building and the apartment for any danger, but all was clear, and he soon came to fetch us in the car.

I stumbled and almost fell coming out of the car. It didn't go unnoticed. "What's wrong with you?" Silva asked.

"Nothing," I said, immediately contradicting myself with another stumble. I had no strength in my legs. "Just feeling a little tired, that's all."

The cop came around and offered me a shoulder to lean on. "You depleted your energy healing Cristina." It was not a question. "You'll have to recharge tomorrow. Maybe you should go and meet Fouchard at the convent. Lots of nature there for you to draw strength from."

Accepting the fact that I would most likely fall before reaching the second floor where my friend's apartment was, I accepted his support. "No need. I can walk on the beach tomorrow before coming to the hospital." After a good night's sleep, I would be at least partially recovered from this, whatever *this* was. It sucked not knowing your own limits.

Silva shook his head and led me inside the building, Vee walking just ahead of us. "No way, too dangerous. The convent is perfect; he won't get you there." I opened my mouth to protest, but he stopped me. "Don't argue with me, or I will give you a matching black eye."

"Well, that's not very friendly, is it?" I quipped, my words jumbling up on their way out. God, I was tired.

"I will pick you both up tomorrow morning and drive you to the convent." He was obviously used to giving commands and being obeyed. "Vee, get an overnight bag for you and this idiot." I made a weird protesting noise and almost slipped out of his hold. "Cristina is going to be okay, and she'd be worried sick knowing you are this weak with a god after your hide. You're going to the convent to recharge."

All right, so apparently I was going to join Fouchard at the convent the next day. With his sister. Part of me was delighted, but I had no strength to even acknowledge it. The other part was disappointed

I wouldn't be able to be there when Cristina woke. The doctor had finally returned after running more tests and told us that, by some miracle he couldn't explain, the laceration causing her heart to fail had healed. She was banged up and would carry scars from the shrapnel on her body for the rest of her life but she was alive, and her heart as healthy as it had been before the attack. I was as confused as the doctor about how I'd managed that but happy; I may not yet understand how they worked or how to control them, but my stupid powers had finally been useful for something worthy.

Silva left after making sure we were in no danger and depositing me on Cristina's bed, from which I had no intention of moving for some time. He was going back to the hospital, and even though he hadn't said as much, I knew he would be sitting by my friend's side all night. The damned warlock had finally earned my respect—he truly cared for Cristina, that much was obvious. I had a black eye and a fat lip to prove it.

I must have dozed off until I heard Vee's soft voice calling me. I popped my eyes open to find her standing by the bed with a steaming mug in her hands. "I made you some tea and toast," she said. The comforting warm scent of toasted bread reached my nose, and I took a deep whiff. "You should eat something before sleeping. You haven't eaten for a while."

I tried to sit, but my head was too heavy and refused to leave the pillow. Vee put the cup down on the nightstand and slid another pillow behind my head to prop it just enough so I could drink without spilling the tea all over myself. Then she ran back into the kitchen and came back with a plate covered in a few slices of toast. The thick kind that dripped with buttery goodness, just like we served in the coffee shop, I noticed with pleasure—those were the best. She sat on the edge of the bed and helped me take a few sips of the hot tea and a couple bites of the bread. As hungry as I was, I was more tired, and after the first couple helpings I couldn't eat or drink any more.

"But you should, Aiden," she protested, her green eyes authoritative like her brother's. "You need your strength."

I smiled what I was sure was a pitiful show of gratitude. "I know, Vee, but I really can't. Sleep will help, but I don't want to leave you alone." The worry that Bob would somehow find Cristina's apartment and break in during the night was gnawing on me so badly, my stomach was tied up in knots. *Fuck, I can't keep my eyes open. How am I going to protect this kid?*

Vee waved her hand, dismissing my worries. "All the doors and windows are locked. We're safe," she said. "I'll be on the couch watching totally inappropriate TV shows while you sleep." I chuckled softly. There was the Vee I had come to know. "Call me if you need anything." She hopped to her feet and, bending down, planted a kiss on my forehead. "Sleep tight."

I did. I fell asleep almost immediately after she left the small room, and I would have slept like a rock all night if it wasn't for the nightmares. In my dreams, Cristina was dying again, covered in her own blood while the ridiculous demigod laughed over her body. At some point during the night, Fouchard joined her, writhing on the sand, the fillet knife of a poacher skinning him alive. My screaming woke me up, drenched in sweat and crying.

"It was just a nightmare, Aiden." Vee was sitting by me again, brushing my head with her small hand. "Just a nightmare."

In the back of my mind I was embarrassed that an eleven-year-old had to be the adult while I sniveled like a baby, but the terror felt too real, too close to home for me to care. "It was horrible," I mumbled, tears still flowing freely down my cheeks. "Horrible."

Vee lifted her legs and stretched over the bed next to me, her arm drawing me closer to her in a mom-like gesture that both surprised and comforted me. "I'll be here with you," she said, her voice steady and mature. "Family sticks together. I won't leave you." Like my parents and every lover I ever had. Like

Cristina and Fouchard had almost done, by no fault of their own. I slipped back into sleep with one thing in my mind: I was going to pull myself together and make sure that none of my loved ones would ever leave me again.

TWENTY-ONE
COMING HOME TO MOTHER

True to his word, Silva was at our door by seven the next morning, blurry eyed and looking like hell.

"You didn't get any sleep, did you?" I asked him as I fought to put my shoes on. I was still extremely weak, my body so heavy I was afraid it would tear through the floor. I was in urgent need of close communion with Mother Nature.

"Enough," he said, his voice suspiciously hoarse. He'd had a rough night. "Did you call Fouchard to let him know you're coming?"

Shit. No, I hadn't. Vee, busy tidying up the kitchen yelled out, "I did. He knows we're coming." Even a child was more efficient than old pitiful me right now. She joined us as Silva helped me by propping my arm on his shoulder so I wouldn't fall. My traitor legs were too wobbly to support me all the way to the car. "He said he has a special corner of the grounds ready for you. He said you'd know what it was, some place called *Cova do Frei Honório*."

I just about choked on my own spit. That was that hole in the ground where we had made love. Alarmed by my coughing, Silva patted me in the back none-so-gently. "Are you okay?"

"I'm fine," I managed to say. "Let's go."

I wobbled my way to his car, thankful for his support, while Vee walked on ahead, a bag with a change of clothes thrown over a shoulder. She spent so much time at Cristina's, she now had a drawer of her own. I, on the other hand, had nothing at her house, and I didn't have time to run home.

Silva went around to the driver side after helping me into the passenger seat. Vee had already made herself at home in the back, a few of her books littering the fine black leather and a giant thermos of a smoothie she had put together herself tucked into the cup holder. My mind wandered briefly to my coffee shop; had the cops closed it properly after they were done with their investigation? How long would it take to fix the damage, and how much was that going to cost me? More pressing, would Cristina be by my side when we finally reopened?

My eyes drifted shut despite my valiant struggle against it, and I fell asleep.

The next time I opened my eyes, we were parked in front of the small building that served as the ticket booth for the convent. It was close to opening time, and the charms that protected the convent from view after hours had been removed already. It was a welcoming sight for my sore eyes. A safe, peaceful haven where Fouchard and I had had some very stimulating and wonderful moments together.

It took me a lot longer than what it should have to slip my jellied body out of the sports car even with the cop's assistance, but when I finally did, I was overcome with emotion; my merman was standing a mere few feet away, waiting for me. His hooded eyes were flooding with worry as he watched Silva help me out of his car, one inch at a time, and then hold me up while Vee closed and locked all the doors.

"Naël," I exclaimed, so softly I couldn't be sure he heard me. Vee ran to her brother, hugged him, and then whispered something I couldn't hear. They both looked at me and I swallowed, embarrassed to be seen in this state.

Fouchard strode toward me, towering over me now that I couldn't stand straight. His stoic countenance was as familiar and dear to me as it had been annoying when we first met. I knew what was beneath that veneer. He bent down, slid one arm under mine and another behind my knees, and picked me up from the ground and held me against his powerful chest.

"Let's make you strong again," he whispered for my ears only and carried me away into the convent grounds as if I weighed nothing at all.

My head, heavy and jumbled, dropped to his shoulder. "I'm sorry, Naël," I said.

"What the hell are you apologizing for, idiot?" My cantankerous merman was back, and I loved it. "You fucking saved Cristina at a heavy cost to you. You have depleted yourself so much, you could have died, fool. Don't apologize for being a hero."

I chuckled softly against him. "I'm no hero, Naël; I did what anyone would have done for a friend."

"Stop belittling what you have done," he scolded me, his voice loud and hard. Then he added gently, "You saved her, sweetheart. You're my hero."

I felt myself drift away to sleep again and snapped my eyes open when my boyfriend slowly dropped to his knees and laid me down on the still dew-damp dirt. With steady hands, he began unbuttoning my jeans and tugged them down my legs. "I don't think I have the strength," I quipped, trying to help him and failing miserably.

With a soft chuckle, he threw my pants to the side and switch his attention to my T-shirt, pulling it gently over my head. "Later, sweetheart," he said, laying a warm hand on my bare chest. "Now, you make friends with the earth and ask her for your strength back." I could feel it already seeping through my pores and running like gentle electric currents through my body. Mother Earth was helping me as I lay there, butt naked and listless. "Silva is setting Vee up with one of the monks, and I am just going to lie here with you until you are totally recharged."

I laced my fingers with his. I needed his strength too. His love. "Thank you, Naël." He squeezed my hand and stretched out beside me. "I love you."

He kissed my cheek and cuddled against me as if we were lying on the most comfortable bed in the world. It might be hard and rough, the jagged rocks poking my skin in uncomfortable places, but at that moment I could not have picked a better place to sleep; I was not only receiving the mercies of Mother Nature but also being nurtured by the man I loved. Bliss.

I woke up sometime later. I blinked to chase away the remaining sleep and turned my face to my boyfriend, still lying beside me in that bed of dirt. Expecting him to be asleep, I was surprised to meet his wide-open brown eyes. "Were you watching me sleep?" I asked, my voice a million times stronger than before. "You know that's a bit creepy."

He let out a soft chuckle. "So is lying naked on the soil, and yet you pulled it off so brilliantly." The snark was back, much to my pleasure. A smile stretched my lips. "Are you fully charged, or do I have to plug you in longer?"

I rose on an elbow and turned my body to him. "I feel a lot better," I told him, brushing a hand over his face. "Thank you." I leaned over and covered his mouth with mine in a long, gentle kiss. I tasted life on his tongue and sighed against his lips.

"As much as I would love to stay and recreate the last time we were here, my sister is probably wondering whether we're alive or dead." Fouchard jumped to his feet and offered me a hand to help me up. My body was reenergized, ready to take life by the horns once more but hoping life would be gentler on me. My boyfriend scanned me from head to toe with a wicked smile twitching the corner of his lips. "I hope you're not considering walking out of here in that getup —or lack of."

I stared down at myself, realizing I was still as naked as the day I was born. Fouchard handed me the clothes he had discarded earlier, and I began to dress. "How long was I out?"

"A couple hours," the merrow said, leaning against the rock wall and watching me pull on my pants. "How do you feel?"

I slipped my T-shirt over my head and sighed. "So much better." Remembering why I had almost lost my life, I asked, "How's Cristina?"

"Silva said she'll be all right," he told me, pushing himself away from the wall. "She's going to be fine."

With a much lighter heart, I walked toward the main cloister, holding Fouchard's hand as if my life depended on it. As soon as she saw me, Vee came barreling down the path to throw herself in my arms. "You're okay," she said, her voice muffled against my neck. "You scared me, Aiden." I may have scared myself too. She let go of me, only to throw herself at her brother, her thin arms knotting behind his neck. "I missed you, Naël." Fouchard kissed the top of her head with that tenderness he always showed his sister.

Silva crossed his arms and smiled—a predatory smile. But I could no longer find fault with him, not after how he reacted once he found out what had happened to Cristina. Remembering the sting of his punch, I touched my lip and then my eye, only to find out they were healed. "How's Cristina?" I asked him.

"I'm heading there right now," he said. "I will call you when I find out. In the meantime, you three stay put until I tell you otherwise." I was about to protest when he lifted his index finger and wagged it. "Don't even think about it. You're not moving anywhere until I am sure you will be safe enough."

"But my store—"

"Your store will be closed until the repairs are done," he said, fishing out the car keys from his pocket. "I will have some witches do their magic on your store, but we can't do it too fast without raising suspicions. A week at least before you reopen."

"And Vee?" I already knew the answer. Without Cristina to watch over her, she had to stay with us until someone trustworthy could be found to take care of her while her brother and I were in forced exile.

Silva left soon after, and, escorted by Brother John, we made our way to the cell that would be our room for the next few days. "We'll look for another cot, but tonight you'll be a bit cramped," the monk said, opening the room door.

Fouchard, still holding on to Vee's shoulders, shook his head and smiled. "It will do nicely, Brother John. We are so grateful you offered us shelter at a time of need. We will make do." I nodded in agreement, and the monk left.

Examining the room with her big green eyes, Vee slowly pivoted, her mouth slightly open. "Wow, this is cool," she proclaimed with a chuckle. "This is straight out of a time travel story. Monks included."

Rejuvenated but still in need of a few more hours of rest, I leaned against Fouchard. "Glad you like it, Vee. This is not a comfy bed." But perfect for love-making, the memory flooding all my senses. There would be no messing around tonight. With the young mermaid in residence, everything had to be kept PG —not that I could have sex anyway, with my blood too busy flooding other vital parts of my body to worry about my naughty bits.

Vee glanced at me and smiled before her eyes drifted to her brother. "Naël, your boyfriend was amazing," she said, catching me unawares. My jaw dropped, and before I could say anything, she continued, "He totally put himself out there for Cristina. He saved her life."

Fouchard pressed me against his side. "I know, Vee, I know," he said, turning his face to me and kissing my forehead. "I've always known that Aiden is a special man. Now if he would only believe that himself."

Tears popped into my eyes, burning and desperate to pour out. Mortified, I wiped one that had managed to roll down my cheek and tried to guffaw, pretending a wave of emotion hadn't just overwhelmed me. "Oh, shucks," I said, mimicking Goofy and hoping they wouldn't notice the catch in my voice. "You guys are too nice."

Not fooled by my pathetic attempt at sounding strong and put together, Vee wrapped her arms around my waist and squashed her face against my chest. "I love you, Aiden, and I know Cristina does too." I couldn't talk. My nose had suddenly filled with snot, and my eyes brimmed with tears that wouldn't be denied.

We stood there for a few moments in silence, cherishing each other's body heat. It was hard for me to believe that just a few months ago, I had no one to love or to love me other than Cristina, and even she had not been part of my life until I moved to Portugal not even two years ago. Hard to believe that I was now loved by all these amazing people. More surprising even was the fact that after a lifetime of denying my magical origins and trying to steer away from anything magical, most of the people in my life, those that mattered, turned out to be magicals too.

"All right. Enough sentimentalism," the merman said in a gruff voice that betrayed his own emotional upheaval. "Time for bed. We all had a very long, difficult day."

Fouchard had piled up a few sleeping bags on the mattress to make it more comfortable, and a mermaid-patterned duvet had mysteriously appeared mixed up with the other plain blankets. Vee smiled that impish grin of hers and winked at me. We did our best to squeeze ourselves into the narrow bed, a task that involved a lot of tossing and turning, groans, and chuckles until we finally found a moderately comfortable fit: Fouchard and me lying slightly diagonally so that our feet pointed at the outside ends of the mattress to make space for the thankfully thin and much shorter mermaid in the middle. It should have struck me as weird, lying there with two other people beside me when I had lived my whole life alone, but instead it felt right, as if it had always been like that, as if we all belonged together. I smiled, watching Fouchard sleeping peacefully, his head just above his sister's, who was also asleep, and realized that this must be how belonging to a family felt like. I wouldn't dare say it out loud, but I whispered it under my breath anyway.

"This is my family. I have a family at last."

TWENTY-TWO
MONK WITHOUT A CAUSE

"Get out of there, Vee. You're not a goldfish."
I had found Fouchard's sister sitting inside the fountain in the main cloister, her mermaid tail flopping
around and splashing water all over the ground. Vee's
tail was a pale blue, so muted it was practically gray,
with none of the iridescence of my boyfriend's
glorious tail. My attempt at authority was not working
too well, and she largely ignored me, reacting with a
stream of giggles instead. "I don't think the monks
will like it very much." I stared at the dirt around the
fountain, bending down to pick up the poor fish Vee
had accidentally dislodged from its home. I threw it
into the water just as a wave came surging onto me.
"Shit, Vee. Now I'm soaked."

"Victoria!" The seriousness of the voice had an
instant impact on the girl, who quit splashing around

and sat upright, her bright green eyes trained on someone behind me. "You will give Aiden the same respect you show other adults, do you hear?" Fouchard stopped beside me, his powerful arms crossed, emphasizing his muscles and the sexy Celtic knot armband tattoo that hugged the top of his bicep. "No, not like other adults," he corrected, his lips barely moving, that forbidding expression on his handsome face. "You will respect and obey him like you do me, do you understand?"

The young mermaid nodded and swallowed a few times before speaking. "I'm sorry, Aiden," she said, her eyes roaming over to me. She folded her arms and rested them over the edges of the fountain, sincerity obvious in her eyes. "I was just having a little fun."

I chuckled, a little uncomfortable but made happy beyond reason by what Fouchard had said. I offered her a hand. "Come on, let's go grab something to eat from the snack bar." I hoped my smile was confirmation enough that I was not offended or upset in any way. I loved the silly monkey and would find it very hard to dig up something she'd say or do that I wouldn't be able to forgive.

Her tail vanished, suddenly replaced by her long legs as she accepted my hand. I pulled her out of the water, dripping and shivering. "It's chilly out here," she said, hugging herself and rubbing her hands on her arms. "I'm going to dry out. Meet you there?" I nodded, and she took off running, stopping momentarily to kiss her brother, whose threatening glare had faded away just as quickly as her tail.

"Cheeky monkey," Fouchard said with a laugh. I couldn't contradict him. He pulled me against him and kissed me. "Don't let her disobey you," he said, his lips on my temple filling my body with that Fouchard electricity I loved so much. "A stern look and a well-placed word should do it."

What did I know about children or even young adults? I had never known a family, and even in the many foster homes I had bounced to and fro throughout my life, I had never had other children around. I deflected. "Have you noticed how grown-up she's looking lately?"

We started walking toward the area where the tourists swarmed every nook and cranny with their cameras and their phones. "Yes, she's practically a teenager," he said, lacing his fingers with mine. "It's going to be hell for the next few years. A teen girl is a challenge, but a mermaid one? We're in for a rough ride."

Not sure whether he was joking or serious, I risked a faint chuckle. We had been in the monastery for three days already. It had been wonderful and horrible all at the same time. Wonderful because being around Fouchard and Vee twenty-four-seven felt like home, and horrible because it had been three days of very cold dips in the tub in the medieval bathroom, followed by hikes in the dark woods at night for a moment of much-needed privacy with my favorite and very eager appendage. If I couldn't make love to my boyfriend soon, I might explode or something equally bad.

"Silva has sent news of Cristina." All thoughts of sex fled from my head. "She's going home tomorrow." Before I could protest, he added, "Silva will stay with her even though he doesn't think she's in any danger now." Because I was the one who had attracted danger. I was the one who taunted the ridiculous but powerful Bob to the point he was willing to attack in front of a regular. I was the reason she had almost lost her life and would bear scars forever.

"I wish I could talk to her," I mumbled, not quite sure I had said it out loud. Fouchard squeezed my hand and smiled. "Do you think it would be okay to call her?"

"I don't see why not."

We were surrounded by people of all shapes and sizes, strolling in between buildings, talking, laughing, oblivious to the fact that magical creatures walked among them. We headed down the path that led to the exit. Halfway down, there was a small cafeteria with simple meals, nowhere near the quality and tastiness of what the monks offered us every morning for breakfast and in the evening for dinner after closing. But it was nourishment and it turned out that an eleven-year-old girl ate just as much as a teenage boy.

I pulled out my cell phone and dialed Cristina's number. I was not sure she had been allowed to keep hers at the hospital, but it was worth a try; I was desperate to hear her voice and assure myself she was alive. The phone rang a few times before going to her voicemail. "Fuck," I exclaimed, stuffing the phone in my pocket emphatically enough to incite some funny stares from the tourists. "I guess I will have to wait until she's home."

Fouchard tugged me closer and kissed my cheek. "Maybe you'll be able to actually see her then." However brief, his kiss left a tingling sensation in my skin that swiftly expanded to my whole face and threatened to take over all my senses. That merman had magic lips, I'd swear. "Let's grab a seat before the princess gets here." I snorted; Vee was not very princess-like; more Energizer bunny, less dainty royal.

After eating at least half of the inventory in the small café—or so it seemed to me—Vee was ready to explore the convent again, energy recharged and curiosity sparked. The Brothers had been very kind and patient, taking her on tours of the grounds many times in the last couple days, but she was insatiable. Today we were on our own.

"I want to go to the *Capela do Nosso Senhor Crucifi-*

cado today," she declared, her hands on her hips while she surveyed the courtyard just outside the cafeteria.

I threw Fouchard a look, my eyebrows arching in confusion. He laughed and whispered, "Our Crucified Lord Chapel." My Portuguese was improving greatly and quickly, but there were things that were still indecipherable to me. "It's up that hill." He pointed to the top of a hill right behind the main buildings. "It's a walk, Vee. Are you sure you want to do it in this heat?"

The stubborn mermaid shook her head. "You're a wimp, Naël." She gave her brother a once-over. "And getting a bit thick around the waist. You need the exercise." I almost choked. Fouchard was in peak condition. The man was perfectly shaped and muscled—no excess flesh anywhere, just the perfect measure in all the right places. Only a sister would get away with saying something like that. "I don't know why you're laughing, Aiden; you're getting a little chubby yourself."

Fouchard rolled his eyes, a habit he seemed to have caught from his sister, and groaned. "All right, slave master, we'll do your bidding." He turned to me and muttered, "Apparently we need the exercise." A chuckle almost escaped me before I could restrain it. Vee's eyes held fire and brimstone, and I had no wish to poke that little dragon.

The so-called chapel was not far, but the wild

vegetation, the rough rocky path, and the fact it was all uphill made it feel as if we had been trekking through the rain forest for days. By the time we arrived, I was sweating like a pig—do pigs actually sweat?—and the soles of my feet were begging for mercy.

"What made me think flip-flops would be the right footwear for this excursion?" I bent down to remove yet another jagged rock that had crawled between my foot and the shoe. The bottom of my foot was dotted with red punctures that smarted enough to make me wince before they healed over within minutes.

Fouchard snickered at my lack of moxie and shoved me gently forward. Vee had already vanished inside what looked like a cave carved out of a massive scarp. "That's the chapel?" My boyfriend sounded as puzzled as I felt. That thing did not look like a chapel at all. "Do you think Vee is safe inside?"

I had no idea, so we both scrambled up to the entrance, worried about what may be lying in wait inside. There was only room for one person at a time to walk through the narrow entrance. I followed my merrow into the semidarkness of the chapel. Vee was standing by what looked like a rock shelf of some kind, worn and jagged by time and the elements. Because the place was very small and we barely fit inside, I slid my arm around Fouchard's waist and pulled him close to me. It didn't help space-wise, but it worked wonders for my need to touch him.

"This does not look at all like a chapel, Vee," I said, lifting my eyes to the ceiling in search of something, anything, that marked this as a place of prayer.

Vee looked at me, raising her eyebrows the way one of my old teachers did when I gave the wrong answer or asked a stupid question. "The Capuchin monks are all about humility." She pointed at the shelf in front of her. "This is the altar. At one time this had a beautiful mural painted on, but time has made it disappear almost completely." Crouching by it, I peered closer, and sure enough, faded colors were still visible here and there along the rough edges and facing wall of the altar. "Also there used to be a wooden crucifix here, but it has long been taken away."

Fouchard humphed. "How do you know all this?"

She shrugged. "Brother Sebastião has been very helpful," she said, staring at us as if we were two ignorant idiots. "He's been telling me all kinds of things about this place. What have you been doing all this time? Staring at the walls?"

I coughed to disguise a chuckle. The first time, we had been too busy getting in each other's pants, and this time I've been too worried about the current state of things—and yes, too busy trying not to think of how I missed fooling around with my boyfriend.

"Let me guess; you spent most of your time making out, haven't you?"

I coughed for real this time. Fouchard's lips tightened into a thin line. "And what exactly do you know about making out, young woman?" he growled under his breath. "You're too young to be thinking about that."

We had been good, we really had. There had been nothing more than a few tame kisses and hugs around her, our hands never straying to private parts of each other's bodies. In fact, we had been so paranoid about Vee witnessing something inappropriate for her age that we had refrained from any PDA even when she wasn't around us.

"You think I don't know what you do when I'm not around?" By all that was holy, I certainly hoped not. There was a time for everything, and she hadn't quite gotten there yet. "All kissing and touching, googly-eyed and dreamy…. God, I hope I don't look that dumb when I fall in love."

A swoosh of air escaped my lips as I allowed myself to release the breath I'd been holding. She did *not* know what we did when she wasn't around after all. Fouchard chuckled beside me, obviously amused with my discomfort. I elbowed him. Hard.

We lingered for a while, examining the worn-out mural and finding bits and pieces of what might have been small chunks from sculptures or, most likely, junk left behind by a clueless tourist. The sun was beginning to fade like the paint on the altar, and we began our descent down to the convent.

The place had emptied of visitors and was quickly returning to its unadulterated state, the one that hid beneath the magic glamors that protected it from the outside world. The setting sun was gifting the sky and everything underneath it with a shower of gem-like colors, and we stopped for a few minutes to watch it. It was then that I heard the tell-tale of a *brahmachakram* charging. I grabbed Vee by her arm and pulled her behind me and Fouchard, raising my arms to protect us from the eminent bolt of energy. I needn't have bothered, though, because before Bob could attack, he found himself surrounded by the monks. Shocked by the sudden appearance of the brown-clad men, the demigod hesitated long enough for the weapon to lose some of its power.

"I have no grievance against you," he yelled at the Brothers. "Move out of the way, or you will get hurt."

The monks said nothing. Instead they stepped forward, closing the circle tighter around the baffled demigod. Their faces were obscured by the brown cowls I had rarely seen them wear since my arrival, and their hands hid inside the wide sleeves. It was rather eerie, a little scary even, a scene from a movie that didn't end well for the antagonist. Bob seemed to realize this too and backed up, only to stumble into more brothers.

"Go away. Are you crazy?" Bob was not very convincing, and the monks were not afraid. A ghostly humming grew louder, and it took me a few seconds to figure out it was coming from the monks. Was that a magical chant? The air began wavering, as if heat was rising from the ground and forming a protective wall around Bob, closing in with each note. "Fuckers, go away. I am a god, and I demand your respect."

He wasn't having much luck with that either. The monks kept on singing, an eerily beautiful sound that tingled in my ears and against my skin, the feeling of magic coursing through me. I watched in fascination as one of the brothers lifted a hand, palm facing the demigod.

"Leave now, or you'll regret it. We don't answer to you or any of your gods, and we have been entrusted with the defense of Aiden Mercer." A rumble punctuated his command just as the circle of magic closed completely, imprisoning Bob within. "We mean you no harm, but if you don't leave, we will take tough measures to prevent you from hurting our guests. Choose wisely."

Bob looked at us, wild-eyed with anger and frustration and then vanished, leaving nothing behind, not even the lingering buzz of magic. The circle fell and was absorbed by the soil from which it seemed to have originated. The Brothers stopped their chanting, and one by one they broke the circle, uncovering their heads and slowly filing away from the courtyard and into the refectory, leaving us alone, dazed, and frozen. Fouchard threw me a worried glance and pulled his sister closer to him, his arms locking over her chest.

"What was that?" Vee asked after a moment of shocked silence.

Fouchard and I exchanged another look. That was an excellent question; what the hell had just happened? I was seeing the monks in a whole new light.

TWENTY-THREE
SISTERLY INTERFERENCE

"I've never seen anyone do that," Vee couldn't stop saying. She had been repeating that same sentence for an hour now, spaced by "That was so cool," and "Who would have thought monks could do that?"

We had joined the Brothers for dinner and were even more surprised by the joviality of the meal. The monks shed their usual somberness and quiet for almost boisterous conversation and laughter. Fouchard and I kept exchanging glances, not quite sure what to think or do. Brother Sebastião, a youngish man who seemed to have taken Vee under his wing, enthusiastically explained to the mermaid how they had gathered the magic to build the protective wall that had defeated—or at least deflated—the ridiculous god. I could still see his face, the nose ring connecting to an ear cuff by a thin silvery chain rising and falling as he flared his nostrils in anger. And possibly frustration. He may have been the son of a god, but he apparently was no match for a bunch of humble monks.

"When exactly did you and your brothers become our protectors?" Fouchard asked, shredding a large chunk of bread with his teeth. The walk to the chapel on the hill and then the excitement of what we had just witnessed had made us ravenous. I raised my eyes from the chicken drumstick I'd been working on, curious about the answer.

"You became ours to protect the minute you came here as our guests," Brother John replied, his elbows on the tabletop and fingers steepled in front of his lips. "We also had orders from the Oracle to keep you safe from all dangers. He said the time would come for you to face Baburaj and his minions—if he has any—but now was not that time yet."

Wait! What? "Was Brother Serafim lucid when he said that?" Considering the Einstein-look-alike was rarely living on the same plane as we were, it was a perfectly sensible question.

The older monk laughed, his time-worn skin wrinkling around his eyes. "He's always lucid," he said. "Just not always ready to talk."

In other words, the damned monks had been lying to me all along. "He made me wait before I could talk to him." I was painfully aware I sounded like a whiny child. "To what end?"

Brother John looked at Fouchard and then back at me and winked. "Well, you had time to reconcile with your lover, didn't you? The two of you make a great team, and Brother Serafim wanted to give you the chance to realize that." It was my turn to stare at Fouchard, my eyebrows arching high. "And of course, he was highly entertained by your sneaking around and creative use of holy spaces."

Fire consumed my face and my neck as the chunk of chicken I had been chomping on got stuck somewhere in my throat. I coughed it out while my boyfriend laughed his head off and patted me on the back. "He watched us?" I managed to say between coughing fits.

"Not on purpose," the monk said, lowering his voice so Vee on the other side of the table wouldn't hear. "But his senses automatically connect with… disturbances of any kind, and you two were pretty loud." I coughed harder, the damn chicken bite refusing to go down or up. Damn monks! "Are you all right there, son?"

I raised my gaze to him with murder in my heart, but something in his voice, in his words, made me still for a moment. I tried to identify the feeling but couldn't quite grasp its meaning or origin. It felt like a strange wisp of recognition, even though I had no idea of what exactly. I swallowed the offending chicken and gaped at Brother John, who was smiling benignly at me, his bright blue eyes twinkling with mischief. I smiled back and focused on my plate where the delicious meal was mostly gone. What was that? That flurry of awareness of something I couldn't put a name to.

I shook my head and sought Fouchard's hand underneath the table. He was there for me as he always was, warm hand enveloping mine in a cocoon of comfort and reassurance. "Maybe it's time to retire to our cell," he said, understanding the unspoken request. He threw a glance at his sister at the other end of the table. "Vee, time for bed."

Vee moaned, her lips twisting into a childish frown. The future teenager in her seemed to be in a constant state of struggle with the child still inside. "Brother Sebastião was going to tell me about the legend of Frei Honòrio. Can I stay a bit longer?"

The young monk looked at Fouchard's scowling face—his you-better-do-what-I-tell-you face—and smiled. "I will deliver her to the cell safe and sound in another half hour, if you'll permit it."

I could almost see my boyfriend's desire to be alone with me for a moment or two and his need to protect his sister at all times fighting for supremacy. "All right, you can stay," he finally said, swiftly adding, "but you better be in that room in thirty minutes or I will tan your hide."

I snorted at his choice of words and he gave me a look. "What? I've never heard you say those very old-fashioned words," I said, shrugging. "It sounded funny. Besides you would never lay a finger on Vee."

He muttered something beneath his breath before saying, "Figuratively speaking." Vee's smirk was swiftly wiped off her face by the forbidding glare her brother threw her way. "Got it, Vee?" She nodded vigorously, and we left the refectory hand in hand.

We walked in silence the short space between the dining space and our cell, savoring the peace and coolness of the night. The room was almost chilly now that night had fallen in earnest but welcoming nevertheless. Strange how I was beginning to think of the austere and rather uncomfortable place as home. Fouchard left me momentarily to use the bathroom, and I sat on the makeshift bed, my back to the hard wall with my knees drawn to my chest and my chin resting on them. There was still a weird flurry of unknown feelings inside me, both comforting and unsettling.

Fouchard stood in the doorway, his powerful arms crossed over his chest and studied me. "What's wrong, sweetheart?" I shrugged, still unable to define what I was feeling. He dropped to the bed and sat next to me, our thighs and shoulders touching. I leaned my head on his shoulder, grateful for his presence. "Did something happen?"

"I can't explain it, Naël. Something about what Brother John said, or maybe the way he said it, made me feel… I don't know what to call it." He covered my hand and laced his fingers with mine. "I felt as if I recognized something, but I couldn't tell you what. It was weird."

My beautiful merrow turned his face slightly to whisper against my temple, "There is a lot of magic energy in the air tonight. Maybe you're feeling its residual energy. We know you're sensitive to that; you can feel the undercurrent of magic when we can't."

True, I was still uncovering things I could do or cause to happen. It seemed as if I was constantly growing in some way, learning about myself.

He was so close, and I missed him so much; I cupped a hand on his cheek and brought his lips down on mine. We had kissed and touched in the last few days, however surreptitiously, but I missed the more intimate time with him. I missed the time we had had in this very room not that long ago. He slipped his tongue between my parted lips and caressed mine, immediately lighting a roaring fire inside me. *How does he do that?* I pushed him down on the mattress and stretched on top of him, my hands crawling under his shirt to feel the familiar ridges and valleys of his muscles. I was so starved for his touch, I swallowed him whole, forgetting that the door had no lock and there was a young mermaid who might walk in on us without warning.

"Missed you," I whispered, intoxicated by his flavor and his heat. His shirt was bunched up under his chin while I drew lazy circles on his chest with my hand.

Fouchard nibbled on my lower lip, pulling it gently with his teeth. "I've been here with you all along," he whispered, his breath caressing my skin.

"I know," I said, sweeping his handsome face with my other hand. "But I missed this, us together, no space between us."

He laughed roughly. "Are you saying my sister has been cramping your style?"

I chuckled, following the movement of my fingers with kisses. "No, I love Vee, and I'm glad we can keep her safe here with us, but I can't wait to be truly alone with you again."

As if on cue, Vee walked in, catching us in our embrace. Her eyes opened wide, but after a moment, she crossed her arms and tapped a foot on the stone floor. "I'm not old enough for this and that, but apparently I am old enough to walk in on my brother having sex with his boyfriend."

Fouchard growled, the angry predator in him coming out with the sound. "Watch it, girl," he warned under his breath while I scampered away from him, straightening my crumpled clothes as I stood. "We were not having sex. Obviously. And I guess we need to sit down one of these days and have the birds and the bees talk, since you seem to be a bit too ill informed about these matters."

She plopped herself next to her brother, who was still lying on the mattress, his torso raised on his bent arms. "What do the birds and the bees have to do with sex?" she asked. A laugh escaped my lips and I disguised it with a cough. Vee gave me a sideway glare. "Brother Sebastião found another small mattress, so I don't have to be squished between you two giants while I sleep."

I noticed the young monk for the first time standing awkwardly by the door with a large, soft roll in his hands, his tanned face a bright shade of red. "I thought you could use it," he said, offering the roll to me.

"Thank you so much." I retrieved it and unrolled it by the wall opposite of ours. It allowed a small space between the two mattresses. "This is perfect," I said, relieved I didn't have to spend another night sharing the bed with her.

The young monk handed me a blanket and a pillow that I staged on the narrow mattress. "Brother John asked me to tell you that the Oracle would like to talk to you, Mr. Mercer. Tomorrow after breakfast."

That was unexpected. What could he possibly

have to tell me now? "I will be there. Thank you, Brother Sebastião."

The young man turned around, waved shyly at Vee, and left the room. Vee stretched and yawned. "I'm pooped," she declared. "I'm going to bed." She got up and crossed the small space in between before throwing herself onto the new bed. I cringed. Those mattresses were not very soft, but she didn't seem to mind; in one fluid move she slid under the blanket and adjusted the pillow under her head, and in less than a minute I could hear her soft snores. Did all kids sleep that easily?

Fouchard was sitting, his long arms wrapped around his knees and his eyes studying me. "Come, we might as well sleep." Since we couldn't do anything else. "It was a long, exciting day." That it was. Between the long climb to the chapel and the Bob attack, my energy was rather depleted again.

I lowered myself to the bed and draped an arm over Fouchard's shoulders. "I could use a good night's sleep," I admitted.

He kissed me briefly, and we both stretched on top of the mattress, Fouchard's giant body spooning mine. The soothing heat from my boyfriend's body and the rhythmic sound of Vee's breath lulled me quickly to sleep, but I still heard my merrow whisper in my ear, "I'm so glad we found each other, Aiden. I love you."

"Too dangerous." Fouchard's words came out as a growl. His menacing expression left little to the imagination. "You're not going."

Feigning a confidence I certainly didn't feel, I crossed my arms and said, "You're not the boss of me." Okay, not a very mature thing to say, but it was all I could come up with. He was right after all; it was dangerous, and I probably shouldn't be going, but it was something I desperately needed to do.

"You can wait until Silva catches the lunatic poacher and then I can go with you." My beautiful merrow's protective hackles were full out. "Bob is still out there, and he is dangerous and has a chip on his shoulder for you." He knew as well as I did that his strength didn't make a difference when it came to the diminutive demigod. As long as Bob, the idiot, was in possession of that powerful weapon, no one was capable of protecting themselves from him. Except maybe the monks. The men in cowls had been an awesome sight, protecting us from the demigod.

Changing tactics, I strode across the space between us and held him against me. The shadow of the gnarled tree behind us enveloped us with a sense of privacy even if we were standing in the middle of a bustling convent courtyard. The tourists were out in throngs, milling around the fountain at the center of the cloister or walking aimlessly, phones in hand, sunglasses and hats obscuring their faces.

"Sweetheart, I have to do this," I whispered, raising my chin toward him. His brown eyes softened, and I took that as a good sign. "Cristina is my best friend, and I got her into this mess."

"You also saved her life, Aiden." It was a weak protest, his resolve obviously fading.

"I wouldn't have had to do it if I hadn't got her in the line of my shit." Yes, this guilt would never go away, and I needed to ask for her forgiveness. I needed to know if she still thought of me as her best friend or if I had become *that* guy, the one you tolerate but can't wait to be away from. "I won't attract any attention. I will just do that weird teleporting thing I do and land right by her side at her house."

Fouchard swept a hand over my head, studying my face. "You're so fucking stubborn, Aiden. I ought to knock you out and tie you to a tree."

A loud burst of laughter escaped my lips. "I could still do it, you know." I pretended to think for a moment. "Maybe we should try that one after I come back—the tying to a tree thing, not the knocking me out." I wiggled my eyebrows and managed to make him crack a smile. "Come on, Naël, I have to do this. You know that."

He hesitated for a moment and then lowered his lips on mine for a long, deep kiss that left me sweaty and wobbly. "You better not get hurt," he said once we came up for air. "I have great plans for you when we get out of here, and I won't take it well if you get yourself killed before that."

My heart fluttered in my chest. "I like the sound of that. Care to elaborate on your plans?" That simple suggestion made me hard as a rock. Without thinking, I rubbed myself against him. "I'm ready."

He laughed softly. "Idiot, you do realize we're in the middle of a crowded courtyard, right?" I had forgotten. Fouchard had that kind of power over me, the type that obliterated everything else in sight. I stopped my X-rated gyration and chuckled. "And no, I won't elaborate, but I can tell you it involves my aqua form."

Intriguing. But then again, he could be talking gibberish and I would still get all hot and bothered. Discreetly, I adjusted my favorite appendage and smiled up at him. "Can't wait." I would now have deliciously wet dreams about this conversation. *Thank you, Naël, for robbing me of restful sleep.* "I'll be back around dinnertime at the latest." I had rescheduled my visit with the Oracle for the next day and was pleasantly surprised when the Einstein-look-alike didn't give me a hard time about it.

Reluctantly, Fouchard freed me from his embrace. "Earlier." It was an order, his cantankerous authoritative side surfacing. "Much earlier."

I smiled, placing my hand on his chest. His heart drummed against my hand, a song now so familiar it spelled home every time. "I'll do my best." I kissed him again and then thought of being beside Cristina's bed at her apartment. My familiarity with her place made it easy to picture it: her small bed against a wall painted in bright sunny yellow and crowned by a large print of an African dusk, a small nod to her family origins. One minute I was still staring at my sexy boyfriend, the next I was surrounded by lemony walls.

"Aiden." Cristina's voice stabbed me with such guilt, tears exploded in my eyes immediately. "What are you doing here?"

Cristina was lying in her bed, covered to the waist

with a golden sheet, her kinky curls spread on the pillow around her head like a dark halo. Her face was bandaged, her lips swollen, and an ugly purple bruise covered her eye. I was paralyzed, standing a few steps away from her, tears rolling down my face and the weight of self-blame crushing my chest. She'd carry scars for the rest of her life, her beautiful face marred by cuts and abrasions, because of me. Me.

"I'm sorry, Cristina, so sorry." The rawness of my voice surprised even me. Cristina opened her mouth to say something, but I stopped her. "Don't say anything, *amiga*. I did this to you, and I deserve your anger." I swallowed a sob. "But I wish you could forgive me. You're my best friend. You're my family."

Cristina slowly propped herself up on her pillow and lifted her arms to me. "*Estupido, vem cá.*" I blinked away the tears, another sob escaping me. "Come here, dummy. Now."

I didn't hesitate. I threw myself in her arms, oblivious to the fact that she was probably sore, and held her against me before exploding into a full-blown sobbing fest. "I should have protected you better. I hate myself."

"As much as I love seeing you this humble for once, and as tempting as it is to use that against you, I'm your friend and I don't blame you for any of this, *estupido*." Strangely enough, being called stupid by her made my heart soar. She pulled me away from her to look me in the eye. It made my heart bleed to see her damaged face. "The only person with any blame here is that idiot who's after you. What's his name? Bob? What kind of name is that for a demigod?"

I tried to control my sobs, wiping the wet mess that was my face with the back of my hand. Cristina frowned and handed me a tissue. I blew my nose and then attempted a smile. I wasn't sure I was one hundred percent successful. She smiled back and gave me a second tissue. "I'm a fucking mess of tears and snot."

With a chuckle, she brushed her hand on my cheek. "You sure are, Aiden, but I'm so glad to see you." I sniffled and wiped another rogue tear from my eye. "I hear you've been hiding in the convent again with your hot man. Has it been a sex marathon?"

I snorted, happy the conversation had turned lighter. "I wish," I told her. "Vee is sleeping in our room."

She let loose a long "ah" and became pensive for a moment. "Another day or so and she can come spend some time with me," she said. "Then you and Naël can put your freak on again." I laughed and sat on the edge of the bed. "I mean it, Aiden. I'm a bit banged up, but I'm okay. The worst of my wounds is fully healed." She looked up at me with her large amber eyes and smiled. "Tó told me I have you to thank for that." I tried to deny it, shaking a hand between us, but she grabbed my wrist and shushed me. "He also told me you almost died because of that. You're totally crazy, *maluco*, but I love you for it."

I didn't fight her then as she drew me in for another hug. "Anything for you, Cristina," I whispered into her thick hair. "You've been my family since I got here, and I love you." We pulled apart and smiled at each other, both with wet eyes and suspiciously trembling lips. "And even though I'm still not happy about you dating the warlock, I see now that he is not so bad."

She guffawed. "High praise coming from you." Indeed. It was still hard to admit that the cop had proved himself to be one of the good guys, but this was Cristina. "He told me he punched you. Hard."

Heat rose to my cheeks. Yes, I remembered his jab, followed at light-speed by an uppercut that made me bite my tongue and hear ringing for hours afterward. "He's stronger than he looks," I said with a snort. "My jaw is still sore." That was a lie. As fast as I healed, the pain had subsided shortly after he socked me.

We sat together in silence for a while. Then she held my hand again and asked, "How in heaven's name did you appear from nowhere?"

"Apparently it's one of my many amazing gifts," I said, rubbing my thumb on the top of her soft hand.

"That and biting sarcasm. I'm quite literally a well of untapped potential magic."

She chuckled. "I don't know about that. I think Naël has long tapped that for sure." I almost choked. Wicked girl. "Come on, tell me things."

For the next hour or so we sat together talking, and with each tick of the clock my heart lightened, guilt evaporating slowly but surely as I assured myself Cristina was and would be all right. And that she was still my best friend.

When it was time to say goodbye, Cristina once again told me to send Vee to her; she could use the company. I was certain Fouchard would not even consider it, as protective as he was of his sister, but I promised I'd try, and after much hugging, I closed my eyes, conjured up the image of a quiet corner of the sanctuary, and teleported myself there while my lips softly uttered, "Beam me up, Scotty."

It was still freaky to do that but cool just the same. A youngster with round-lensed glasses and a face covered in acne welcomed me with a stunned, wide-eyed frown. I smiled at him, but the poor boy couldn't believe his eyes, his mouth wide open and body frozen in place. "Are you okay there, buddy?" I asked him, pretending nothing was out of sync. "You look like you've seen a ghost."

I didn't wait for him to start asking questions and strode away in the direction of the granary where tourists were not allowed, our meeting point if we needed some privacy. I texted Fouchard to let him know I was back, and he replied immediately. He was not at the granary but having a picnic out in the woods with Vee. I wanted to run but thought I would attract too much attention, so I walked as fast as I could, weaving through the droves of people who still wandered around the convent.

As soon as I rounded the trunk of a large chestnut tree, my eyes met with my boyfriend's, who bounced to his feet in a feline move that belied his size. I did run then, crowds left behind and the world fading into the background as my senses focused solely on the magnificent and beloved body of my merrow. We threw ourselves into each other's arms and hung on as if to a life buoy. The whirlwind of emotions that had been gathering inside of me all day burst out in that desperate embrace.

"Thank God you're okay," he whispered, his lips buried in my hair, his hands flattened on my back pulling me tighter. "I couldn't even think straight all day knowing you were out there."

I wanted to tell him I was doing fine, that now that I knew Cristina didn't hold me responsible for what happened, I could breathe a little easier. I wanted to tell him that even though I still had a demigod chasing me with a deadly weapon, I felt nothing but relief. No danger on earth compared to the pain of losing a friend, a loved one. And for now at least, all those whom I loved were safe and sound. These tears choking me weren't tears of pain or anger; they were tears of joy. For the first time in my life I was part of something, I was loved. Happiness in a nutshell.

TWENTY-FIVE
ROTTEN SMELLS AND REVELATIONS

"Did she really say that? How is she? Will she have to be in a wheelchair?" The questions kept coming like an unstoppable force of nature, over and over since Aiden had returned the day before. Vee couldn't be more excited at finding out her friend Cristina was well and asking for her. "Will we still be able to hang out?"

Fouchard placed a finger across her lips. "Shh, girl. You're wearing me out." I snickered, and he gave me the look. All right, I wouldn't undermine his authority by laughing at their interaction. But they were truly entertaining at times. "You will see her tomorrow."

"Tomorrow? We're going home tomorrow?" Vee took hold of her brother's wrist and hopped like a jackrabbit. "What about the poachers?"

Fouchard threw me a look, and I stepped in. "Silva called. They caught them. You'll be safe now." Unless you were around me, of course, since Bob hadn't given up yet as far as I knew. "You were right, Naël, one of them was a cop." Which only reinforced my belief that you couldn't trust anyone. Of course my circle of trust had expanded significantly in the past few months, a fact that was drilling a major hole in my theory of mistrust. But I wouldn't mention that to anyone. Let them think I was still the jaded what-ever-I-was with a serious chip on his shoulder for everything magical.

We finished eating breakfast with the brothers who then quickly vanished to wherever they went during the day. Only Brother John remained, waiting patiently to take me to see the Oracle before the monastery opened its doors to the public.

Silva had called first thing in the morning to give us the news. "We got two of them," he said. "We believe there is at least one more at large, but we are confident our jailbirds will be easily persuaded to sing." Gotta love police jargon. Or maybe this was just Silva trying to impress us with his old gumshoe lingo. "I think it's safe for Fouchard and Vee to come back home. You, on the other hand, should still be in hiding. That crazy god is still after you."

I wouldn't mention that last bit to Fouchard.

Better to steer away from the vexing subject of Bob and his weapon of mass destruction.

I was looking forward to going back to semi-normalcy, running my totally repaired café—courtesy of the local coven—and lying on the sand to soak in the sunshine. It was high season, and I was losing quite a bit of money having my store closed. Not that I was worried about money, especially when the lives of those I loved might be in danger, but a man had to eat, and I couldn't let my best friend go without income either.

"Are you ready, my son?" Brother John asked, that funky man-bun in such stark contrast with his humble brown habit. "The Oracle is waiting."

I couldn't resist. "Let him wait. He made me wait the first time while everyone lied to me about his mental stability." Well, some of that had not been too far from the truth, but still. "He can wait a few more minutes." The older monk gave me the look, the same look I often saw Fouchard give his sister when she was being disrespectful or disobedient. I surrendered. "Okay, okay, let's go. Sheesh, I thought monks were supposed to be patient and kind."

"I think you probably already wore out all their patience, Aiden," Fouchard said, a threat of a chuckle in his words. "Go, we'll be in the main cloister. Go."

I gave him a peck on the lips and hightailed out of there. The quicker I talked to the Einstein look-alike, the quicker I would be back to my family. I savored that word in my head: family. What a wonderful combination of letters, one that made me warm and fuzzy inside and brought a smile to my lips every time. I had a family. How freaking amazing was that?

The Oracle was in his usual position in the library, and I wondered where he went during the day while the tourists crawled through that space, trying to imagine how it may have looked many years ago. His eyes opened as I walked in, leaving Brother John outside. Without a word, he offered me a seat on a cushion set in front of him. I guess I had been promoted to whatever level you had to be to not have to sit on the cold stone floor.

"You wanted to talk to me, Brother Serafim?" I asked him as I dropped to the cushion, shifting a bit to find a comfy spot. The monk's hair was even messier than the last time I'd seen him, if that was possible. His thin lips stretched into a smile, but he didn't utter a word. I flared my nostrils. "Well?"

The old man stayed quiet for a while longer before asking, "Remember that woman a few months ago who was asking questions about you and your merman?"

That was totally out of the blue. Did I remember her? Yes, of course. She still appeared in my nightmares frequently as Pescado's accomplice, plotting against us. "Yes. The police haven't been able to locate her. They think she might have left the country." As much as I mistrusted Silva, the warlock had been an invaluable and willing source of information.

The oracle shook his head. "She's in Portugal." That made me feel really good; yet another thing to worry about. "She was an accomplice to the serial killer and more recently the poachers."

I almost jumped out of my skin. "What? She was in with the poachers?" Who the fuck was this woman and what did she have against us?

"You have a mutual acquaintance; someone she loves dearly—at least, as much as her cold heart allows her to." Who could that be? And what did that have to do with anything? She was free to love whoever she wanted. I was all about personal freedoms. "Someone who wants you dead."

Another one? *Join the waiting list, lady.* "If she wants me dead, why bother with Naël and Vee?" Made zero sense.

Brother Serafim clicked his tongue. "*He* wants you dead," he said conversationally, as if we were discussing the weather. "She wants you to suffer first."

I was guessing my magical origins had everything to do with that. One more strike against it. "Why? Do I even know her?"

He shook his head again. "No, she doesn't know you, but she knows about you." Well, that was helpful. I was just about to ask him to stop speaking in tongues when he added, "She knows who and how powerful you are."

I wished people would stop telling me I was powerful. Yes, granted, I had a few interesting and useful gifts; some I'd had all my life and others had recently surfaced. But powerful? I could hear at a distance, teleport, heal myself and others, and see magicals for what they were. I was yet to smite an enemy with one glance or stop a train in its track. I was no Superman.

"Even if that's true, that I'm as powerful as everyone keeps telling me I am, why would she care? It's not like I'm trying to take over the world or eradicate all magicals from the earth." Okay, in the not-so-distant past, I probably would have found that kind of power attractive. I'd been so angry at my parents—whoever they were—for leaving me alone in a world I didn't understand and had no skills to navigate that eradicating them all had been a frequent fantasy of mine. But I would never do it. Hell, I had a hard time knocking Pescado out to rescue Vee; how would I be able to wipe out a whole population?

"She's Baburaj's mother." He could have knocked me out with a feather. The diminutive demigod had a mother? "She's still pissed your mother got her man."

The story kept getting weirder and weirder. "Her man?" My mouth went dry, and I closed it, realizing I was gaping like a fish out of water. "What do you mean?"

"Your father is a mighty druid whose magical talents caught the attention of the gods," he explained in a soft voice, the tone of someone telling a child a bedtime story. "It was widely believed that if he mated with a goddess, he would produce a child with powers never before seen on earth." No, I didn't like where this story was headed. "When he fell in love with your mother and was out of the mating pool, so to speak, a lot of other divinities were disappointed. A few, like Baburaj's mother, were outright mad with jealousy. Jhanvi is a yaksha who was not satisfied with her own limitations and wanted to mate with someone capable of impregnating her with a powerful being, strong enough to rule over all others."

My head was beginning to throb. "Yaksha? What the hell is that?" I blinked a few times, hoping the dull pain behind my eyes would fade. It didn't.

"A yaksha is a nature spirit whose job is to guard treasures of the gods," the old man explained. "Most are benevolent and harmless, but others, like Jhanvi, are ravenous for power." Awesome. "And sex. Some are definitely what humans would call nymphomaniacs." Having been a man-whore until recently, I couldn't fault her for that. "Jhanvi set her eyes on your father, and when he picked Lakshmi instead of her, she lost it. It didn't matter to her that even if she got your father, she would never produce someone powerful as you, her own powers being mediocre at best."

A thought occurred to me then; could that be the reason why my parents abandoned me in a world I didn't fit in? "When you say she lost it, what exactly do you mean?" The small monk was now busy sipping from an old crockery mug that another brother had just brought in for him, a nasty, almost rotten smell wafting from it. I wrinkled my nose. What the hell was he drinking?

"She couldn't do anything against your father or mother; she was not powerful enough. In fact, she possesses very few magical powers, mostly basic stuff." He took another sip of the reeking concoction in his mug and let out a sigh of delight. The old man was nuttier than a chipmunk. "But when you were born, she saw it as her opportunity for revenge. You were just a babe, and your powers would not start manifesting themselves until much later. So she tried to kidnap and kill you." His pallid eyes become more distant, the dark pupils expanding. Was he getting high on that drink? "As you may imagine that didn't sit well with your parents, who decided to hide you somewhere she would never be able to find you—right in plain sight."

My stomach clenched, half from the horrible smell but also from the emotions his story was stirring up in me. So maybe my parents actually loved me, but hadn't they realized that by dropping me among the regulars without a clue of who or what I was, they were condemning me to a life of loneliness and self-doubt? "How did she find me now then?"

Brother Serafim yawned so wide, I swear I saw the inside of his stomach. "Your powers have been strengthening and manifesting themselves. You can't hide that kind of magic," he said, his eyes closing. "Magicals like you have a very definite signature, one that can be tracked once the powers are deployed. She found you and sicced her idiot son on you."

The monk was falling asleep as he spoke. Soon I wouldn't be able to get any more answers from him. "How come he has that weapon? Did he steal it?"

He released a hiccupping chuckle. "Hell no, his mother did. It was not very hard for her to get Brahma to fuck and impregnate her." I cringed at his words; they sounded very wrong coming from a monk. "While he was sleeping it off, she stole the weapon and hid it until her son was of age and able to wield it."

Much to my surprise and dismay I watched as the monk slowly lowered himself to the mattress and fell asleep. *Shit.* I still had questions. After waiting for a few moments, thinking that maybe he would wake up, I gave up and left, thanking the monk outside the door. Brother John was nowhere to be seen.

As I made my way to the cloister where Fouchard and Vee were waiting for me, my mind filled with questions. If my true identity was out of the bag, so to speak, why hadn't my parents made themselves known to me? It would be nice to know what other tricks I had up my magical sleeve instead of constantly being surprised by them. I was obviously not a god, not even a demigod, so what was I exactly? This whole conversation about my unique talents didn't come any closer to answering that question. Okay, I was a magical, but what kind? What was my role in the magical world? Did I even have one? And more pressing, what the fuck was the Oracle drinking?

TWENTY-SIX

THE SCOOBY GANG IS ALL HERE

"No wonder we haven't been able to locate her," Silva said, his onyx eyes rimmed in red. It seemed as if the warlock hadn't been getting enough sleep. Cristina's recovery had hit him hard. That knowledge made me like him a bit more. Just a smidgen; let's not go crazy. "She has nothing to connect her to the serial killer, or the poachers for that matter." Yes, my devil-spawned nemesis had been busy keeping track of me and those I cared for, making sure that information reached the ears of those who wished us ill. No way to track her—diabolical but freaking smart. A tiny part of me admired her cunning even as the rest of me hated her everything else.

"The question is, how do we catch her?"

Fouchard, ever practical, said. "I mean, we can't just let her roam free, doing her worst to get us all killed."

I took a sip of my coffee and watched the exchange without saying a word. My mind was still reeling from the Oracle's revelations about my family. No, not my family—my progenitors. Fouchard, Vee, and Cristina were my family, not these distant magicals whom I'd had no contact with or knowledge of until recently. Shared genes did not a family make.

"We're looking for her, I assure you," the policeman said, his hand firmly attached to Cristina's. My friend was still bruised and paler than I had ever seen her, but she was slowly going back to her normal daily routine. "She's a slippery one. Every time we think we have her, she manages to vanish."

"Follow her idiot son," I said. Every eye around the table turned to me. I had been quiet for so long, my voice seemed to have startled them all. "He's not so good at hiding, and she won't be too far from him."

Fouchard smiled at me. "Yes, that's it. He'll be hanging out at bars; anywhere where there is plenty of alcohol." Bob was indeed a lush, and there was no doubt in my mind it wouldn't be too hard to find him. "Just follow the rumors of ghostly activity involving drinks, and he'll be there."

Cristina threw me a worried glance. "How are you doing with all these developments, Aiden?" I was numb, I think. To find out that my parents were indeed protecting me by abandoning me was hard to swallow and not as comforting as you'd think. They hadn't left me behind because they didn't love me, but they *had* ditched me all the same. I shrugged. "You know I'm here if you need to talk, right?"

I nodded. "I know, *amiga*." I didn't think I was ready to talk about this, not even with my boyfriend—who had been very gentle around me for the past two days since we came back from the monastery. "Same here." I wasn't sure my smile reached my eyes, but I was in a strange mood.

"Can I have another *nata*, Cristina?" Vee had been unusually quiet as if even she could tell I was not up to any shenanigans. Cristina dropped Silva's hand and followed the girl to the kitchen to get her one.

"Why am I never invited to your parties?"

I almost jumped out of my skin. Taz had once more managed to sneak up on us. She stood behind Silva, her skinny arms crossed and her high-heeled foot taping furiously on the tiled floor. "I'm beginning to think you don't like me."

If there was something I liked about the red-haired witch, it was that she always made me laugh. "Stop being such a drama queen and sit your skinny ass down." She pouted but did what I told her. "We couldn't find you, witch. Where the hell were you?"

We hadn't seen or heard from her since the attack, which in itself was worrisome, considering she was always showing up uninvited.

"Cristina, good to see you up and about," she yelled. Cristina waved at her from the counter where she was filling a plate with all sorts of goodies, Vee right by her side, offering her expert advice. The witch then turned to me. "For your information, Aiden, I've been busy looking for your stalker friend."

I groaned. "She's not my friend." Fouchard chuckled, and I threw him a killer look.

"Whatever," Taz continued, unfazed as usual. "You can start by thanking me, you ungrateful lout." She reached for a pastry even before Cristina had set the plate down on the table.

"Thank you for what? For being an insufferable busybody?" I guessed I could start by thanking her for giving me an out from my numbness. My snarkiness was finally resurfacing.

"The pot calling the kettle black," she mumbled as she took a bite of a *bola de Berlim*. With her lips covered in sugar and cheeks bloated, she added, "You can thank me for finding your nemesis's whereabouts."

What? How had she figured out what the High Warlock of Lisbon couldn't? "Bullshit. You found nothing." Yes, I still had trouble trusting her.

She feigned outrage, flattening a palm on her

chest and leaving a huge sugary stain on her dark blue shirt. "You hurt my feelings, Aiden. I may not tell you where she is after all." She took another giant bite of the sugary confection and puffed up her cheeks like a chipmunk collecting hazelnuts.

"Ignore the angry barista," Silva said, a rare smile dancing in his lips. "We need that info so no one else gets hurt."

Taz huffed and slumped her shoulders. She swallowed her mouthful and said, "Okay, fair is fair. You're not going to like it though." Uh-oh, what was she hinting at? Why wouldn't I like it? "She has been hiding under the city."

I think we all gasped at the same time. Taz was well known for saying preposterous things, but this topped them all. Under the city? How did one hide under the city? Did she mean the subway? "What the hell are you talking about, Taz? How can she be under the city?"

The witch brushed a storm of crumbs off her shirt and what was showing of her impressive bosom. "The evil duo has been hiding right under the streets of downtown Lisbon."

That could not be; even I knew that downtown Lisbon was stolen from the river, built over sand and water. No chance of tunnels or anything built underneath.

"You mean they're hiding in the Roman

galleries?" Silva's eyes had opened to wide circles. "That's quite brilliant and stupid all at the same time."

I was so confused. "Wait, what are the Roman galleries? Never heard of them." I scratched my head, feeling a headache coming.

Cristina, now sitting beside her boyfriend, explained, "You would have heard of it if you watched TV once in a while, my clueless friend." She touched the bandage on her face and cringed. Damn, the wounds on her face were still sore. "About two thousand years ago, our friends the Romans wanted to build a city where Lisbon now stands but couldn't because you can't build on sand and mud, at least not something that will last. Being the smarty pants that they were, they figured out a way around; they built this underground maze of tunnels with arched ceilings which now not only support the whole of downtown but keep the city from flooding."

Fouchard whistled. "Fuck. Those ancients had smarts. And skills." I stared at him, loving his expression of awe and fighting the urge to kiss the crap out of his lips. "But how is that brilliant and stupid?"

Silva answered, "Brilliant because no one will bother them until the fall when the place is drained for one of only two public openings of the year." Cristina nodded. "Stupid because the tunnels are mostly flooded this time of the year and not exactly a safe place to live. Unless you're a fish."

We all stared at Fouchard, who furrowed his brow and shook his hands. "No merfolk live there, I assure you. I doubt it if anyone even knows about it." Maybe Pescado had known about the tunnels, but then again, the evil duet would probably prefer to leave their hiding spot a secret from everyone. Safer in the long run.

"If the place is flooded most of the year, how are they surviving down there?" I asked.

Surprising everyone, Vee answered, "They're using magic. Duh!" She didn't even spare me a look and continued to munch on a pastry while we all gawked at her. When no one said anything, she looked up and said, "What? Why are you looking at me like that?" We all burst out laughing. "You guys are so weird." She shook her head and went back to eating, paying no attention to our laughter.

Once we all managed to get our hilarity under control, Fouchard said, "You know what that means, right?" I had no idea and told him so with my gaping mouth and furrowed brow. "We're due for a swim."

I hoped he didn't mean what I thought he meant; I was in no mood to go chase my nemesis inside flooded underground tunnels. Swimming with my merrow in the beautiful ocean waters was one thing, paddling through narrow, dark, cavernous hallways was another. I shook my head emphatically. "No way. I'm not doing it."

Fouchard turned to Silva and said, "I will talk him into it."

Jerk. Who did he think he was? As if he had any power over me. Okay, maybe he did; not power as in magic but the kind that came from being loved so fiercely. I loved him with an almost frightening intensity and was therefore willing to do just about anything for him.

After Taz left and we had cleaned up the store in preparation for its reopening in a few days, Vee threw a fit when her brother told her she had to come home with us instead of spending the night with Cristina.

"She can stay with me," Cristina said. "Tó has been staying over to keep an eye on things, so she'll be safe. And I do miss girls' night."

Vee looked up at her brother, eyes shining in anticipation and fear. "Please, Naël. I'll be good, I promise." She looked at me as if begging for backup. "And that way you can spend some time with Aiden and do all the lovey-dovey crap you do when I'm not around."

My cheeks burned, and I had to lower my eyes for fear she could see how much I wanted to be alone with her brother. It had been too long since our kisses and stolen touches had led to anything more than that.

"I'll keep the ladies safe," Silva said, holding Cristina's hand and smiling. "They'll be okay."

I saw the resolve in my boyfriend's eyes soften and dwindle away. He ran a hand over his face and sighed. "All right, you can stay with Cristina." Then he looked at me, and my heart started a frenzied tap dance inside my chest. "There is something I've been wanting to do with Aiden." His voice hadn't risen over a whisper, and I was sure I was the only one who heard that last comment. My face burned hotter. What was he planning? Whatever it was, I was so on board. My body missed his; I missed the intimacy that came when we were totally vulnerable with each other, physically and spiritually.

After goodbyes and closing the store, Fouchard drove us to his place. We had been staying in my condo since we came back from the monastery so we could be closer to my store and to Cristina. It hadn't been that long since I'd been at his house, but I was still awed by the massive size and beauty of the architecture. Crossing the wide threshold to the foyer brought me a sense of being home again and, having a one-track mind, I immediately headed to the stairs to go up to Fouchard's room. He stopped me.

"Aren't we going upstairs?" I was surprised to see the predatory glint in his eyes. "Don't you want to have crazy monkey sex now that we are finally alone?"

"I have a surprise for you." The whisper made my whole skin break into goose bumps. Whatever it was, the simple promise made me hard. "We're going down to the beach."

That *really* surprised me. We had made love on the sand a few times, but sex on the beach was not as smooth as the cocktail by the same name. Getting it on on the sand meant a lot of uncomfortable grains in unseemly places. At one point during one of our love-making sessions, I actually took a choking gulp of sand. No, I much preferred less silty settings.

At my hesitation, he grasped my hand and pulled me behind him, heading down to the basement beach. "You know how many times you've asked me how merfolk make love in their aqua form?"

I nodded. I was curious about a lot of things to do with the merrows, especially sexual things. He had never told me, always skirting around the subject as if it was taboo or something. The merfolk must be able to mate underwater, right? Fouchard lived mostly landside but Neptune, for example, rarely came to the surface and yet he had several children. How had he impregnated his wife?

"What does that have anything to do with us going to the beach?" I asked, feigning ignorance while more than a little turned on by what I expected the surprise was.

Fouchard stopped halfway down the stairs to look

up at me. "I figured that instead of telling you about it," he said, the predator in his eyes still shining through, "I'd just show it. Better yet, I'll demonstrate it."

I gulped. Hard. At that moment, Pinocchio and his long wooden nose had nothing on me.

TWENTY-SEVEN

MERMEN DO IT BETTER

THE SOFT LIGHTS ALONG THE HIGH WALLS WERE already glowing even though there was still some natural light coming from the narrow exit into the ocean beyond. I had been struck dumb by my boyfriend's words and all the erotic fantasies playing in a loop inside my head.

Fouchard led me to the edge of the water and began stripping me. After he pulled my shirt off, closely followed by my pants and underwear, he asked me to undress him. I didn't waste any time, and soon we were standing as naked as the day we were born, facing and drinking each other in with our eyes. How long had it been? Three, four days? It felt an eternity since I had seen him like that. For a moment I was tempted to just give up on the whole thing and make him mine right there and then, as the mild ocean waves lapped and teased the sand. But my merrow didn't give up; he held my hand tight and pulled me behind him into the water.

"We're really going to do this?" I didn't know what to expect since he had been so secretive about it, and that made me as nervous as excited. I trusted him completely. Nothing he did to me would harm me in any way. But his words from some time ago haunted me: *Merrows are predators, Mr. Mercer.* "You're not going to eat me after we have sex, right?" I asked him.

Fouchard tilted his head back and laughed. "I'm not a black widow, Aiden." He pulled me closer until our bare skin was touching and his breath warmed my face. "I love you, idiot. I won't be hurting you in any way. Much to the contrary." He wiggled his brows and I chuckled, relief washing over me. "You're in for a treat, sweetheart."

I meekly followed him then, the saltwater rising to caress my shins, my knees, my upper thighs and cover my favorite appendage. Thankfully, the water was warm, as it normally was this time of the year, only a few degrees below my body temperature. Pinocchio gave the ocean a silent thank-you, and I moved on, deeper and deeper until there was no other way to go but underwater.

As he had done a few times before, Fouchard covered my mouth with his as soon as we were submerged and breathed inside, filling my lungs with magical air. He had explained that one of the few magical gifts merrows had was the power to temporarily allow gill-less creatures to breathe under water. It was fascinating to suddenly open my mouth and inhale only the life-giving oxygen in the water. I could also talk, even though sound didn't carry well in liquids.

I watched in fascination as my boyfriend's beautiful and muscular legs and his other delicious male parts transformed to a mesmerizing iridescent blue tail. As beautiful as his mertail was, it was just as powerful, propelling him through the water as surely as a boat engine but much more gracefully. We swam for a while, our hands still attached so I could stay by his side while he navigated around kelp and fish, heading somewhere I was not yet privy to.

When he began heading toward the surface, I couldn't help but be disappointed; was that it? The big secret was that merfolk did not have sex in the water? We broke the surface to find ourselves inside a grotto of some kind. It was a large gallery with no visible exits other than the one we had just come from. "No one will disturb us here," he said, cupping my wet cheek with his hand. "I placed a glamor over the entrance, and no merfolk, fish, or any other creature will come to interrupt us."

That sounded definitely much more promising. I

couldn't hold it any longer; I practically leaped at him, my arms knotting behind his neck and my lips latching on to his in a hungry kiss. He didn't seem surprised and immediately opened his mouth to allow my tongue in. His salty flavor was ambrosia, intoxicating and nurturing. Frantically, I wrapped my legs around his hips, feeling the velvety softness of his tail against my arousal. I groaned inside his mouth and tightened my embrace. Fouchard had his hands flattened on my back, pulling me closer while his lips were creating havoc on mine.

"I want you," I moaned against his lips and then groaned as he pushed me away from him. "What? No—"

Without a word he devoured me with his eyes, hinting of his innate wild side, and then dove under the surface. Confused, I looked around me, trying to find him beneath the water without success. "Naël, where are you?"

I needed not worry. Warmth enveloped me as my merrow, hidden under the darkness of the grotto, wrapped his lips around and slid up and down the length of me. I writhed in pleasure, a soft groan escaping me while below, underwater, my boyfriend kissed and suckled me into ecstasy. With nothing to support me, I reached out behind me to grab hold of the large rock that jutted out from the wall, its surface mostly submerged. My moans echoed in the cavernous space as the pressure in my core grew to astronomical heights.

Just as I thought I was going to explode, Fouchard pulled away and broke the surface. He had a satisfied smile on his face, and so he should; those lips were magical. Closing his hands on both sides of my waist, he lifted and set me on the edge of the rock lip, my legs and lower body still submerged. I must have looked confused because a low, sexy grunt came from deep in his throat. "Patience, sweetheart, patience."

I had never been known for that virtue, so I folded forward to take his generous lips between mine. "Can't wait much longer, Naël."

He pushed my upper body away and, holding on to my hips, pulled my lower body closer to him. My ass was now half hanging off the ledge of the rock, and I had to support myself with my arms so I wouldn't topple off. Fouchard braced himself on either side of me and pulled his body out of the water, the lower half of his tail still swinging gracefully in the ocean. My eyes roamed to the part of his tail where his crotch would have been, and I couldn't believe what I was seeing; the surface had opened to reveal a part of his body I had gotten pretty familiar with for the past few months. He followed my eyes and a smile curved the corner of his lips. "Surprise."

Wicked man. "That's it? A zipper-type opening? The rest is the same?"

He let out a roar of laughter. "It's more like a Velcro-type opening, and you seem disappointed," he said, amusement belying his words. "I thought you like my—"

I interrupted him. "Yes, of course I do. You're beautiful and have the power in all the right places." My eyes roamed down to the part in question, and I swear my mouth watered at the memories of my lips wrapped around it. "I was just surprised."

He chuckled again. "Our tail is more of a protection than an actual body part, Aiden. Underneath it, everything you know is still there." He winked.

"Then why did you tell me you had a surprise for me?" The whole conversation had not distracted me from the fact we still hadn't made love.

That wicked smile I had grown to love so much made an appearance as he gently pushed me back until I was lying on the rock and slid a finger inside me. I yelled as a mix of surprise and pleasure filled and almost undid me. *Bastard.* But what a lovely bastard he was. I pulled myself up on my elbows and ran a hand over his rough short hair, trying awkwardly to close the space between us. He pulled my bottom further off the rock ledge, and I was now practically hanging by the small of my back. I closed my fingers on the edges and held on so I wouldn't fall off just as he teased me with that expertise I had come to expect from my lover.

"I brought no lube," he whispered, kissing one of my hips, now totally submerged. I was so far gone, I couldn't care less. "No need for it; mermen produce their own under the water." As if to prove it, Naël dipped a hand under water and ran it over the tip of his erection. Holy shit! My merman was a walking bottle of lube. He looked up at me for a moment, heat and amusement dancing in his eyes, and slipped his now well-lubricated fingers inside of me again. I moaned, pleasure building as he diligently worked on me. "Are you ready?"

Was I ever. I nodded, unable to say anything. The pressure inside me threatened to explode at any moment, but he made me wait no longer. Holding on firmly to my hips, he buried himself in me. I think we both screamed at the same time. It was difficult to tell, because the echoes bouncing of the walls created a wonderful melody of sorts, our two voices entangled in ecstasy. He drove me hard, but I couldn't get enough of him as he filled me completely. I had never been a romantic fool but here I was in tears over how close we were, body and soul.

"Am I hurting you?" he stopped and asked, an expression of alarm on his face.

I shook my head, a large knot in my throat. "No, not at all, Naël. I'm just happy," I said, a sob-chuckle escaping along with the words. "I have never felt this close to anyone, my love. I just can't believe my luck."

He cupped my cheek with a hand, and his lips stretched into that smile he saved only for Vee and now for me. My heart soared. "Not luck, sweetheart, not luck. Fate. We were fated together." That was the first time I had heard him say that, but as curious as the comment made me, I was too turned on to explore it. Instead I urged him into his stormy ebb and flow motion again.

Later, much later, after we had both reached the stars and rested together on top of the cold, wet rocks, bodies entwined and hearts beating in unison, his words finally hit me; what did he mean by that? What did he mean by fated together?

"Something Penelope Moreno, the High Priestess, told me when we were in Óbidos," he said when I asked him, his warm breath tickling my nose. "She said that our relationship was fated, that it was written in the stars. She didn't tell you?"

No, she had said nothing of the sort to me. And what exactly did that mean? Taz was going to be drowned in questions, but for now I just wanted to enjoy my boyfriend's warm body, still in his aqua form, exquisite tail stretched against my legs. There was no doubt about it; this man-whore was well and truly retired.

TWENTY-EIGHT
FEAR AND FIREBALLS

"It reeks of death and rodents." I was not a happy camper, standing in the main nave of the Sé, the cathedral of Lisbon, its high arched ceilings looming over us. "I don't like this a bit."

Taz slapped my arm. "Will you stop being a baby and shut up?" I rubbed the sore spot on my arm and made a childish face at her. "There are no rats down there. The city keeps it squeaky clean since they open it to the public twice a year."

Fouchard was putting all his muscle mass to good use, lifting the ledger stone from the floor in the transept. The slab of marble screeched when my boyfriend, with the help of the warlock, pulled and slid it to the side. As if it wasn't spooky enough to be going down under the city, we were entering the tunnels through a grave.

I shivered. "You're not the one going down into a dark, flooded hole in the ground, witch." My chest hurt from the pressure of anxiety and, I'll admit it, fear. I had never been too fond of small enclosed spaces, and now I was going to go inside one where two creatures who wanted nothing more than to see me dead lurked.

"You've been underwater many times, Aiden," Fouchard said, winking at me. Memories of our little adventure in the grotto of love—yes, I named it and was hoping to go back frequently—just a week ago flooded me with toe-curling tingling. I might have salivated a bit. "I won't let you drown, idiot."

I adjusted my pants discreetly. "I'm not afraid of drowning. I'm afraid of what those two assholes who hate me might do to me. And you, Naël. I don't want them hurting you."

Fouchard snorted. "I'm a lot stronger in the water, Aiden. I may not have a lot of magical powers landside, but in the water it's a different matter." I disagreed with him; he did have some skills landside—but admittedly not something that would help us fight the deadly duo. "I can hold my own." His biceps bulged from under his sleeves as he pulled on the heavy slab one last time, and my pants shrank. Why couldn't we just go back to my place and forget about this in each other's arms?

I knew I was being childish. Bob and his mommy

dearest had to be dealt with before somebody else got hurt. They had already done enough damage. I sighed, resigned. "At the first sign of a rat, I'm high-tailing out of there," I warned, only half joking. Fouchard laughed, and Taz clicked her tongue in disapproval.

Cristina was home with Vee while we undertook this dangerous and, in my not-so-respected opinion, ill-advised adventure. "We'll be waiting out here with a dry towel and some hot tea for you," teased the witch, patting me on the back as she would a kid. I mumbled a profanity under my breath, and she gave me the evil eye.

"Right, it's time," Fouchard announced, his smile belying the somber tone of his voice. He was not too happy about going down the hole either. He turned to Taz and Silva. "You wait for us here. If they try to run out this way, you get them."

I was pretty sure they didn't need an actual exit to escape. Bob had powerful magic on his side, though poor compared to that of the god who had spawned him.

The only known entrance to the tunnels was smack in the middle of a busy city street, which didn't lend itself to a furtive entry, but Silva had the perfect solution—a secret passage, hidden inside a tombstone on the floor of the city's cathedral. Leave it to a warlock to find the spookiest gate to the city's under-belly. The opening gaped at us, dark and ominous like the jaws of a monster ready to eat us alive. A shiver ran through my body, and I tried in vain to swallow the knot that had formed in my throat.

"Well, see you in a bit," Fouchard said, taking the first step down the gloomy staircase heading to the bowels of the city. I grabbed his wrist and stopped him. "What's wrong?"

I licked my dry lips. "I'm going ahead," I said, not quite sure where this bravery—or stupidity—was coming from. "This is my war, and I prefer to take the first blow."

For a moment I thought my boyfriend was going to be pissed by my not-so-me hero attitude, but he smiled and stepped out from the hole to allow me to go first. As I stepped past him, he whispered, "I love it when you get this protective." The fear in my gut melted instantly, and a tiny smile curled my lips. Yes, the giant merrow had magic for sure.

I climbed down the uneven stone steps, closely followed by Fouchard, who held on to my shoulder, feigning fear when I knew all he was trying to do was comfort me. Soon we were completely buried in dark-ness, and I wished there was some light. As if on cue, several soft candles flared along the walls to illuminate our way. I guessed that was another one of my powers

—creating light where there was none. Cool, even though I would much prefer having the gift of physical strength so I could kick Bob's ass from here to hell.

The stairs sloped and curved deeper into the ground, too dark at the bottom for us to see what was coming. The Sé was built on a steep hill, away from the plateau where downtown Lisbon was standing. We were in for a long descent. Even my boyfriend's warm hand on the crook of my neck couldn't dissipate the feeling we were descending into Hades. My body was assailed by shivers. Fouchard squeezed my shoulder gently. The noise of city nightlife had long been replaced by an oppressive silence—the silence of a tomb.

After what felt like an eternity, the steps became slick with moss and moisture tickled our noses. "We're close." My whisper didn't echo as I had feared, but on the other hand, my mind was echoing my anxieties tenfold. *We're going to die down here, entombed like the monks buried on the church's nave.* I took a deep breath, trying to get rid of the voices. Fouchard, always attuned to my feelings, stopped and hugged me, his strong arms crossing over my chest and his lips nestled into the space between my neck and my shoulder. I could feel his heart beating against my back, and that life rhythm soothed me, enveloping me in a sense of peace so in contrast with the way this situation made me feel. I leaned on him, allowing his heat to warm my fear-iced body and closing my eyes to shy away from this dank and dark place.

"Better?" Fouchard asked, his mouth moving over my skin and sending tiny shivers of a different kind to other areas of my body. "Together we can beat those two. We're close to the water, and my magic is already strengthening. Together, Aiden; we'll do this together."

The one good thing—and possibly the only one—about where we were was that my energy was strengthening and growing. Here I was not only in proximity to nature but buried in it. The power of the earth humors was seeping through my skin, tingly like bursts of static electricity, making me stronger. Pity it wasn't making me any braver though. I opened my eyes, straightened as Fouchard let go of me, and resumed the way down.

Soon I could hear the gentle lapping of water against rock, a sound that normally brought me peace. Now it stirred nothing but anxiety inside me. I inhaled sharply as my feet sank into wetness. And so it began. I turned slightly to Fouchard and nodded. We were walking in the tunnels. Confirming my suspicions, the stairs turned into a flat slab of rock, still slanted but no longer steeply dipping into the ground.

As we walked down the slope, the water, cold and dark, climbed quickly, and soon it had reached our chests. Fouchard stopped me, nodded, and as we had planned, dove with me under the water. The light I had wished into existence also shone below the surface, and I was surprised to find that the water was clear, inhabited only by fish and not the scurrying creatures I had expected.

Fouchard pulled me close to him and covered my mouth with his, blowing his magic air into my lungs so I could continue to breathe once we were submerged. My mind went to the last time he had done that, and heat ran through me despite the coldness of the water. I longed to recreate that day, but first we had two naughty magicals to catch.

A few more feet in the tunnel and we could no longer hold our heads out the water, so we swam. It occurred to me I wasn't sure how to find Bob and his mother in this maze of tunnels that branched out in all directions, the water running under the arched ceiling through hallways and corridors that never seemed to end. I was just about to ask Fouchard the question when I felt it—the unmistakable prickling of approaching magic. I grabbed my boyfriend's arm and mouthed, "They're close." He nodded and, as I had made him promise beforehand, he fell behind me, still close enough to jump into action but a bit more sheltered from immediate danger. I could self-heal; he couldn't.

The prickling soon turned to throbbing, a live presence inside of me. I could feel the magic running wild through my veins, malicious and threatening, unlike the magic I felt when close to Taz or Silva. It was also much stronger, acrid as it burned its path through me. I stopped swimming and, allowing my feet to float down to the floor, I began walking instead—less movement of the water and slower progress. I wondered whether they could feel my energy just as I felt theirs. A few yards farther, the water level dropped, and we were breathing air again, my body submerged to right below my neck. Fouchard, being taller, waded in water that rose up to the middle of his chest. I could hear voices, first indistinguishable but becoming clearer as we approached; the high-pitched female voice rising above the male's. We slowed down even more.

When the voices became so close we could hear the words, we peeked around the corner to find the tipsy god and his mother involved in a heated argument. Fouchard touched my shoulder gently, his face hovering beside mine.

"It has to be done, Baburaj," Jhanvi said, both her hands clamped over her son's forearms. Bob didn't look happy, slouched over his own legs as he sat cross-legged on a step. The whole gallery where they were standing had been drained, and only a trickle of water ran over the stone floor. "Stop going after the *mac druid*. I want the merman first." My gut twisted and I had to control the urge to run to her and snap her neck in two. Frightened by my own anger, I leaned against Fouchard, trying to absorb some of his soothing heat. "*Mac druid* loves the fishman, Fouchard. We catch and kill him first. I want the *mac druid*'s heart to be torn into shreds before we kill him."

Guessing she was referring to me and not some druid I didn't know of, I clenched my hands into fists, nails piercing the skin of my palms. Warm blood trickled down to my wrists as an uncontrollable anger I had never felt before grew inside my chest; like a ball of fire, it burned and yearned to be released. I took a few deep breaths and managed to control the anger long enough to step away from our hiding place and face the deadly duo.

"No…." Fouchard made a move to hold me back, but it was too late; I was already in plain sight of the magicals.

"You wanted me?" I said, my voice dripping wrath, an ancient anger that didn't wholly come from me. Inside, I felt as if generations before me were all rising up against those two. "I'm here. Come and get me." I couldn't believe my own words. I had somehow distanced from my own self, and I was watching the scene rather than participating in it. I threw a quick glance at Fouchard, making sure he was still hiding. I knew it was killing him, not being able to jump in and protect me, but he had promised not to do it.

Jhanvi and Bob both turned their heads toward me, paralyzed by the shock of my presence. Mother Dearest was the first one to snap out of the trance. "How dare you come to us, cursed *mac druid*?" she spat out, her eyes shooting fire in my direction. "How dare you address us?"

I laughed. Cackled, actually. Like the freaking Wicked Witch of the West, I propped my hands on my waist and cackled. Was I stuck in a bad B-movie? It was as if I had no control over my own body, my own words. "Attack is the best defense, hag." Oh, my God. Had I actually used the word "hag"? What the hell was wrong with me?

There was a flicker of worry in the woman's eyes, but it didn't last long. "Why, aren't you going to hide behind your daddy's skirts this time?" What did she mean?

I shook my head, retrieving a slice of self-control. "What the fuck are you talking about? I don't have a father." At least, I didn't know who or where he was. Same difference.

It was her turn to laugh like the Mad Hatter. "You stupid creature. Who do you think protected you in the monastery when my son came to kill you?"

I blinked several times. "The monks, obviously.

What are you implying?" Was she trying to distract me?

Bob jumped to his feet, the chains hanging from his ear and nose clinking in the empty gallery. "Your father is one of the monks, idiot. He's one of the druids."

What? My father was a monk? The monks were druids? My head swam with confusion. "Now you're just making things up in hopes I get distracted and let you go."

Jhanvi stepped forward, her modern clothes in sharp contrast with the Roman construction. "Baburaj speaks the truth; one of those monks, those druids, is your father. Interesting how he didn't tell you that," she purred, malice tainting her words. "Could it be that he still doesn't want you, that he prefers that you stay far from him? Poor, unwanted creature that you are."

I lost it. I lost all control. The anger swelling inside my chest materialized in my hands as bright red flaming balls of energy. I raised my palms in their direction, and they both screamed at the same time. They weren't expecting that. Hell, *I* wasn't expecting that. They scrambled for the exit, a dark tunnel behind them, but I was faster. With a primal scream that sounded nothing like me, I released the fireballs in their direction. Jhanvi screamed again and threw herself on top of her son, pushing him out of the balls' trajectory. A burst of fire lit up the gallery as the fireballs exploded against the wall. White stone exploded into a million fragments, flying and falling around us like heavy snow. Within the space of a heartbeat, I summoned another energy ball. This time, before I could release it, their crouched bodies disappeared from sight. Magic; they had used magic to vanish. Frustrated, I stood there, holding the throbbing fireball, anger still growing in my chest.

"Aiden, sweetheart." I turned to the voice, hand raised to attack. Fouchard was standing there, vulnerable against my anger. "Put that away, Aiden. They're not here anymore. Put it down."

I held my hand up for a moment longer and then lowered it in horror. I was pointing it at my lover, the man I loved more than anything or anyone in the world. I had allowed this foreign anger to blind me. I dropped to the wet floor, breathing heavily, tears flooding my eyes. "I'm sorry, Naël. I'm so sorry."

Fouchard kneeled beside me, his arms enveloping my shoulders, and kissed me, a loving touch of the lips, a gentle reminder of our love. "Are you okay?"

"I almost shot you." Disbelief replaced the anger inside. "I could have killed you."

My boyfriend shook his head. "No, you couldn't." He smiled. "You would never be able to destroy this masterpiece," he said, gesturing at himself. A chuckle climbed my throat. "Not after what I did to you in that grotto. If you killed me, who would do that to you again?"

The sound of my laughter bounced off the walls and was soon joined by Fouchard's. I laughed until the chuckles turned to sobs. My boyfriend drew me into his arms and kept me there while I emptied myself of all the anger, the frustration, and pain. Jhanvi's words had hit a nerve, the one that flared up every time someone reminded me that I had been left to fend for myself, that my parents hadn't cared enough to take care of me. The lifelong sense of neglect and abandonment poured out of me all at once.

I wasn't sure how long we sat there, Fouchard holding me and me crying my eyes out, but eventually the tears dried out. My wonderful merrow took my lips with his and made me feel loved again. How had I lived a whole life without him? "Are you ready to go back?" he asked me quietly.

I nodded and scrambled to my feet, Fouchard supporting me. That's when I remembered. "Did you hear what she said?" I asked him. His eyes narrowed. He'd heard it too. "She said my father is one of the monks."

He slid an arm over my shoulders and coaxed me into a walk. "I guess it's time for another visit to the convent," he whispered as we walked back the way we had come. "I have a few chosen words for the man who fathered you. Not all nice."

I leaned against him, feeling depleted of energy. "The damned Oracle has a lot of explaining to do."

Together we walked and then swam toward the stairway to the Sé where my world had suddenly changed forever.

TWENTY-NINE
DADDY DEAR

"Why is he pacing around and growling like a lion?" Taz said in a tone way too loud to be considered the whisper she'd intended.

I stopped in my tracks, dust puffing up where I had carved out a rut with my nonstop pacing. "This lion can hear you, witch." I growled again for effect. "How would you feel if you just found out that once again you've been lied to about your parentage?" The anger that had caused me to turn into a human weapon in the tunnels was gone, but I was still fuming at the fact that my father had apparently been under my nose all this time and never bothered to tell me. "What if it's the crazy Oracle? What does that say about my genes?"

Fouchard approached and cautiously draped an arm over my shoulders. I had been a bit prickly for the past few days, ever since Mommy Dearest had revealed that my father was one of the monks. Three days had passed, and yet this annoying anger, however faded, still burned inside me. I had been betrayed by some of the few people in the world I trusted. "Sweetheart, the Oracle is not your father," my boyfriend said.

Taz giggled. "Aww, that's so sweet that you call him sweetheart." Both Fouchard and I blasted her with our eyes, and she had the good sense to step back and busy herself staring out into the sky.

"Think about it, Naël. My father probably sat with us for breakfast several times, talked to us about the weather and other trivial things, and never once had the decency to tell me we shared more than just the bread." That familiar pain that had followed me my whole life was gnawing at my heart. "I can't, I just can't."

Fouchard pulled me closer and kissed my temple. "I love you. Don't forget that." I wouldn't. Not ever. His love was the one thing that made me wake up with a smile on my face and filled me with warmth.

Taz, always the sneak, appeared by our side, her bright red lips puckered and a look of remorse in her emerald eyes. "For what it's worth, Aiden," she said, "I love you too." She threw a look at Fouchard and quickly added, "As a friend. I love you as a friend."

Despite the pressure in my chest, I burst out

laughing, and so did my boyfriend. Looking confused at first, the witch soon joined us. "Thank you. As witches go, you're not half bad." We brought her into a three-way hug. It was true, I considered Taz a friend, as weird as that sounded to me. I trusted her and even looked forward to her visits.

"Sorry to break up this love fest, but Brother Serafim is ready to see you now." One of the younger brothers—younger than me, so not my father, for sure—said, an amused smile dancing on his lips. "Are you coming?"

The hug broke apart, and I threw Fouchard a last glance before following the monk. "We'll be waiting here, Aiden," my boyfriend yelled before I stepped inside the building that housed the Einstein look-alike.

Brother Serafim was in his usual position, legs crossed, bottom settled on a large, comfortable cushion over a mattress. He raised his eyes to me and smiled, pointing at another cushion placed in front of him. I had definitely gone up the ranks.

"Sit, Aiden." He stared at me for a moment and then blinked. "You are angry, and not about those who pursue you and wish you ill."

Duh, that much must be obvious to everyone who looked at me. My jaws were sore from clenching them for days now, and my neck stiff with tension that not even my boyfriend's gentle touch had been able to smooth away.

"There is no reason for that."

Excuse me? No reason to be upset about being kept in the dark about my own father? I kept my cool. "I beg to differ, Brother. I've been lied to multiple times when I visited the convent."

He clicked his tongue and shook his head. "Why do you think you were allowed in our sanctuary for more than a day visit?" *Don't know, don't care.* I took a long deep breath. "Only those who are related to us are allowed to stay overnight and bring guests." How was I supposed to know that? "Your father has not revealed himself to you because it was paramount that you focused on the vexing issue of Jhanvi and her son. If he was to tell you he was your father, you'd be distracted, and things could go badly very quickly. Love sometimes veers you off the right path."

What the hell was he going on about? Out of nowhere, Taz's words of months ago came to my mind. She had warned me about not getting distracted by love, but I thought she had meant Fouchard. Was this what she had been talking about?

"News flash: things went badly anyway. I almost destroyed Lisbon's oldest patrimony and killed my own boyfriend. All because I have no clue about my own magical power, what I can and cannot do. This learning on the spot is becoming dangerous."

"Your powers are manifesting themselves now because there is a need for them, unlike before."

Again, I disagreed. I could have used a slice of those powers when that troll held my head inside a toilet or when that mobster about killed me with his fists. "Your father is now ready to introduce himself to you. Are you ready to talk to him without unnecessary angst?"

Was I? I couldn't be sure. A lifetime of fending for myself left traces of anger behind. "I'm not promising anything," I mumbled like a moody teenager.

The Oracle waved at the young monk by the door, who opened and sidled behind it to make room for Brother John. The monk filled the doorway, tall and powerful. I had seen him battle Bob along with his brothers, and there was no doubt about it; there was powerful magic in the unassuming monks.

"Brother John," the Einstein monk said, "care to be the one breaking the news to our young, befuddled friend?"

The monk brushed a big hand over his hair, which was still caught at the top in a small man-bun, and cleared his throat. "Certainly, Brother." Was there a hint of hesitation in his voice? He turned his eyes to me. "Aiden, by now you know that your father has been living here in the convent for a long time. This order of monks is made up of druids from around the world. Our power combined was what allowed us to protect you and your family from Babu-raj." *I know that. Get to the important part.* "There is no easy way to say this, so I'll just say it. Aiden, I'm your father."

I must've been losing my mind, because amidst such a revelation all I could think of was *Star Wars* and the scene between Darth Vader and Luke. Hopefully my father was more of an Obi-Wan than a Vader, but it still gave me pause. I stood there dumbfounded and paralyzed, staring at the monk who claimed to be my father, the same man I had needed so many times in my life and had never been there for me. I didn't know how to separate all the different and warring feelings that erupted in my heart; there was love and joy mixed with anger and an immense sense of loss— loss for what I could have had as a child and didn't.

"I know you must hate me, and I don't blame you," the monk—my father—continued, eyes shimmering. Were those tears? "But you must know that abandoning you in the world was not an easy choice for me or your mother."

The bubble of rage growing in my throat burst, and I jumped to my feet. "Then why did you? If you are both as powerful as everyone tells me you are, why not just protect me?" My low growling voice echoed inside the library, words that reeked of pain and anger, the poison I had carried inside me for a lifetime. "Instead, you left a baby to his own devices, helpless and unloved. What kind of fuckery was that? You were supposed to love and protect me, not abandon me to grow up feeling like a piece of refuse no one wants around for long." An overwhelming need for my mate flooded me. I needed his touch to soothe me, to calm me down, to remind me I was loved.

My so-called father had the good sense, or the nerve, to look distraught. "I know, son, but you were born too strong, too powerful, and as long as your location was known you'd be in danger no matter how much we wanted to protect you," he said, choking on the words, hands stretched in my direction in a silent plea. "Cutting you off from the magical world was the only way we knew to protect you until you came into your full potential. We have kept a discreet eye on you through the years but didn't dare intervene for fear you'd be spotted by the likes of Jhanvi and her son." His blue eyes sought mine, pleading. "We both love you, son. We did this out of love, not neglect or indifference. I hope you'll find it in your heart to forgive and allow us to guide you from now on."

Now he wanted to be in my life? I snorted, tears burning in my eyes. *I need Naël.* "I'm not sure I can do that. You'll forgive me if I need to digest all this news." Would I ever be able to forgive him? I wanted to. Even in my fury, I had that kernel of need to have him in my life, to experience what it was like to have those who made me in my life. But not yet. "I need time."

My father dropped his arms along his body, jaw clenched. "Take all the time you need, Aiden." I turned to leave, desperate to be with my man and out of the suffocating aura of the room. He grabbed my arm on the way out. "And son, I'm so happy you found someone who loves you like Fouchard does."

I pulled away from his touch and left the library for the coolness of the night. I sighed, glad to finally be able to breathe.

"Aiden!" Fouchard was striding toward me, his long legs devouring the space between us. I didn't hesitate; I threw myself in his arms and burst into tears. The tears I had been keeping under control ran free as I sobbed against my mate's chest. He held me tight, cooing into my hair, his warm breath anchoring me to the here and now. "It'll be all right, sweetheart, it will be okay." I squeezed him harder, my face buried in the crook of his neck. "I love you. Vee loves you. All your friends love you. You're not alone anymore, sweetheart."

Another warm body sandwiched me from behind —Taz. She flattened her cheek against my back and laid her hands on my shoulders. "Hey, Aiden, you know I love you, right? We're practically siblings by now."

I had never ugly cried before but now knew why it was called that; snot bubbled out of my nose as the torrent of tears ran down my cheeks and puffed up my eyes. I remained the ham in that sandwich for a while, absorbing their love and their heat, allowing my aching heart to soften and return to its regular rhythm. The tears finally stopped, and the anger blurred into the background.

"Taz?" I whispered, in control again.

My witch friend was still glued to my back, her chin propped on one of my shoulders. "Yes, Aiden?"

"Just because you think of me as your brother now, it doesn't mean I like witches." I braced myself for what I knew was coming.

She didn't disappoint. Letting go of me, she snorted and swatted my neck, Cristina-style. "Sheesh, I guess you're back to normal. And you're not so much like a brother as like a sister." Amusement was obvious in her voice, and we both burst out laughing. "I guess we're staying here tonight."

The monks had arranged for another room in the visitor building for Taz to sleep in while we took our usual one. "You're sure you didn't bring your broom? You could just fly home."

"Funny, Aiden, very funny," she said, beginning her walk to her room across the yard, her red hair flowing loose behind her. She flipped us the finger, never bothering to look back.

Fouchard and I also retreated to our room, his arm over my shoulders. The silence of the night was broken only by the sound of the crickets and our own steps.

"Are you okay?" Fouchard asked me right before we entered our room, his eyes seeking mine under the light of the moon. I nodded. I was, strange as it sounded even to me. I was okay. Crying had released a lot of the anger and pain trapped inside, and I knew I could face a world that had radically changed for me in the few days. I was not ready to fully forgive my father yet, but I knew in my heart that I would some-day. Maybe tomorrow, maybe in a year. I just needed time to adjust to my new reality.

I sighed, rose on my toes, and kissed him. "I'm better than okay because you're here with me." He smiled and kissed me again, his tongue lingering over my lower lip. "But there is one thing I'm not okay with at all." I said it deadpan, and Fouchard threw me a worried glance. "I'm not okay with going to that hellish bathroom again. Every time I have to sit on those latrines, I'm afraid some creature will get a bit too intimate with me."

My boyfriend let out a loud chuckle, and I smiled. All was well in the world tonight despite the earlier emotional explosion. I had my merrow with me, and that was all I needed. The world was my oyster, and Fouchard was my pearl.

THIRTY

THE GANG IS ALL HERE

Cold drops of water snapped me out of slumber, and I sat up, confused and alarmed. Everything sent my heart into red alert after all that happened. But it turned out it was only my boyfriend, dripping ocean water from every inch of his lovely body. "You scared the shit out of me, Naël." I flattened a hand against my chest where my heart was going bonkers.

He laughed and dropped on the towel next to me. "You should have come and swum with me," he said, leaning over and planting a brief kiss on my lips. "The water is nice and cool today."

"The sand is nice and warm," I said, kissing him again. "Stalemate."

Fouchard chuckled and cupped my face with his big wet hands. "You're adorable when you act stupid." I scoffed at his usual lack of finesse. "And I love it when you're adorable. If we weren't on this crowded, very public beach, I would ravish you right here, right now."

"Hold that thought. I could use some good ravishing later." My whole body immediately reacted to his words as his hand dropped from my cheek to my upper thigh.

We lay back on the towels, tiny grains of sand scratching my exposed skin as my hand snaked across the space between me and my boyfriend to hold his. He sighed. "We have to go soon. The others will be waiting for us."

We were meeting with the whole gang later at the coffee shop, since we hadn't really been all together since before our stunt in the underground tunnels. Things had changed dramatically for me, from being fatherless to having one, a fact I hadn't been able to digest properly yet. Bob and Mommy Dearest were still at large and, one would guess, still holding a huge grudge against me. And let's not forget my newly acquired destructive and deadly powers. The monks had already offered to teach me how to summon and control all these new *gifts* I didn't know I had. I certainly didn't want to risk killing someone I loved, or anyone for that matter; I had never been nor ever would be a killer.

For another half hour or so we ignored all our

problems and lingered on the warm sand, soaking in the soothing rays of the sun. Then we shook ourselves and our towels free of all the sand, took a quick icy cold shower in the *paradão,* and decided to walk along the beach for a while before going back to reality. We hadn't planned it, but our legs took us to the same bench where Fouchard and I had shared our first kiss. The memory filled me with a mixture of nostalgia and desire. He had been such a tease back then, kissing me as if there was no tomorrow, only to walk away afterward, shedding his clothes in the sand and diving into the dark waters of the ocean.

"Want to sit here for a while?" Fouchard asked me, pointing at the bench. His wicked smile told me he was also remembering that night. "We should send a petition to the powers that be to have this bench named national patrimony. That kiss was epic."

I couldn't agree more.

We sat, Fouchard's arm draped behind my shoulders, thighs glued together. Back then, we had been wearing jeans, but now we were both in our bathing suits, and our skin touched and melded together. "Did you ever think we would end up together?" I asked. "You didn't start on the right foot with me." In fact, he had started very much with his foot in his mouth, and yet, I hadn't been able to get him out of my mind. I had wanted him so bad I couldn't sleep at night.

Fouchard's lips stretched into a beautiful smile. "I knew we would end up together." I furrowed my brow, surprised. What did he mean by that? Back then, he had done nothing but insult me while turning me on constantly. "You haven't guessed yet?" I stared at him stupidly. "Come on, Aiden. I thought you had finally seen it. Have you been thinking of me as your mate lately?"

Now that he mentioned it, yes, I had caught myself thinking of him as my mate. Not boyfriend, not lover. Mate. "Yes, so what?"

"Didn't you ever wonder why we were drawn together no matter what we said about each other? That we couldn't keep our hands off each other?" Not really. I had just assumed it was my man-whoring hormones playing with me. What was he saying? "Fuck, Aiden. We're mates. You know, as in fated to be together?"

My mouth dropped open, and I blinked furiously for a moment or two. "Is that even a thing?" I had read it in books, of course, but I always thought that was something invented by a romance writer some-time in history. A disturbing thought popped into my mind. "Wait, does that mean we had no choice? That we are together not because we fell in love but because the universe wanted us to be?"

Fouchard burst out laughing, and I crossed my arms, annoyed. "You lovable fool. Of course we had a choice. We could have walked away from each other, but we did fall in love. Us, not the universal forces, *we* fell for each other. Hard."

Without giving him a chance to say anything else, I slid a hand behind his neck, pulled his face toward mine, and kissed him. He moaned inside my mouth, his tongue gently caressing mine and making me tingle all over.

By the time we arrived at the coffee shop, all our friends were already there, sitting around a table in a corner and eating half of my pastry supplies. Cristina was taking an order outside on the patio, but the shop was suspiciously empty of customers at a time when we were usually at our busiest. I smelled a rat; a magical rat.

As if to confirm my suspicions, Taz greeted us with an impish smile. "Sorry, Aiden. You may not make much profit today." I scowled, not really mad at her. I was glad she used her magic to keep the customers away for a while. I was looking forward to communing with the people, magical and regular alike, that I was now happy and proud to call my friends and family.

Before I could sit down, Vee tackled me, whooshing the air out of me. For such a puny kid, she sure had some muscle power. "Whoa, kiddo, that's a mighty hug you have there," I said, encasing her thin body with my arms. She held on as if for dear life, her face flattened on my chest and hands tightly wrapped around my waist. "What's up, mermaid?"

"Nothing," she said, voice muffled by my shirt. "I just thought you may need a hug."

Touched, I peeled her off me and looked into her unusual eyes. "You're way too smart for a mermaid," I said, brushing her wild white-blond hair with my fingers. "I did need a hug; how did you know?"

"Don't indulge her," Fouchard said, pulling out a chair and taking a seat next to Taz, "or her head will swell even more."

Vee turned to her brother and propped her hands on her waist. "You're just jealous that I am hugging Aiden instead of you." I smothered a chuckle with my hand. Fouchard's lips were curved into a smile, his eyes soft as they always were when addressing his sister. Vee turned to me again and grinned. "There are some advantages to being a mermaid. We are more attuned to other creatures' feelings."

Fouchard snorted, almost spitting out the mouthful of coffee he had just drunk. "What are they teaching you in that mermaid school? Lessons in how to be even more full of yourself than you are already?"

Cristina, newly arrived from the patio, the warlock, and even Taz followed the exchange with interest. None of them had siblings and, just like me, found this friendly, however barbed, banter between my boyfriend and his sister fascinating.

With a loud humph, Vee stuck her lower lip out in a pout. "You are such a pain, Naël," she said, taking her seat at the table. "You should take lessons from your boyfriend, who is much nicer than you." I turned my face away from them to hide the grin stretching my lips. "You're a typical merman with no respect for the female of the species."

For the first time ever, I watched as Fouchard's face morphed from one of amusement to surprise— or maybe shock. "Whatever gave you that idea?"

It sounded as if our eleven-year-old was already afflicted with some teenage-isms, those pesky germs that make teens say and do very unwise things.

"T.J. told me that, and I totally see it now." *Oh, girly, you are setting yourself up for grief.*

Fouchard's eyes had darkened, his lips stretched into a thin line, a muscle in his jaw twitching. "And who might this wise woman be?" His voice was deceptively gentle, the calm before the storm.

Vee thrust out her chest and crossed her arms, her chin defiantly jutting out. "She is one of the girls in my circle of friends."

I was never part of a clique, since I was more of a loner, but I knew what they were. I had always thought of them as a tepid gang where the leader manipulated the other members into doing some seriously stupid shit.

My boyfriend made a valiant effort not to explode by taking a gigantic slurp of his hot coffee. "We will talk about this later, young lady." Vee had the good sense to look nervous at his choice of words and dropped her arms and the attitude.

Cristina sat next to Vee and draped an arm over her small shoulders. "We have to talk, Vee. Your friend is not giving you accurate information," she said, amusement barely disguised by her somber tone. "Your brother has never shown any disrespect for females of any species, so I think you owe him an apology, don't you?"

Vee stared at her shoes for a moment before raising her eyes to her brother. "I'm sorry, Naël. That was not fair," she said with a loud sigh. "I know you are not like that at all." She licked her lips. "Will you forgive me? I love you."

The corners of my merrow's lips had already begun to turn upward, but he hid them behind his hand. "I don't know, those were pretty serious allegations."

He was evil. I loved it.

Vee opened her mouth in surprise, and then, jumping out of her seat, wrapped her arms around her brother's neck in a hug. "You are so mean," she said, giggling. He laughed and kissed the top of her head.

"Siblings," Taz exclaimed, shaking her head. "I'm glad I don't have any." She sounded so serious, we all burst out laughing. After all the seriousness of the past weeks, it was nice to be able to laugh about silly things like this. It was comfortable; it was home.

We talked for a while, the store magically closed to new customers. My friends had a lot of questions, and I did my best to answer them. My own questions had to go unanswered for the moment, but I had many; I had questions about my mother's whereabouts, my father's powers, the druid monks. First, I had to adjust to my new reality.

"Baby steps," Fouchard had said the night before after we had made love in our bed. "Brains can only take in a certain amount of information at a time. Digest this first before asking for more." It was good advice, and I was more than willing to follow it.

After my friends had devoured nearly all my food supply for the day, Fouchard and I retreated to the kitchen to wash the dishes. I washed, he dried while we watched the others through the small window to the coffee room where they still lingered, talking and joking around. My mind went back to the day I had been injured by Bob and how I had almost crawled out of my skin watching Silva touch Cristina. They had been almost in the same position as they were now, but my feelings toward their relationship had radically changed.

"The warlock has proved to be a great ally, right?" Sometimes it felt as if Fouchard could read my thoughts. Maybe this mate thing connected us in more ways than one. He leaned against my back, his chin resting on my shoulder and his hands, still holding the kitchen towel, knotted around my waist. I rested against him, enjoying the way his breath caressed my neck. "He's good for Cristina."

I had to agree. "I hate to admit it—and don't you ever dare tell him I said that—but yes, he has surprised me." I turned my face to plant a kiss on his cheek. "I'm glad Cristina found a good one. He's been amazing with her."

Silva had practically moved in with my friend so he could be at her beck and call any time of day or night. Now that she was mostly recovered, he had loosened the grip a bit, but I knew he still kept watch over her house at night, getting very little sleep as he sat in his car until the wee hours of the morning. Cristina would most likely be furious if she found out, but I knew where he was coming from— a place of fear and love—and I had no plans to rat him out.

My guilt swelled every time I stared at my beautiful friend's face, now scarred. I knew it wasn't my fault, but that didn't make me feel any better about it.

"Do you think Cristina will let me finance plastic surgery?" I asked.

"I don't think she'll want the surgery at all," Fouchard said, kissing my neck. "She's the kind of girl who is proud of her battle scars. I personally think it makes her even more beautiful, and it's obvious Silva agrees with me." Silva was following my friend's every move, his eyes tracking her lips as she spoke, an expression of awe on his face.

I smiled and turned all the way around in Fouchard's arms to kiss him properly. Our lips melded, tongues dancing together, hearts setting the rhythm of our movements. We were both panting when we pulled apart. My mate's desire for me was poking me in a tantalizing way.

"Should we give them the slip?" I asked, tilting my head in our friends' direction.

"That would probably be wise," he murmured against my lips. "I can tell Pinocchio wants to play."

I laughed. "Pinocchio is a very playful guy." I wanted to get lost in the dark eyes of my man. "I love you, Naël. Thank you for giving me what I missed my whole life. Thank you for loving me and letting me love you."

Fouchard pulled me closer, our bodies completely fused together and lips less than a hairbreadth apart. "Same here, sweetheart. And once we capture the deadly duo, I may even ask for your hand in marriage." I raised my chin so quickly, I almost slammed my head into his. He chuckled. "But for now, I was wondering whether you would like to officially move in with me. That house doesn't feel like home anymore when you're not there."

My heart might have stopped for a second. My breath caught, rendering me speechless for once.

"Are you going to answer me, or are you just going to stand there with your mouth open like a dead fish?" That wicked smile of his was dancing on his lips again.

I swallowed, licked my lips where his taste still lingered, and said, "Of course, Naël. Of course I'll move in with you."

With my heart tap dancing in my chest, I sealed our deal with a long, hard, delicious kiss. Fouchard slipped his hands all the way down to cup my ass and pull my pelvis against his. "Can't wait to get you home."

Home. Such a tiny, common word that meant the world to me.

"There is only one rather vexing question," I said, breathless as he suckled on my lower lip. He stopped and furrowed his brow. "If I move in, will you be able to gather the necessary stamina to keep up with my god-gene-enhanced sex drive?"

Fouchard's luscious lips opened in a sexy smile that held the promise of many pleasurable years to come. "Are you kidding me? You know me, I'm always ready for a challenge."

And for the first time in my life I was too. I was not running away ever again.

Never fear, Aiden and Naël's story is far from over. Be sure to check out the final book in the series, ***Of Fire & Bone***.

As if having a powerful druid and a goddess for parents doesn't suck enough, throwing a vengeful god into the fray certainly doesn't do Aiden any favors.

Looking for more M/M romance from Natalina? Be sure to check out shifter Romance, ***Infinite Blue*** today!

Thanks for reading *Of Scales and Fire*. I do hope you enjoyed this story. I appreciate your help in spreading the word, including telling a friend. Before you go, it would mean so much to me if you would take a few minutes to write a review and share how you feel about my story so others may find my work. Reviews really do help readers find books. Please leave a review on your favorite book site.

Don't miss out on New Releases, Exclusive Give-aways and much more!

Join my newsletter: http://bit.ly/reisnewsletter
Join my reader group: http://bit.ly/RebelsOutcasts

I'd love to hear from you directly, too. Please feel free to e-mail me at

catarinadeobidos1@gmail.com or check out my website http://bit.ly/WebNatalina for updates.

Natalina wrote her first romance in collaboration with her best friend at the age of 13. Since then she has ventured into other genres, but romance is first and foremost in almost everything she writes.

After earning a degree in tourism and foreign languages, she worked as a tourist guide in her native Portugal for a short time before moving to the United States. She lived in three continents and a few islands, and her knack for languages and linguistics led her to a master's degree in education. She lives in Virginia where she has taught English as a Second Language to elementary school children for more years than she cares to admit.

Natalina doesn't believe you can have too many books or too much coffee. Art and dance make her happy and she is pretty sure she could survive on lobster and bananas alone. When she is not writing or stressing over lesson plans, she shares her life with her husband and two adult sons.

twitter.com/TichaB

instagram.com/reisnatalina

bookbub.com/authors/natalina-reis

pinterest.com/lisboeta62

ACKNOWLEDGMENTS

I spent most of 2019 writing this series. Little did I know what awaited all of us in 2020, the year of the Great Pause. If Aiden and Naël had their adventure in 2020—well, they wouldn't, would they? Because my little country, like most of the world, closed down several times throughout the year to try and contain the microscopic monster that is Covid-19.

As I write this, new cases and deaths from the pandemic are yet again spiking in Portugal, and hospitals and medical personnel are overworked and overwhelmed. People are being told to stay home as the country once again shuts down.

I think I speak for most bookworms when I say that books (and yoga) have kept me sane throughout this madness, and I am hoping that by the time this book is published things have gotten better around the world. But if they have not, I hope that my book will bring readers a moment of pleasure at least, a sliver of heaven in a world that is everything but.

Thank you to all my readers, my wonderful publisher who believed in this series, her amazing staff, my family and friends, and all of those who stuck it out with optimism and a smile on their lips. Better days will come.

ABOUT THE PUBLISHER

Hot Tree Publishing opened its doors in 2015 with an aspiration to bring quality fiction to the world of readers. With the initial focus on romance and a wide spread of romance subgenres, Hot Tree Publishing has since opened their first imprint, Tangled Tree Publishing, specializing in crime, mystery, suspense, and thriller.

Firmly seated in the industry as a leading editing provider to independent authors and small publishing houses, Hot Tree Publishing is the sister company to Hot Tree Editing, founded in 2012. Having established in-house editing and promotions, plus having a well-respected market presence, Hot Tree Publishing endeavors to be a leader in bringing quality stories to the world of readers.

Interested in discovering more amazing reads brought to you by Hot Tree Publishing? Head over to the website for information:

www.hottreepublishing.com

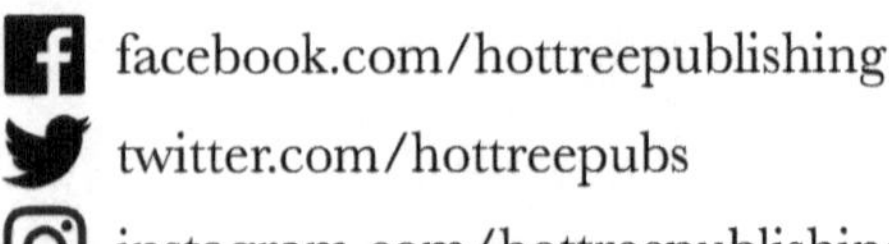

facebook.com/hottreepublishing
twitter.com/hottreepubs
instagram.com/hottreepublishing

www.ingramcontent.com/pod-product-compliance
Lightning Source LLC
Chambersburg PA
CBHW060746190726

48285CB00002B/322